AVA AND THE BEAR

THE SHIFTERS SERIES BOOK TWO

ELIZABETH KELLY

EK PUBLISHING INC.

Cover art by
The Final Wrap

Published by
EK Publishing Inc.

AVA AND THE BEAR

He'll risk everything to save her.

Grizzly shifter, Bishop King, has two loves – sex and food. So, when he meets Ava Lewis, a curvy redhead with the intoxicating scent of sex and chocolate, he knows he's in trouble.

Ava's looking for love, not a one-night stand, and grizzly shifters don't do relationships. It doesn't matter how attracted she is to Bishop or that every time she's around him, she loses her damn mind and ends up half-naked and in his arms. There's no future for them, and she wants her happily ever after.

But when an unstable shifter targets Ava, Bishop's vow to stay away from the beautiful, fragile woman is forgotten. Ava doesn't want his help, but Bishop's grizzly wants her, and he'll stop at nothing to claim her – even if that means battling an ancient and powerful enemy.

AVA AND THE BEAR

He'll risk everything to save her.

Grizzly shifter, Bishop King, has two loves – sex and food. So, when he meets Ava Lewis, a curvy redhead with the intoxicating scent of sex and chocolate, he knows he's in trouble.

Ava's looking for love, not a one-night stand, and grizzly shifters don't do relationships. It doesn't matter how attracted she is to Bishop or that every time she's around him, she loses her damn mind and ends up half-naked and in his arms. There's no future for them, and she wants her happily ever after.

But when an unstable shifter targets Ava, Bishop's vow to stay away from the beautiful, fragile woman is forgotten. Ava doesn't want his help, but Bishop's grizzly wants her, and he'll stop at nothing to claim her – even if that means battling an ancient and powerful enemy.

CHAPTER 1

"Heads up, Mr. Chambers is behind curtain number four," Ginger said as Ava walked up to the nurse's desk.

Ava groaned and rubbed at her forehead. Her shift was over in a half-hour, if only he had waited just a little longer. She wondered if she could simply ignore him until her shift was done. Then he'd be Ginger and Ronda's problem, and she could go home and climb into a nice hot bath.

"If you're thinking of ignoring him, think again." Ginger grinned at her. "He's been here ten minutes and has already asked for you twice."

"The guy's a hypochondriac." Ava twisted a lock of her bright red hair around her finger. "There's never anything wrong with him. I'd say he was just here for drugs, but he doesn't even ask for painkillers."

Ginger laughed. "He's not a hypochondriac or a druggie, Ava. He's smitten with you."

"Smitten? The 1950s called, they want their lingo back," Ava replied.

Ginger whacked her lightly on the arm. "You know what I

mean. He's got a crush on you. You should think about dating him."

Ava shook her head. "No, thanks. He's not my type."

"Why, because he isn't a handsome lion shifter or a big old grizzly shifter?" Ginger raised her eyebrows at her.

"How much has Willow told you?" Ava asked.

"Enough. After that offhanded comment about riding the grizzly shifter's face, you know I had to find out more," Ginger said.

"So that's why you wanted to take Willow out for coffee last week, just the two of you."

"Yep," Ginger said shamelessly. "And in case you're wondering – my vote is for the commitment-phobic grizzly. I mean, Keegan is handsome and totally charming, but do you really want him wearing your underwear?"

"Ginger, keep your voice down," Ava said.

"Uh oh. Has he already worn your underwear? It's cool if he has, but I didn't think you'd seen him lately."

"I haven't," Ava said. "He wasn't my type either."

She supposed that wasn't particularly true. Not that she wanted to pass her underwear around, but Keegan might have been her type. Unfortunately, he hadn't contacted her other than a brief coffee date with him.

So, who cares? It's Bishop you really want, anyway.

She shut down her inner voice in a hurry as Ginger rested her elbows on the desk and sighed. "Willow told me how Bishop keeps saving your life. It's so romantic. The guy took a table to the back for you and killed a man for touching you."

"He didn't kill anyone!" Ava said. "He just scared the guy into wetting his pants and then knocked him out."

She sighed inwardly. Her best friend, Willow, had a special

knack, one that involved seeing ghosts and helping them move on to the light, but this time her willingness to help had nearly gotten her and Ava killed. Luckily Willow's new bosses, a wolf shifter named Mal, and Bishop, a huge and formidable grizzly shifter, had followed them to the abandoned barn.

They'd arrived just in time for Bishop to save Ava from a nasty man with a knife. She'd been nearly weak with relief and gratitude toward the giant grizzly.

Gratitude? Is that why you let him pull off your shirt right there and kiss you senseless?

She blushed as Ginger said, "But he did take a flying table to the back when that ghost attacked you at the party."

"It wasn't me the ghost was attacking. It was Keegan and his brother. But yes, he did," she admitted. "and it was very nice of him."

"Yes, very nice." Ginger laughed. "And from what Willow says, the make-out session you had with him in the bathroom afterward was also very nice."

"I'm going to kill her," Ava said.

"You know Willow can't keep a secret," Ginger said. "Besides, what's wrong with having some fun? When was the last time you even went on a date?"

"I went on that date with Keegan to the paranormal only bar," Ava said.

"Right. That's when Bishop showed up and nearly killed Keegan for kissing you."

Ava flushed again. "He was just being irrational."

"Whatever, Ava. I haven't even met the guy, and I can tell he has it bad for you."

"Yeah, well, he doesn't do relationships, remember? Grizzly shifters don't mate with humans. Hell, they don't even really mate with their own kind. They get together to have sex and make babies, and that's it. The males don't help raise their children."

"Willow says Bishop is different."

"Willow's wrong. Bishop is only interested in sex," Ava said. "And I know it's true because I haven't heard a word from him in over two months."

"Well, have you -"

"Ginger, I love you, but I don't want to talk about this, okay?" Ava said.

The small brunette nodded sympathetically. "I'm sorry. I just want you to be happy and find someone. Then we could all double date! Robbie and Mal are getting along great."

Ava knew for a fact that Mal thought Robbie was an idiot. Hell, they all did, but Ginger seemed to love him, so Ava and Willow had vowed to be supportive.

She grabbed Mr. Chambers' chart and scanned it absent-mindedly. Nearly six months ago, Willow had taken a reception job at a security firm owned by Mal, Bishop, and a jaguar shifter named Kat Frost. It didn't take long before Willow and Mal were involved, and after a bit of a rocky start, the two of them started dating despite Mal's belief that shifters and humans shouldn't interact. The two of them had been happily dating for the last two months.

Ava was happy for her best friend, but there was a part of her that was disgustingly jealous. She glanced down at her chubby body and pulled self-consciously at her scrub top. In the last month or so, she had vowed multiple times to eat right and get her body active more often, but the lure of chocolate and the couch was too strong. She cursed her lack of willpower. She would never find a man if she didn't get into shape.

Bishop likes you just the way you are. Remember? He

likes your curves and your freckles. He said he wanted to fuck you and that you belonged to him.

Yeah, well, she wasn't a piece of property that he could just claim. Besides, he might find her attractive and want to have sex with her, but she was looking for a relationship. She was tired of dating men who only wanted one thing from her, and after the fiasco with Clint, she'd vowed she would never be someone's booty call again.

"Ava?" Ginger said. "I can take Mr. Chambers' vitals if you want to skip out a bit early."

"Thank you, but it's fine. Mr. Chambers isn't that bad," Ava said.

She walked down the hallway toward curtain four. It was quiet in the ER tonight. Of course, it was just before seven on a Wednesday night, but still, there was only Mr. Chambers and a woman suffering from stomach pain in the ER.

She took a deep breath and ducked behind the curtain. "Hello again, Mr. Chambers."

"Ava! How many times have I told you to call me Sean?"

She smiled as her fingers found the pulse at his wrist, and she glanced at her watch. "Not feeling well again?"

He shrugged and waited patiently as she finished taking his pulse. "I think I tweaked my back a bit."

"That's a shame. What was it last week? Your leg?"

He nodded. "I do a lot of marathon training. Always hurting something."

As she wrapped the blood pressure cuff around his arm, she surreptitiously studied his body in the thin hospital gown. He certainly had the body of a marathon runner. He was on the shorter side and very lean, but the muscles bulged in his arms and legs, and he looked to have what her mother referred to as a 'wiry strength'. His red hair was thick and cut short with odd streaks of darker red throughout, and, unlike her pale, freckle-covered skin, his skin was a golden brown. He also had the coolest looking eyes she'd ever seen. They were a light gold with flecks of red in them. Contacts, obviously, but still cool.

He was handsome enough, and Ginger was probably right about him having a crush on her, but there was something about him, something she couldn't quite put her finger on, that made her uneasy.

He smiled at her, showing even white teeth, and she slightly blushed. "Sorry, I was being rude. You have beautiful eyes, Mr. Chambers, but it's no excuse for staring."

"I don't mind at all, my dear Ava. How is your shift tonight?"

"Oh, fine. I'm off in about fifteen minutes, so you'll be well looked after by Ginger and Ronda."

Sean frowned. "I thought you were on night shift this week."

"I was," she absentmindedly answered as she wrote some numbers on his chart, "but I switched with Tina."

Sean frowned again as she gave him a brief smile. "The doctor will be in shortly, okay?"

"Yes, thank you. Ava, I was wondering if you'd like to -"

"Ava?" A handsome dark-haired nurse, Brody stuck his head behind the curtain. "We still on for tonight?"

She stared at him blankly, and he grinned. "Dinner and a movie, remember? You promised me."

"Oh right, I forgot. Listen, I'm pretty tired, and I -"

"You're not ditching me again, girl," Brody said. "I'm finished work, but I'll wait for you. We can go back to your place, and you can shower and change."

"Sure," she said even though she really was tired, and the last thing she wanted to do was go out. "I'll see you in a few minutes."

Brody winked at her before waving at Sean. "Good to see you again, Mr. Chambers. It's been a few days."

Sean gave him a strained smile as Brody disappeared behind the curtain. Ava frowned. For the first time, Mr. Chambers actually appeared sick. She touched his forehead. "Is your back very painful? We can set up an IV and give you some morphine if you need it."

He shook his head and stared down at his lap. "No, thank you."

She hesitated a moment longer before patting his arm. "Have a good night, Mr. Chambers. I hope you're feeling better soon."

He didn't reply. She walked away, feeling oddly uneasy. Just before she ducked past the curtain, she glanced over her shoulder. A soft red glow appeared beneath the thin gown covering Mr. Chamber's upper chest. His cheeks were reddening, and her eyes widened when smoke drifted from his nostrils.

"Mr. Chambers? Are you all right?"

"Ava? You're done. I'll take over with Mr. Chambers." Ronda touched her shoulder, and Ava jumped and twisted around.

"What?" she said.

"I said your shift is done. Brody's waiting at the desk for you. Have a good night, and I'll see you tomorrow, okay?"

"Sure, right."

She glanced back at Mr. Chambers. The red in his chest, if it had even been there, had faded, and no smoke lingered around his face. He smiled benignly at her. "Have a good evening, Ava."

"Thanks, you too." She hurried away, her stomach in twisty knots.

"AVA, HURRY UP! WE WON'T HAVE TIME FOR DINNER BEFORE the movie if you don't move your ass," Brody hollered from the living room.

"Yeah, yeah. I'm ready. How do I look?" She twirled for him, and he made a low whistle.

"Your tits look super in that shirt."

She laughed. "Thanks."

"Although," he stood, "why you even care what you look like is beyond me. We've sworn off men, remember? We made a pact last month."

"We were also drunk as skunks, and, if I remember correctly, you drunk dialed Tito as I was in the process of passing out and had phone sex with him."

Brody shrugged. "I'm a whore. What can I say?"

She laughed again. "Thank God I passed out before he answered."

"You could have picked up some valuable tips, sweetie." Brody raised his hand and ticked off the points on his fingers. "I'm excellent at phone sex, blow jobs, rim jobs, making the boys cream their -"

"Yeah, yeah, I get the picture," Ava said. "I'm ready. Let's go before we really do miss the movie."

"CRAP! WE'VE GOT TO HURRY IF WE WANT TO MAKE THE late show." Ava tugged on Brody's arm as they left the restaurant.

"Hold your horses, woman." Brody smacked her on the ass. "I'm stuffed to the gills and can only walk so fast right now."

She laughed. "I told you not to have an appetizer and dessert."

"I've got to fuel the machine." Brody patted his flat stomach. "C'mon, I know a shortcut."

He grabbed her hand, and she followed him down the street. He took a left into an alley, and the two of them moved quickly past the large trash bins pushed up against the wall.

"Ugh." Ava held her hand over her nose. "Could you have found a more repulsive smelling shortcut, Brody?"

"It's not that bad," Brody said, but he threw his hand over his nose as they passed the largest of the bins. "C'mon, almost there. Once we're out of the alley, it's just a hop, skip, and a jump to the theatre."

"Excellent. And we're likely to have an entire row to ourselves thanks to our Eau de garbage smell," Ava said.

He laughed. "Oh please, it's not that bad."

A lid clattered to the ground, making Ava jump. "What was that?"

"Cat, probably," Brody said. "Don't worry. I'll protect you."

"Thanks." Ava took his hand. "But with your cat allergy, I'll be the one saving -"

"Mr. Chambers?" Brody squinted into the darkness. "What are you doing here?"

Ava stared at the redheaded man. He stood in the alley with his hands in his pockets, and a ripple of unease went through her.

"Mr. Chambers?" she said. "Are you okay?"

"It's a lovely evening, isn't it?" he said.

"Yes." Brody gave Ava a *what the hell* look. "How are you feeling?"

"Fine, just fine."

He continued to stare at them, and Brody's hand tightened

around Ava's. "Well, that's good. Listen, we don't mean to be rude, but we're late for a movie and -"

"You don't deserve her, you know."

"What?" Brody frowned at him. "What are you talking about?"

"Brody, let's go." Ava tugged on his hand. Tingles of alarm raced through her nervous system, and she tried to make Brody move backward with her. He pulled his hand free.

"What are you doing here, Mr. Chambers? Did you follow us?"

"She deserves better than you. You're nothing but a foul-mouthed cretin who shouldn't even be allowed to breed."

"Excuse me?" Brody scowled. "I don't know what your problem is, but get the hell out of our way."

"Brody, don't."

Brody ignored her. "Go on, Chambers. Get out of here."

"You dare to tell me what to do?" Sean's face darkened, and that reddish tinge glowed beneath his t-shirt. "You? A puny little human? You're not fit to lick my feet."

"Fuck you, you crazy asshole," Brody said. Before Ava could stop him, he stormed toward the smaller man. "I've had just about enough of your attitude."

His face bright red and his body swelling, Sean took a deep breath. Ava watched in horror as he blew a wave of bright flames from his mouth. They engulfed Brody, and Ava screamed as Brody shrieked in agony. He turned toward her, and her horrified scream cut off abruptly at the sight of his melting skin.

He took two stumbling steps forward and then fell flat on his face. His entire body engulfed in fire, she stared in sick terror as his hands clenched and unclenched before falling still. The smell of burning flesh filled the air. Sean stepped around the burning corpse and smiled at her.

"Don't be afraid, Ava. I would never hurt you."

"Get away from me." She staggered back.

He frowned. "I had to do it. Don't you see? He would have corrupted you. He would have taken you in all sorts of terrible ways and ruined your sweetness. I did it to save you."

"What are you?" she moaned.

"I am the bringer of fire, the creator of chaos, and your true love." He smiled gently at her. "You will be my bride, and I will fill your belly with my children. We'll be together forever."

Ava turned and ran for the opening of the alley. Behind her, Sean growled with anger, and there was a strange flapping noise. The wind ruffled her hair, and she looked up to see Sean, large wings sprouting from his back and breathing fire from his nose, flying over her.

She stumbled to a stop as he landed in front of her. His skin turned a rich, vibrant red and scales appeared on his face and neck. His body swelled, and his fingers turned to thick, black claws.

"Why do you run, Ava?" His voice deepened, and his eyes glowed with a hellish light. "Why do you run from your chosen one?"

"Stay away from me!" she cried out as he stepped closer. His wings were enormous now. They were a light red, and she made another moan of terror when the tip of one brushed across her arm. It had a leathery texture, and she could sense the power in them as he folded them against his back.

"Come with me, Ava. We will be together forever."

"No!" Panic buzzing through her veins, she shoved him as hard as she could. He stumbled back, his wings unfolding to help him catch his balance, and anger flashed in his eyes.

"Why would you deny me? Do you not understand who I am? I am your destiny, and you are mine. There is no denying that."

When she didn't reply, more anger rippled across his face. He yanked her into his embrace. He was hot, so hot she thought she would catch fire just from his nearness. She screamed again as he shook her roughly. His hands dug into the tender flesh of her arms, and a burning sensation shot through her skin.

"Do not deny me!" he shouted. "Do not ever deny me what is rightfully mine!"

He picked her up and threw her across the alley with an angry scream. She hit the wall of the building with a jarring thud. Her head bounced off the hard brick, and she crumpled to the dirty ground. Her ears ringing and her vision blurry, she squinted up at Sean as he knelt beside her.

"I'm sorry, Ava," he said. "I didn't mean to hurt you. Please, believe me. But you shouldn't deliberately upset me like that."

Through a haze of fear and pain, she heard the shouts of others. A small trickle of relief went through her when Sean stood and glanced at the mouth of the alley.

"You'll be okay," he said. "You'll be just fine, and when you're better, we'll talk again."

Her vision darkened, and she struggled to stay conscious as Sean's body swelled and his clothes tore apart.

"I'll see you soon, my bride." He shifted completely, and she watched as he leaped into the air, wings beating, and disappeared into the dark sky.

A few seconds later, a young woman and man knelt beside her. "Lady, are you okay?"

"Help me," she said before she slipped into the darkness.

CHAPTER 2

Bishop stared at the woman sitting across from him. She popped the last of her steak into her mouth and chewed happily before taking another swig of beer. She wiped her mouth and smiled at him.

"Having a good time?"

"Yes," he lied.

"Good. Are you going to finish that?" She pointed to his half-eaten steak.

He handed the plate to her. "I'm full. Help yourself."

"Thanks." She hesitated. "You know, for a bear shifter, you don't eat that much."

He cleared his throat. "I had a big lunch."

"Oh."

The woman dug into the remainder of his steak as he took a drink of beer and studied her silently. Like most females of his kind, she was tall with wide hips and large breasts, but she had a toned look. There would be no soft curves to sink into, no touch of velvet skin against his.

She'd give him a hell of a ride in the sack. Female grizzly shifters loved being in control, and the bedroom was no exception. He'd yet to sleep with one who hadn't, at some point, handcuffed him to the bed.

He supposed it was why he hadn't slept with many female grizzlies. He wanted to be in control. A woman's breathless cries of need, their helplessness as they shuddered under his skillful hands and mouth, made his cock so hard it nearly hurt. Only when the woman in his bed was screaming his name with pleasure, and her body was warm and pliant from hours of ecstasy did he allow himself to find his own release.

Female grizzlies didn't want to be controlled. It wasn't in their nature. Because of that, he'd often sought out other types of shifters or the occasional human who not only enjoyed giving control to him but understood it was about sex and nothing else.

He watched the grizzly shifter devour her steak with a single-minded determinedness that a few short months ago would have turned him on like a house on fire. He loved a woman with an appetite, loved when they enjoyed their food and made no apology for it. Hell, any woman who spent any time with him needed to love food. When he wasn't at work, he was eating or thinking about eating. Food was as pleasurable to him as sex.

In fact, if pushed, he'd be hard-pressed to decide what he loved more – food or sex.

Sex, his grizzly growled immediately. *More accurately – sex with a certain voluptuous redhead who smells like chocolate.*

He shut his grizzly down with a harsh snarl. Thinking about sex with Ava was a bad idea. A very bad fucking idea. He'd spent the last two months doing his best to forget her completely, and tonight wasn't the night to allow thoughts of her to creep back in.

But she's ours. His grizzly had a plaintive, pleading note in his voice that Bishop had never heard before. *Why won't you take what belongs to us?*

She's not ours! Get it through your thick skull. She doesn't belong to us. For all we know, she and that asshole lion shifter, Keegan, are having sex every damn night.

That brought a grumble of anger from his grizzly and an emotion remarkably close to pouting.

I want her. Give her to me.

Bishop had no idea what the fuck was going on with his grizzly, but he was ready to strangle him.

You want her too.

Yeah, so maybe he did. But he couldn't offer Ava anything but sex, his kind just didn't do relationships, and that wasn't what she was looking for. Of course, he'd never felt this strong of a pull toward a woman before. He'd never felt such an immediate need to possess a female - human or shifter - but he chalked that up to her smell. Ava had the most intoxicating scent of any human he'd ever encountered. It practically screamed sex to him, and that was why he and his grizzly were so obsessed with her. Who wouldn't want a woman who smelled like chocolate and - hot and sweaty, fingernails down your back, screams until she's hoarse - sex?

"Bishop?"

He shook himself all over as his grizzly retreated with the mental image of a naked Ava under him, all of her limbs clinging to him and moaning his name.

"Yes?"

"I asked if you were ready to go." The female gave him an odd look.

"Oh, of course. I'm ready whenever you are...."

He trailed off, realizing with absolute panic that he had forgotten her name.

The woman waited for a beat before rolling her eyes.

"Doreen. My name is Doreen."

"Right, right. Of course. Sorry," he said hurriedly. Blushing a little, he signaled the waiter for the bill.

"You're not much of a talker, are you?" Doreen said.

"No, not really."

"That's fine. There are better uses for your mouth, right?" She grinned at him.

He'd joined the 'Bear With Me' dating site on a whim three days ago. Half-convinced his obsession with Ava was because of his recent dry spell, he'd barely even checked Doreen's profile when she messaged him. They'd sent a couple of messages each before agreeing to meet for dinner.

Dinner was just a formality, of course. The real purpose of 'Bear With Me' was to assist grizzly shifters in finding the perfect - no strings attached, I definitely won't call you in the morning – relationship they were after.

Doreen finished her beer as he paid the waiter and gave him another wide grin. He forced himself to return her smile as she leaned back in the booth and stretched. It pushed her full breasts against the thin shirt she wore. Her smile grew when his gaze dropped briefly to her chest.

"Your place or mine, Bishop?" she asked.

"I'm sorry, what?"

He tried to stall for time. He'd gone on this date intending to take the shifter to his bed and relieve some of his pent-up need, but now he was nearly repulsed by the thought of sleeping with her.

Find Ava. She has what we need. His grizzly made a reappearance that he ignored.

She rested her elbows on the table. "Your place or mine?"

"Actually, I'm pretty tired. I think I'll call it a night. If you don't mind," he said.

Her mouth dropped open, and her hands curled into fists.

"What? Are you blowing me off?"

"No," he said. "I really am tired, and you know how we are when we don't get enough sleep."

"You're blowing me off," she said softly. "You do get the purpose of 'Bear With Me', right?"

"Yes."

"Then what the hell, jackass?" She was growing angrier by the second.

"It's not you. It's me," he said.

"Oh, you did *not* just say that to me," she snarled. "If you weren't interested in fucking tonight, then you shouldn't have invited me to dinner."

She growled, and a few of the other patrons in the restaurant gave them nervous looks.

"Calm down, Maureen, okay? Take a deep breath and -"

"My name is Doreen! Not Maureen – DOREEN!"

She slammed her fists into the table, invoking a startled scream from the woman sitting in the booth behind her.

"Doreen, I apologize, but -"

She slid out from the booth, grabbed his half-full glass of beer, and threw it in his face. As the cold liquid dripped down his face and into his shirt, she snarled at him a final time.

"Fuck you, Bishop King! I'm great in the sack. I would have rocked your fucking world, you stupid ass!"

She turned and stomped out of the restaurant.

BISHOP OPENED THE FRONT DOOR OF HIS SMALL HOUSE AND dropped his keys on the side table before kicking off his boots.

"Princess? Where are you? Daddy's home."

He smiled when the large calico cat appeared in the hallway, meowing softly. She weaved around his feet as he reached down and petted her with one large hand and then shrugged out of his jacket. He hung it on the hook, grabbed a beer from the fridge, and wandered into the living room. The couch groaned under his weight when he sat, and he swallowed a mouthful of cold beer as Princess leaped onto his lap. Purring, she rubbed against his chest before sniffing at his beer-soaked collar.

"Did you miss your daddy, Princess? Hmm?" He stroked the cat's soft fur as she butted her head against his chin before licking his beard with her rough tongue. "Daddy missed you. Yes, he did. Who's my good baby princess? Hmm? Is it you? Yes, it is."

He clicked on the TV and channel-surfed aimlessly as the cat settled onto his chest with a contented meow. His mind wandered to what Ava might be doing at this very moment. She worked shift work at the hospital, so she could be there. Or maybe she was at home. Maybe she was running a bath. Maybe she was undressing and climbing naked into the tub. Maybe every inch of her delectable freckle-covered skin was wet as she relaxed in the water. Maybe she was thinking about him and sliding her hand between her legs to –

He stood abruptly. The cat slid from his chest with a disgruntled hiss, and Bishop drank the rest of his beer in three large gulps before heading toward his bedroom. He would have a shower - a very *cold* shower - and go to bed.

WILLOW WALKED QUICKLY DOWN THE DARK ALLEY. IT WAS close to nine, and the sun had set hours ago. She could see her breath, but the icy cold air had little to do with the missing sun.

"Are you sure this is the right place, Alma?" she said. "I don't see the box."

She paused and listened intently. "Okay. If you're sure."

She moved deeper into the alley and clicked on the small flashlight she held. She swept the light across the alley and made a small noise of triumph when she saw the large cardboard box.

She crouched in front of it and opened it carefully, her face lighting up when she saw the two tiny kittens huddled on a dirty and torn blanket. "Hi, babies. Don't you worry, Willow's here."

She turned and smiled at nothing. "You can go to the light now, Alma. I found them. Yes, I promise I'll take good care of them. You don't have to worry."

She waited, squinting at a light that only she could see, before reaching into the box. The kittens hissed at her, their tiny teeth glowing in the light of the flashlight.

"It's okay, babies. I'm not going to hurt you. You don't have to -"

The hair on the back of her neck stood up when the low growl came from deep within the alley. She stood and shined her flashlight in the direction of the growl, gasping when two pairs of eyes glowed in the light.

"Who are you?" she said, ignoring the way her nervous system screamed at her.

"Hello there." Two small and compact men drifted into the weak light. "What's a little girl like you doing all alone in a place like this?"

"None of your business," Willow said. "Go on. Shoo."

"Did she just shoo us?" The larger of the two men said to his companion.

"The little bitch did," the second man said.

"You know what the problem is with humans, Rocky?" the larger man asked.

"Why don't you enlighten me, Dino?"

"Dino? Rocky?" Willow burst into loud laughter. "Please tell me those aren't your real names."

"Shut up, bitch," Dino said.

The two stepped closer, and Willow took a step back. "You should leave. This isn't going to end well for you."

Dino laughed an ugly sound that echoed down the alley. "Yeah? What are you going to do? All ninety pounds of you looks pretty dangerous."

Rocky eased forward, then stopped and sniffed the air before whining nervously. "She's been claimed by a wolf, Dino."

"Has she now?" Dino raised his eyebrow at her. "A human as a wolf's mate. I've never heard of that before."

"Like I said - you should probably get going."

Dino stared around the alley. "Where is your mate? He leaves you to wander alone at night in an alley?"

"He knows I can take care of myself," Willow said.

"Can you? I guess we'll find out," Dino growled and lunged forward.

Before he could grab her, angry growling echoed down the alley. Rocky whined again. "Dino, wait. I can smell -"

A grey wolf came out of the darkness. His green eyes glowed, and he bared his teeth in an angry snarl. Rocky screamed when it leaped onto him and knocked him flying.

Dino barked harshly, and his clothes tore from his body as he shifted to his animal form. Willow backed away as he barked at Rocky. Rocky shifted quickly, and the two crouched in front of Willow and the large grey wolf.

"Hyena shifters?" she asked the wolf.

He barked in reply before standing protectively in front

of her.

"I can help, Mal," Willow said.

He barked again, and she sighed. "Fine."

Mal snapped his teeth at the two hyenas and bounded toward them. He snarled when Rocky tried to sink his teeth into his shoulder but was thwarted by the thick fur. Mal sank his teeth into the hyena's front leg. He crunched straight through to the bone, and the sound made Willow wince.

"Oh, God, I'm gonna puke," she said.

Rocky shrieked and danced away on three legs.

Dino launched his body at the wolf. Growling ferociously, Mal hit him mid-air and knocked the hyena to the ground. He pinned him down with his mouth around the hyena's throat and sunk his teeth in until blood trickled out. The hyena squealed in pain and went limp as Mal growled again. After a moment, Mal backed away and shifted to his human form.

"Shift," he snarled.

With submissive whimpers, the two hyenas shifted into their human forms. Dino backed away, holding one hand to his bleeding throat as Rocky clutched his broken and bleeding arm.

"Go. Before I lose all patience and kill you both," Mal said.

The two hyena shifters turned and ran from the alley with a frightened look at each other.

Mal faced Willow. She grinned and wrapped her arms around his naked waist, hugging him and placing a loud kiss against his chest.

"My hero. Thank you, honey."

"This is why you shouldn't be doing this alone," he said heatedly. "Do you know what would have happened to you if I hadn't been here, Willow?"

"What are you doing here, anyway? I didn't ask for your

help with this one."

He didn't reply, and she frowned at him. "Were you following me, Mal?"

"I had to, Willow. Okay?"

"You said you would give me my freedom to help the spirits, remember? You said you would only join me on the ones that I asked you to help me with."

"I know," he said. "But I worry about you, honey. And this is the perfect example of why you shouldn't do this alone."

"How many have you followed me on?" she asked.

When he didn't answer, she poked him lightly on the chest. "You've followed me on all of them, haven't you? Tell me the truth, wolf boy."

"Yes. I can't help it, Willow. You're my mate. I have to protect you."

She squeezed him tightly and smiled at him. "I love you, Malcolm Burke."

"I love you, Willow Blossom Tanner."

She kissed his chest, and he leaned down and placed a soft kiss on her mouth. She parted her lips, and he deepened the kiss, stroking his tongue against hers as she made a soft sound of need.

"Keep making those sweet little noises, and I'm going to take you right here in the alley," he growled into her ear.

She grinned at him before untangling herself from his embrace. "Why, Malcolm Burke, I had no idea you were such an exhibitionist."

She crouched in front of the cardboard box as Mal jogged to where he'd shed his clothes and quickly pulled them on. She plucked the kittens out of the box as they hissed again.

Behind her, Mal growled lightly.

"Pay no attention to the big bad wolf," she said to the

kittens. "He's not nearly as mean as he sounds."

"Willow, tell me you aren't holding a cat in your arms," he said.

"I'm not." She smiled at him over her shoulder before turning around. "I'm holding two cats."

"Ugh," he said as she showed him the two tiny black kittens in her arms.

"Mal, meet Johnny Cash and Dolly Parton."

"You named them?"

"Of course, I named them. They can't go without names. Can you, little cutie-pies?" She made a kissing noise, and the two kittens hissed at her.

"They're a bit scared," she said cheerfully, wincing when one of them sunk its tiny fangs into her arm.

"This is what the ghost needed help with? Kittens? Are you kidding me?" Mal asked.

"Nope. Alma was a homeless lady who lived in this alley. She died of a heart attack two days ago. She asked me to rescue the kittens she found the day before she died."

Willow walked down the alley. "C'mon Johnny and Dolly. We'll get you something to eat and some toys to play with."

"You can't keep them, Willow." Mal followed her.

"Of course, I can't. I'm not allowed to have pets at my apartment," she said.

His sigh of relief turned into a groan when she smiled cheekily at him. "But you, on the other hand, have a perfectly good house that has no pet restrictions at all."

"I'm a wolf, Willow! I can't have cats!"

"Says who?" She grinned again at him. "I have a feeling you're going to get along very well with Johnny and Dolly."

"EXPLAIN TO ME AGAIN WHY I'LL HAVE CATS POOPING IN MY house when they have a backyard to poop in?" Mal grumbled as he followed Willow into the house.

He was loaded down with a plastic litter pan, a large box of litter, and a bag of kitten food. Willow carried a bag of toys and the two kittens in their new crate and gave him a horrified look.

"The kittens can't go outside, Mal! You heard the vet. They're too little. Besides, indoors is best for cats."

"Can you also explain to me why I just sat for nearly two hours in the emergency vet and then paid them three hundred and fifty dollars to have two kittens – who I hate, by the way - vaccinated and dewormed? How many worms will they be getting rid of?"

"Oh hush," Willow said. "Pets cost money, Mal. You have to be prepared for that if you're going to be a responsible cat owner."

"I don't want to be a cat owner!"

"He doesn't mean that," she said to the two kittens. She stuck her finger into the grate and flinched when one of the kittens bit the tip of it.

"Just remember that you still have to pay for their other two sets of vaccinations, rabies -"

"Rabies? They have rabies?"

"No, silly. It's to protect them against rabies." She opened the crate and stepped back. "Plus, you'll have to get them neutered and spayed, so they don't have more kittens."

Mal winced. "I don't feel right taking Johnny's manhood like that."

"Oh, please. He'll be much happier, trust me. Besides, you don't want to add to the pet overpopulation problem we have, do you?"

As she talked, she filled the two newly purchased pet

dishes with food and water and opened the box of kitty litter. She poured some litter into the litter pan and pulled the two kittens from the back of the crate. They hissed and scratched at her hands as she plopped them down in the litter pan.

"This is where you poop, babies," she said.

"This is where you poop?" Mal said. "That doesn't seem like an effective way to potty train."

"That's the brilliance of cats. You don't need to potty train them. They know instinctively," Willow said as the two kittens crawled out of the litter pan and crept under the couch.

"Don't worry. They'll be running around like crazy in no time."

Mal crouched and stared at them. Their eyes glowed, and they hissed at him. He growled in return, and the one on the left arched its back as high as it could and hissed again.

"Don't frighten them, Mal," Willow scolded. "Leave them alone for now. Let them get used to their new environment."

"I had no idea you were such a cat lover," Mal said.

"I love all animals." Willow grinned at him. "And this is why we're taking it slow. Who marries someone without knowing if they like animals or not?"

"I was pretty sure you liked animals." Mal pulled her into his embrace and squeezed her ass. "You sleep with me on a regular basis."

She laughed. "Is that your way of asking me to spend the night?"

"Yes," he said. "Stay the night with me, Willow."

"I don't have any work clothes here."

"I cleared out space in the closet for you a month ago. You know I don't mind having your things here, but you keep refusing," he said.

"I have a toothbrush here."

"Stay with me." He brushed his lips across the curve of her collarbone. "I'll drive you home tomorrow morning before work. You can shower and change, and we'll drive in to work together."

"This will be the third night in a row that I've stayed here." She trembled under his warm touch as he cupped her breast.

"Will it?" He rubbed his thumb over her nipple. "I haven't been keeping track."

She moaned and pressed her petite body against his. "You're making it very difficult to say no."

"Then don't. I want you in my bed with me, Willow." He licked the curve of her ear, smiling happily when she sank into his embrace.

"Fine. But you'll be grumpy when we have to get up extra early tomorrow."

"I won't." He kissed the tip of her nose as her cell phone rang. "I'm not the grumpy morning person, remember?"

"I believe I've mentioned a few times not to talk to me in the morning until I've had at least one cup of coffee." She slapped him on the ass before grabbing her cell phone from her purse and answering it. "Hey, Ginger. What's going on?"

Her face paled. Mal slid a steadying arm around her waist as she gave him a frightened look. "Okay. No, I'll be right there. I'll try calling her parents, but they're on some safari in Africa, and I doubt they'll answer their cell phones. I'll see you soon."

"Willow? What's wrong?" Mal said.

"Ava," Willow said as tears slid down her cheeks. "She was attacked tonight, and she's in the hospital. I have to go, Mal. I'm sorry, I can't stay here tonight."

"I'm coming with you, honey." He grabbed his keys and took her hand, leading her out the door.

CHAPTER 3

When Bishop walked into the office the following day, Mal and Kat, a jaguar shifter and the third partner in their security firm, stood at the reception desk with their backs to him. Willow was missing, and he frowned when Kat said, "She still hasn't woken up?"

Mal shook his head. "Not really. They thought she was starting to wake up at around two this morning. She opened her eyes for a few moments and squeezed Willow's hand, but that was it."

"Shit. Any idea who did this to her? Do they -"

"What's going on?" Bishop asked.

They turned and gave him identical guilty looks. "Morning, Bishop."

"Morning, Mal. Where's Willow?"

"Oh, um, she's not going to be in today."

"Is something wrong?"

"What? No. Why?" Mal gave Kat another one of those oddly guilty looks.

"What's going on? Is Willow okay?" Bishop asked.

"She's fine."

"Who were you talking about?"

"Who was I talking about?"

"That's what I said."

"I was talking about Willow. She won't be in today," Mal said.

"You mentioned that."

"Right. Well, I need to make a phone call." Mal walked toward his office, and Bishop growled at him.

"Tell me what's going on, Mal."

Mal glanced at Kat, who shrugged. "He'll find out sooner or later."

"Listen, don't freak out, but Ava's in the hospital," Mal said.

Bishop's stomach dropped a few feet. "What's wrong with her?"

"She was attacked last night and -"

A roar burst from Bishop's throat, and his grizzly surged forward.

Mal held up his hands. "Calm down, Bishop."

Bishop snarled at him as his clothes tore. Mal said, "If you shift, they won't let you into the hospital to see her."

Bishop stared at the floor, willing his grizzly to chill the fuck out. It retreated after a few tense minutes, and he didn't miss Mal and Kat's looks of relief. Without speaking, Bishop headed for the door of the office. He needed to see Ava before his grizzly lost his mind.

"I'M SORRY, SIR, BUT IF YOU'RE NOT FAMILY, YOU CAN'T GO into the ICU," the silver-haired nurse said frostily. "You're welcome to wait until -"

"I'm her boyfriend," Bishop lied.

"Is that right?" The nurse clearly didn't believe him.

"Yes."

The nurse continued to stare at him, and Bishop tried to rein in his grizzly. It growled and snarled with a frantic need to be free.

Be calm. We'll see her soon.

He tried to smile at the nurse, but it came out as a grimace. Her eyes narrowed, and she said, "I don't think -"

"He's her boyfriend, Greta."

A small and dark-haired nurse stopped beside him. Bishop had no idea who she was, but he could have hugged her.

"I'll take him to her room," the nurse said.

Bishop followed the woman down the quiet hallway. "Thanks."

"You're welcome, Bishop."

"I'm sorry, have we met before?"

"No. My name's Ginger. I'm a friend of Ava's."

"What happened to her?" Bishop asked.

"We don't know. She and Brody were attacked last night on their way to the movies. The people who found her said she passed out just after they got there. She hasn't woken up since."

"Who's Brody?"

"He's another nurse at the hospital." Ginger's voice broke. "He was a nurse. He was dead when the paramedics got there."

"How did he die?"

Ginger wiped at the tears that slid down her face. "He burned to death."

Bishop swore under his breath as he followed Ginger into the last room on the right. Ava laid motionless on the bed, hooked up to beeping machines. His grizzly's soft whimper threatened to spill past his lips.

Willow sat beside the bed, holding Ava's hand. Her usual cheerful face was pale and pinched with worry. "Hi, Bishop."

"Hi, Willow." He pulled a second chair up to the bed and sat down, picking up Ava's hand and rubbing it gently. "How is she?"

"Not very good. She woke up, sort of, around two this morning, but she didn't talk or anything. She just squeezed my hand and closed her eyes again."

Willow made a soft sobbing noise. "The doctor said there isn't any brain swelling or anything like that, but I'm so afraid, Bishop."

"She'll be okay, Willow. She's tough." Bishop studied the bandages on Ava's arms. "What happened to her arms?"

"Burn marks." Willow stroked Ava's forehead. "She was with Brody, and he was burned alive."

"I told him," Ginger said. She stood behind Willow and squeezed her shoulders before kissing the top of her head. "I have to get back to the ER. My break is almost over. Do you want anything? I can bring you a cup of coffee or a sandwich."

Willow shook her head, and Ginger frowned. "You have to eat something, Willow."

"I'm not hungry."

"Okay. Just tell the nurses to call me if you need me." Ginger said.

"Thanks, honey."

"Does she have any family?" Bishop asked as Ginger left the room.

"Her parents and her younger sister are in Africa on a safari. I left a voicemail on their cell phone, but they haven't called me back."

She stroked Ava's face again. "Please wake up, honey. Please."

"She will," Bishop said.

"What if she doesn't?" Willow said. "What if -"

"She will," Bishop said with a conviction he didn't feel.

They sat in silence for nearly an hour. Willow stood and stretched, rubbing her eyes as Bishop studied her.

"Have you been here all night, Will?"

"Yeah."

"Why don't you go home and get some rest? I'll stay with her."

"No, I don't want her to be alone," Willow said.

"She won't be. I won't leave her side."

"Bishop's right, honey. You need to get some sleep." Mal entered the room, and Willow smiled at him.

"I see you made it past the nurse," Mal said to Bishop.

"How did you get the nurse to let you in?" Willow said.

"I said I was her boyfriend."

Another faint smile crossed Willow's lips. "Clever bear."

"She didn't believe me," Bishop said, "but Ginger told her I was Ava's boyfriend."

Willow squeezed Mal's hand. "And you?"

"Ginger told the nurse I was her brother."

"Ava's always wanted a brother," Willow said. She started to cry again, and Mal hugged her gently.

"Let me take you home for a little while. You need sleep and a hot shower, and something to eat. Bishop will stay with her."

"What if she wakes up?" Willow asked.

"I'll call you right away if she does," Bishop said.

Mal took her hand and tugged her to her feet. "Come with me, honey. I'll bring you back this afternoon."

Willow leaned over Ava and kissed her forehead. "I'm just going home for a little bit, honey. Bishop's here with you."

Bishop studied Ava's face. Her freckles stood out even more than they normally did and, after a guilty look at the door, he leaned forward and kissed one pale cheek.

"Wake up, Ava," he whispered into her ear as his grizzly made another unfamiliar whimper.

He'd been sitting with her for nearly five hours, and Ava hadn't woken up or even changed positions. He stroked her long red hair before, with a second guilty look at the door, burying his face in the soft curls. He inhaled deeply, breathing in her sweet scent, before straightening.

She'll wake up soon, he soothed his grizzly. She had to. He couldn't –

He jerked, his hand squeezing Ava's when he realized her eyes were open, and she stared at him.

"Ava? Honey, can you hear me?" He touched her shoulder and squeezed her hand again.

She stared unblinkingly at him. He reached for the call button, but she said, "Bishop?"

"Yeah, honey, it's me."

"Don't call me honey," she said.

He gave her a wide grin of relief. "How do you feel?"

"My head hurts. And my arms." She glanced at the bandages on her arms. "What's wrong with my arms?"

"You were burned, hon – Ava. Do you remember what happened?"

"No," she said with fear in her voice. "I can't remember, Bishop."

"It's okay," he said. "It's okay, Ava."

She took a deep breath and cleared her throat. "I'm thirsty."

"I'll get you some water."

"Ice chips are best."

He pressed the call button and then immediately held her hand again.

She glanced at their linked fingers but didn't say anything as Bishop said, "Willow was here earlier, but we made her go home and get some rest. She was here all night."

Greta entered the room. She smiled at Ava and touched her shoulder. "I'm so glad you're awake."

"Thanks, Greta."

"Thirsty?"

Ava nodded, and Greta left and returned with a plastic cup filled with ice chips. She raised the bed into a sitting position. "Do you feel light-headed?"

"A little."

"That will pass. I'll let the doctor know you're awake. She'll be in soon, okay?"

As Greta left the room, Ava took a few ice chips before staring at Bishop. "You were sniffing me again."

He blushed furiously. "I'm sorry."

She closed her eyes, and he stroked the top of her hand with his thumb. After a few moments, she said, "We were in an alley, I think."

He squeezed her hand, and she opened her eyes and stared up at the ceiling. "We'd finished dinner, but we were late for the movie." She hesitated. "I think. It's so hazy."

"It'll come back to you. Maybe you should just rest for now," Bishop said.

"Brody wanted to take a shortcut through the alley, and so we did. It smelled bad."

He ignored the way his grizzly growled with jealousy over a dead man. "Don't think about it for now, okay?"

She ignored him, her brow furrowed in concentration. "We were almost at the end of the alley when a patient, Mr.

Chambers, showed up. He was acting weird and insulted Brody and told him he wasn't good enough for me. Brody got so angry and then…."

Her frown deepened, and he squeezed her hand a little tighter. "Ava, honey, don't -"

"Oh my God." She stared at him in sick horror. "Brody, he – he's dead. He died in front of me. He was burning, and I could smell his flesh, and I -"

She broke off into choked sobs. Bishop jumped out of the chair and sat beside her on the bed. He gathered her into his arms. She stiffened and then relaxed in his embrace, crying quietly as he stroked her back with his warm hands.

After a few minutes, she took a wavering breath and wiped at the tears on her face. "I can't believe Brody is dead."

"I'm sorry about your boyfriend," he said.

"He wasn't my boyfriend," she said. "He was my friend, a good friend, and now he's dead because of me."

She broke into harsh sobs, her body shaking. Bishop repeatedly kissed the top of her head as he rocked her. "It's not your fault, honey."

"It is," she said. "Brody's dead because of me."

"No, that's not true. Don't think that way." He rubbed her lower back, trying to stop her shaking.

She continued to sob, and he held her closer. His grizzly had retreated, completely unarmed by Ava's crying. Bishop tried his best to comfort her. "Honey, you can't -"

"Ava?" Willow and Mal entered the room, and Willow ran to the bed.

"Oh, honey." She climbed onto the bed. Ava pulled away from Bishop and clung to Willow.

"Shh, honey. Shh." Willow stroked Ava's hair and kissed her forehead. "It's okay."

"Brody's dead, Willow," Ava said.

"I know, sweetheart. I'm so sorry."

"It's my fault."

Willow wiped at the tears on Ava's face. "Why do you say that?"

"Mr. Chambers killed Brody because he thought we were dating."

"Who's Mr. Chambers?" Willow asked.

"He's a patient. He comes in all the time for nothing. Ginger said he had a crush on me, but I didn't believe her. Only, I guess he does. He said I was his destiny and that he'd fill my belly with his children."

Bishop growled as Willow stroked Ava's hair. "It'll be okay, honey."

"He was a shifter," Ava said.

"What kind of shifter?"

"I think he was a dragon." She shuddered all over as Mal stared at Bishop in surprise.

Willow glanced at Mal. "You never told me there were dragon shifters."

Mal cleared his throat. "Dragon shifters exist, but they don't reveal themselves to humans."

"Why not?" Willow asked.

"They're one of the few shifters who decided not to reveal themselves to humans. There aren't very many of them, and they tend to keep to their own kind."

"Are they afraid that the humans would hunt them?" Willow asked.

Mal shook his head. "No, honey. Dragon shifters are the most powerful shifters. It's extremely difficult to kill one."

"So then why are they in hiding?"

"They believe that humans will try to hunt them, and if they do...."

"The dragons would destroy the human race, Willow," Bishop said.

"What?" Willow blinked in surprise. "But you said there weren't very many of them."

"There aren't, but they're so powerful, Willow. Humans have no idea how lucky they are that dragon shifters decided to stay hidden. In fact," Mal glanced at Bishop, "most shifters believe they are extinct."

"But they aren't," Willow said.

"No." He glanced at Bishop again. "But there's no way that a dragon shifter would reveal itself to a human. Ever. What Ava saw, it had to be something else."

"He breathed fire," Ava said. "He burned Brody by breathing fire on him, Mal. He told me that I was his bride and when I disagreed, he picked me up and threw me into the brick wall like I weighed nothing. His hands burned my skin. He started to shift, and there were scales."

"You hit your head pretty hard, Ava," Bishop said.

"I know what I saw," Ava said.

"It's impossible, honey," he said. "He's something else."

"Like what?" Willow frowned. "What else has scales and breathes fire in the shifter world?"

"It could have been a darthen lizard," Mal said thoughtfully.

"A what?"

"A darthen lizard," he repeated. "They're a type of lizard that, if provoked, can breathe a small amount of flame."

"This wasn't a small amount," Ava said. "He completely engulfed Brody in flames."

She closed her eyes, and Willow squeezed her arm. "It's okay, honey." She glanced at Mal. "I've never heard of a darthen lizard."

"They're pretty rare, and, like dragons, they keep to themselves."

"Are they violent?" Willow asked.

"No, but there are always exceptions."

"Can they fly?" Ava asked. "Can darthen lizards sprout wings and fly away because Mr. Chambers did."

Mal shook his head. "No, they can't fly."

"The real issue is what Ava's going to tell the police," Bishop said. "They won't believe you if you say it's a dragon."

"There are shifters on the police force," Ava said.

"Yes, but again – most shifters believe that dragons are extinct," Mal said.

"Why don't you two?" Willow asked.

Mal glanced at Bishop, who nodded. Mal checked the door to the room before saying, "Bishop knows one."

"Oh. Well, you can talk to him then and find out if there are any, like, rogue dragons flying around," Willow said. "Then we'll know for sure that -"

"No, I can't speak with her about this," Bishop said. "Not unless we're absolutely certain it is a dragon."

"It was," Ava insisted wearily. "Why won't you believe me?" She pulled away when Bishop tried to take her hand.

His grizzly whimpered with misery as Mal said, "You hit your head pretty hard, Ava, and your friend died in front of you. Panic and pain can mess with a person's mind."

"I know what I saw," Ava said. "Would you mind leaving? I'm exhausted."

"We still need to talk about what you're going to say to the police," Bishop said. "If you say it's a dragon, if you even give the humans an idea that they exist, then -"

"I won't say anything," Ava said. "I'll tell them I don't

remember anything that happened. I have a head injury. They'll believe me."

"Are you sure that's -"

"Bishop, you and Mal should go. Ava needs to rest," Willow said.

"I'll stay with her," Bishop said. "She shouldn't be alone."

"She won't be," Willow said. "I'll stay with her."

"I think I should stay." Bishop frowned. "What if this Chambers guy comes back and -"

"I don't need a babysitter," Ava said. "You should leave, Bishop."

The coldness in her tone made his grizzly let out an undignified whimper. "I just want to keep you safe, Ava."

"That isn't your responsibility." She closed her eyes and turned to her side.

Bishop reached to touch her, but Mal shook his head and took his arm. "C'mon, Bishop. We need to get back to the office."

He led Bishop toward the door as Willow trailed after them. Mal kissed her lightly on the mouth. "I'll come back in a few hours."

AVA STARED AT THE WALL, IGNORING HER URGE TO GLANCE AT Bishop as he left. Willow sat down in the chair next to the bed. "Ava? Honey, are you okay?"

"He thinks I'm lying," Ava said. "I haven't spoken to him for nearly two months, and then I wake up in the hospital to find him holding my hand and sniffing my hair. He called me honey and held me while I cried, and then he called me a liar to my face."

Willow stroked her arm. "I'm sorry, Ava. Bishop means well, but I think he's confused about his feelings for you and -"

"He doesn't have any feelings for me," Ava said. "He wants to have sex with me, and that's it."

Willow winced. "You're wrong, Ava."

"I'm not. I told Bishop specifically that unless he wanted to date me, to stay away from me. And he has."

"He was worried about you. He sat with you all day today and -"

"I don't care," Ava lied. "Even if he does feel something more for me than lust, he thinks I'm a liar. I don't want to be with someone who doesn't believe me."

"He doesn't think you're a liar," Willow said. "It's just – Bishop and Mal, they're not like us, honey. They have a hard time believing in things they can't see, touch, or feel. And if dragon shifters don't reveal themselves to humans, I can see why they think you were confused."

"Do you believe me?" Ava asked.

"Of course, I do," Willow said. "If you say you saw a dragon, then you did."

"Thank you, Will." Ava stared silently at the ceiling for a moment. "Brody has a sister who lives here in the city. Do you know if anyone has spoken to her? They were super close, and I know she...."

She squeezed her eyes shut to stop the tears as Willow rubbed her hip and said, "I'm sure they have, but I can find out for you."

"Thanks," Ava murmured as a woman wearing a white lab coat entered the room. She took the chart from the holder at the end of the bed and looked it over before smiling at Ava.

"Hello, Ava."

Ava opened her eyes. "Hey, Dr. Alvez. How are you?"

"Better than you," she said with a cheerful smile. "How are you feeling?"

"Tired."

"I bet you are. Let's have a look at you." Dr. Alvez smiled at her. "We need you better and back in the ER. The place is falling apart without you."

CHAPTER 4

Bishop parked his truck in the driveway and stared at the tiny house. The front yard needed mowing. A wave of guilt washed over him. She would be angry with him for missing his visit last week. Of course, she was always mad at him, so what difference did it make?

He rubbed at his forehead, willing himself to get out of the truck and go into the house. He didn't want to. He wanted to go back to the hospital and force the nurses to let him see Ava. He winced and rubbed at his head again. It didn't matter if he could convince the nurses to let him visit - it was Ava who didn't want him there.

He clenched the steering wheel tightly in his large hands. He'd returned to the hospital last night after work, but the silver-haired nurse informed him that she knew he wasn't Ava's boyfriend. He'd glared at her, and a soft growl slipped out before he could stop it. The nurse was surprisingly unafraid. She'd threatened to call security before informing him that Ava had requested no visitors and specifically instructed her not to let Bishop visit. His grizzly had snarled angrily, and it was all he could do to control it and leave the hospital without tearing the place apart.

Now, he forced himself to leave his truck and enter the small house. It was dark and musty, and he navigated around the stacks of books that littered the front hallway.

"Mom? Are you home?"

"Where else would I be?" she called irritably.

He entered the kitchen and smiled tentatively. "Hi."

"You missed your visit last week. Too busy fucking around, I suppose," she said. She was cleaning the kitchen sink, and he watched her arms flex as she scrubbed at it. She might be old, but she was still powerful, and he felt that familiar combination of anxiety and anger as she glared over her shoulder at him. "Well, were you?"

"No, Mom." He dropped into the kitchen chair. It was solidly built and didn't make a sound as his bulk hit it. He tried to smile at her. "Just really busy at work."

"How many times have I told you not to call me mom?" She turned back to the sink. "You know I hate it."

"Sorry," he said automatically.

"The grass is way too long," she said. "And most of the leaves have fallen, which means it'll have to be raked before it can be mowed."

"That's fine. I'll do both tonight."

"It's bad enough that you only visit once a week." She added another squirt of cleaner to the rag and scrubbed compulsively. "Now I have to do all the outside chores as well?"

"No, of course not."

"Don't get lippy with me." She turned and pointed her finger at him. "I wasted the best years of my life raising you, and this is the attitude I get in return? Did you know that Alice Peterson's son bought a house with a suite in the basement so she could live with him? It's obvious that he loves his mother and worries about her. You couldn't give a shit about me. Visit once a week, barely say a damn word, and now you won't even help out around the house. What kind of son are you? Do you even care that I -"

"I said I would do it." Bishop stood up so quickly that the heavy chair toppled over, "and if you want to live with me, you're more than welcome. I have a second bedroom."

"You'd like that, wouldn't you? Your own personal slave to cook your meals and clean your goddamn toilets. Do you think I'm stupid?"

"No, *Leslie*, I don't think you're stupid, but I'm tired of you accusing me of being a bad son. I love you, and I only want what's best for you."

"What do you know about love?" she said. "The apple doesn't fall far from the tree, does it?"

"I am not like my father," Bishop said as his stomach churned.

"No? Then you've settled down, gotten mated and just haven't told your own damn mother about it?"

"I told you, I'm not interested in mating with someone," he said. "I thought that would make you happy. If I don't mate with someone, then I'll never leave them and destroy their life as my father destroyed yours."

"It wasn't your father who destroyed my life," she said.

"Mom, I -"

"Don't call me that!" She screeched as her body swelled and thick fur grew on her cheeks.

Despite how much larger he was, fear twisted through him. His grizzly made a soft snarl and retreated.

"I'm sorry, Leslie. Listen, I'll start the yard work now, okay? As soon as I'm done, I'll make us dinner, and we can have a nice visit."

"Whatever," she muttered before turning away and staring out the window. "Make sure you rake all the leaves before you mow."

"I will."

He trudged outside and waved to the neighbour as he wheeled the lawnmower out of the garage, then grabbed the rake. He raked at the leaves, ignoring his desire to just get in the truck and drive away.

WILLOW STARED WORRIEDLY AT AVA AS SHE HELPED HER INTO her t-shirt. "Are you sure you should leave?"

"Yes. Dr. Alvez cleared me to go this morning," Ava said.

"You just woke up yesterday. What if you have a fractured skull or something?" Willow said.

"I don't. They did a CT scan, and everything was normal. I want to go home, Willow."

"I know, honey, but -"

There was a knock on the door. Willow drew back the curtain to see a dark-haired man standing in the doorway. "Ava Lewis?"

"Yes?"

"My name is Detective Matthews. May I come in?"

"Oh, of course." Ava glanced at Willow as she sat on the side of the hospital bed. Willow perched beside her, and the detective sat in the chair next to the bed.

"How are you feeling, Ms. Lewis?"

"Better. I'm on my way home."

"Good." Detective Matthews said. "Would you mind answering a couple of questions before you go?"

"No, but there were a couple of police officers here yesterday, and I told them everything I could remember."

"I know," he said. "But I'm the detective working on Mr. Miller's murder, and I had a few follow-up questions."

"Okay," Ava said.

"You look awfully young to be a detective." Willow smiled brightly at him.

He grinned. "I'm older than I look. And you are?"

"Willow Tanner. Ava's best friend." Willow held out her hand, and he shook it firmly.

"You have an amazing aura. Did you know that, Detective Matthews?" Willow asked.

"It's not the first time I've been told that."

"Really?" Willow asked.

"No, not really."

Willow laughed as the detective pulled out his phone and glanced at the screen. "So, you and Mr. Miller had just finished dinner and were headed to the theatre. Is that right?"

"Yes." Ava willed her hands not to shake.

"How long have you and Mr. Miller been dating?"

"We weren't. We were just friends," Ava said.

"Do you know if Mr. Miller was dating anyone?"

"I don't think so. He and his boyfriend broke up a few months ago. Why?"

"Just wondering if that might have anything to do with it," the detective said.

"It didn't. Mr. Chambers killed Brody because of me," Ava said.

Detective Matthews consulted his phone again. "You knew Mr. Chambers through the hospital, is that correct?"

"Yes. He was a patient here a few times."

"More than a few times," Detective Matthews said. "He's been making weekly visits to the ER for the last three months."

Ava nodded. "He came in a lot."

"And was it always during your shift?"

"I guess. I mean, I know I saw him every week."

"How did he know your schedule?"

"I don't know," Ava said. "I guess I just thought it was a coincidence."

"You've never dated Mr. Chambers?"

"No. I... he wasn't my type."

"You were cutting through an alley when Mr. Chambers appeared, correct?"

"Yes." Ava clutched Willow's hand as the detective gave her a sympathetic look.

"I know this is difficult, Ms. Lewis, but I appreciate your cooperation," he said. He glanced at his phone again. "Mr. Chambers said that Brody didn't deserve you. That you were his destiny?"

"Yes," she said.

"Brody told him to get lost, Mr. Chambers got angry, and then?"

"Then I can't remember," Ava said. She squeezed Willow's hand, and Willow squeezed back reassuringly.

"You can't remember anything. Nothing at all?" The detective asked. He had clear, light blue eyes, and Ava flushed before glancing at the floor. She hated lying, and, unlike the police officers from yesterday, she had a feeling that Detective Matthews could see right through her flimsy attempt.

"That's right."

"So, you aren't sure how Mr. Chambers set Brody on fire or how your arms were burnt?"

"No."

"Witnesses said that you were awake when they found you. That you spoke to them and asked for help."

"I don't remember that." Ava cleared her throat.

"Do you remember seeing anything in Mr. Chambers' hands? A can of gasoline perhaps or a bottle of lighter fluid?"

"No."

"I'm not surprised. There was nothing left of Mr. Miller but a pile of ash. Even his bones burned, Ms. Lewis. It would take a lot more than gasoline or lighter fluid to do that."

Ava didn't reply, and the detective glanced at the bandages. "Did you receive the burns trying to help Mr. Miller?"

"I don't remember," Ava repeated.

"You remember nothing after Mr. Chambers showed up in the alley?"

"That's right," Ava said. Her stomach felt like it'd been put through the spin cycle of a washing machine.

Willow put her arm around Ava. "Is that everything, Detective Matthews? I really should get Ava home."

Detective Matthews stood up. "Yes, that's good for now."

"I'm sorry I couldn't be of more help," Ava said.

There was an awkward silence before Willow said, "So you haven't found Mr. Chambers yet, I'm assuming?"

"No. We went to his apartment, and most of his personal belongings were gone," Detective Matthews said. "I understand you've turned down the police protection offered to you."

She nodded, and he said, "Probably not wise, Ms. Lewis. I'm not trying to frighten you, but there's the possibility that Sean Chambers will go after you again."

"I work for a personal security company," Willow said. "We already have some of our people watching her apartment, and we'll keep her safe."

The detective nodded but didn't say anything. He studied Ava carefully for a moment, his eyes roaming over her hair before he said, "Thank you for your time, Ms. Lewis. Could I get your phone number before I leave?"

Ava blinked at him. "My phone number?"

"In case I need to ask some more questions later. I could take you for a coffee when you're feeling better. Maybe you'll remember more once you've recovered," he said.

"Oh, right. Of course." Ava recited her phone number, and he added it to his phone.

"I'll be in touch soon, Ms. Lewis."

"Goodbye, Detective."

He left the room, and Willow let out her breath. "Woo, he is handsome."

"What?" Ava said distractedly as she slipped into her shoes.

"Detective Matthews is hot, Ava. Don't tell me you didn't notice the way he was eyeing you up."

"He wasn't," Ava said.

"The man took your phone number."

"As part of his investigation, Willow," Ava said.

"Right. I've never had a detective tell me he wanted to take me for coffee," Willow said.

"Xavier did."

Willow rolled her eyes. "One, Xavier flunked out of the police academy and two, he made me coffee at his place right before we had a two-day sex marathon. I think Detective Matthews is interested in you."

Ava just shrugged and headed toward the door. "Let's go, Willow. I really want to be home."

CHAPTER 5

"Kat's late again," Bishop grumbled as he stepped into Mal's office.

"She'll be here." Mal didn't look up from his computer screen.

"She'd better be. I'm not getting stuck with doing the interviews like I did the last time."

Mal shrugged. "You did fine. Willow agreed to work for us, didn't she?"

"All I'm saying is that we need to talk to Kat about her habit of strolling in late every morning," Bishop said.

Mal finally looked up from his computer. "What's going on with you, Bishop? Since when did you start caring about Kat's punctuality? Hell, half the time, you're later than she is."

Bishop sat down in the chair with a heavy thud before rubbing at his temple. "Sorry, Mal. I have a bad headache."

"You look like shit. Did you get any sleep?"

"Not really. I went to see Leslie last night."

"Ugh," Mal said. "That's a guaranteed bad night."

"It was uglier than usual because I missed last week's visit."

Mal frowned. "You should just stop going over there, Bishop. It's not good for you."

"She's my mother, Mal. I can't just abandon her no matter how terrible she was as a parent."

"She was beyond terrible," Mal said. "Besides, if it's a mother figure you're craving, you know my mom thinks of you as her kid. You don't need Leslie and her nastiness."

"She's still my mom." Bishop stared at his hands before clearing his throat. "How's Ava doing?"

"Better. She went home from the hospital yesterday. Willow stayed the night with her and will be in shortly. I told her to take another day off, but she knows we'll be busy with the interviews."

"Who do we have watching Ava?" Bishop asked.

"Right now, it's Garth. He's posted outside her apartment. Fenton's going over there later this afternoon."

"I can take a couple of shifts."

"Not a good idea."

"Why not?" Bishop asked.

"You know why. You can't concentrate when you're around Ava."

"Yes, I can," Bishop said with a scowl.

"No, you can't. And besides," Mal's voice softened slightly, "Ava doesn't want you there."

Bishop swallowed down his pride. "I know, but we don't have to tell her. Please, Mal, I can't just sit around knowing that she's in danger."

"I know, buddy. But lying to Ava isn't the solution." Mal hesitated. "Why don't you just ask her out, Bishop? You've been miserable the last two months."

"I can't," Bishop said. "You know I can't."

"You're not like your father. I don't care what your mother says – you aren't."

"You don't know that for sure," Bishop said. "What if I hurt Ava the way my dad hurt my mom? What if Ava becomes like her? I would never forgive myself."

"You're not like him," Mal repeated. "Don't let her poison you that way."

"It doesn't matter. I just want to sleep with Ava and nothing else."

"Bullshit," Mal said bluntly. "You can lie to Willow and Ava all you want, Bishop, but don't lie to me."

"I don't want to hurt her, Mal," Bishop said.

"I know."

KAT GLANCED AT HER WATCH IMPATIENTLY. THE MAN IN front of her was a shifter and based on the way he moved, he was a sloth shifter. She stifled a sigh of frustration as the man scanned the board in front of him.

"I think," he spoke slowly, "I'll try a mocha today."

"Is that everything?" The barista wasn't doing a great job of hiding her own frustration.

Kat couldn't blame her. The line for coffee snaked out the front door, and she could hear the low grumbling of people behind her.

"Do you have any of those, oh, what do you call them, oat bars?" the man said thoughtfully.

"Yes, sir. That will be -"

"Hold on, now." I need to make sure I have enough cash." The man reached behind him for his wallet. He moved at roughly the speed of a snail. He jerked in surprise when Kat tugged his wallet from his back pocket and practically shoved it into his hand.

"Here you go!" she said with forced cheerfulness as the barista stared gratefully at her.

"Thank you." The man's watery eyes perused her chest through her silk shirt. She rolled her eyes, wishing she hadn't left her jacket in the car.

"You bet." She tapped her foot impatiently as he turned to the barista and counted out his money.

"Good God," she muttered under her breath before yanking her cell phone from her purse. Quickly she texted Mal and Bishop. Their first interview was in five minutes, and she was nearly ten minutes away. If the sloth in front of her didn't hurry up, she'd miss the whole damn thing.

"Next."

She hissed when a man darted in front of her and placed a quick order for coffee.

"Hey!" She poked him in the back. "No butsies."

"Did you just say butsies?" The man turned around, and Kat's breath caught in her throat. He was, quite simply put, gorgeous with short, reddish-brown hair and bright green eyes. He was smooth-shaven, and she studied the small silver hoop in his eyebrow before dropping her gaze to his mouth. He had nice lips, and her cat made an undignified purr when he grinned and revealed a deep dimple in his left cheek.

She took a glance at his body. Although not by much, he was taller than her, and he had the lean build of a swimmer. He wore jeans and a short-sleeve golf shirt that revealed muscular arms. Her heart beat a little faster. She had two weaknesses – dimples and tattoos - and the man standing in front of her was covered in tattoos. At least, she thought he was. Both arms were covered in tattoos, and she was confident the rest of his body would be too.

Why don't we find out? Her cat purred loudly as the man's grin widened.

"See something you like, Kitten?"

She jerked her head up and glared at him. "You butted in line."

"So, I did. But you look like one of those fancy coffee type of girls, and I just need a plain old, black coffee."

He handed the barista some cash and smiled at her as she passed him the steaming cup of coffee. The barista smiled weakly in return, Kat could almost see her drooling, and he winked at her before taking a sip.

"Delicious. Thanks, sweetheart."

"You bet," the barista said faintly.

He turned back to Kat and raked his gaze up and down her body in a shameless display of interest. She glared at him as her cat sat up and made a soft, pleased meow.

Knock it off! she snarled. *He's a bird shifter! Have some pride, for God's sake.*

"Sorry, Kitten. I'm in a bit of a hurry this morning," he said before heading past her.

"Asshole!" she shouted after him.

He raised his coffee in acknowledgment, and she tore her gaze from his ass before nearly snarling her order at the barista. The girl made a frightened squeak, and Kat mumbled an apology. This day couldn't get any fucking worse.

"I KNOW, I KNOW. I'M LATE." KAT SHOVED THE OFFICE DOOR open with her hip. She juggled her purse, her laptop case, and her cup of coffee, and she swore loudly when coffee surged out of the hole in the lid and splashed onto her shirt.

"Fuck!" she repeated as Willow hurried around the desk.

"Here, let me help." She took Kat's coffee and set it on the reception desk as Kat dropped her bags and hurried to the kitchenette.

"Do we have any soda water?" Kat called as she opened the cupboards.

"Top left cupboard." Willow ducked around her and, standing on her tiptoes, snagged the soda water. "Hold still."

"Thanks, Will. Is the first interviewee here?"

"Yes. Bishop and Mal are with him." She dabbed at the spots of coffee on Kat's shirt.

"I've had the worst morning," Kat grumbled. "First I'm running late, and then this asshole with a dimple and tattoos and a disgustingly great ass, butted in line in front of me at the coffee shop and -"

Willow jerked in surprise, splashing Kat's face with soda water. Kat wiped it away impatiently. "What?"

Willow looked to her right, and Kat followed her gaze. The asshole sat in one of the chairs in the small sitting area, drinking his coffee and grinning at her.

"Good morning again," he said politely.

"What are you doing here?" Kat said.

"He's here for an interview," Willow said. "Ronin Smith, this is one of our partners, Katarina Frost."

"Nice to meet you, Mrs. Frost."

"It's Ms. Frost." She glared at him. "I bet you're regretting butting in line now, aren't you?"

He laughed. "You don't seem like the type of woman who would deny a man a job just because he occasionally plays the butsies game."

Willow snorted laughter. Kat hissed under her breath

before snatching the dishtowel from her and blotting at her shirt. "Are they in Mal's office or Bishop's?"

"They're in the conference room. Mr. Taslen is an elephant shifter and, uh, pretty large."

"Thanks." She snagged her coffee from the reception desk and, ignoring Ronin's stare, stalked past him and slipped into the conference room.

"Mr. Smith? Nice to meet you. I'm Malcolm Burke." Mal shook Ronin's hand. "These are my associates, Mr. Bishop King and Ms. Katarina Frost."

"It's nice to meet you." Ronin shook Bishop's hand and then Kat's. He held on to it a little longer than necessary, and she glared at him before tugging her hand free.

Kat didn't miss the way Mal glanced at Bishop as Ronin sat down across from Kat.

"Mr. Smith, it says you worked for the New York police department for ten years." Kat stared at his resume.

"That's correct."

"Why did you leave?" she asked.

"I was looking for something different."

"Indeed." She arched her eyebrow at him. "You moved to Hawaii and taught scuba diving for three years."

"I did."

"Why did you move here?" Mal asked.

"I grew up here. Well, in a small town just outside of the city. Mavenburg, have you heard of it?"

"Yes." Mal nodded. "My father's from there."

"It's a nice place."

"Why didn't you move back to your hometown then?" If

Kat's jaguar didn't knock it off with the purring, she'd strangle it.

"Not enough excitement for me," he said with a grin.

"You're a bird shifter, is that correct?" Kat sniffed the air delicately.

"I am. That's a pretty good sense of smell you have, Ms. Frost."

"What kind of bird?"

"Oh, a little of this, a little of that," he said. "I'm kind of the mutt of the bird world."

She didn't reply, and Mal cleared his throat after a moment. "So, let me tell you what we do. We provide personal security, mostly for shifters but the occasional human as well, and we've recently started providing security for corporations. We've been asked to take on a few more corporate clients, and we're short-staffed as it is."

He glanced at Bishop and Kat. "The job isn't super excit-ing, but the work is steady, and we offer competitive pay. You'll mostly be providing security for a few office buildings downtown, and there may be the occasional private security gig we'll need you to do. The hours can be odd from time to time. We have a vampire client at the moment whose daughter is a bit of a wild child. If you're assigned to keep an eye on her, you'll be working a night shift."

"That's fine with me."

"Do you have a licence to carry?"

"I do. Will I need a gun?" Ronin asked.

"Not normally, but there may be some jobs that require it." Mal glanced at Bishop again. "We have a human client right now who is having some trouble with a shifter. If we ask you to take a shift watching her, it may be a good idea to carry a weapon."

"What kind of shifter?" Ronin asked.

Mal hesitated. "We're not certain yet. But we know he's dangerous and obsessed with our client."

"Okay."

Mal nudged Kat under the table. She glanced at him before giving Ronin a stiff smile. "I think that's everything, Mr. Smith. Thank you for your time. We'll be in touch."

She stood and held out her hand. Ronin shook it briefly and then shook Mal's and Bishop's.

"It was nice to meet you. I hope to hear from you soon," he said politely and left the conference room.

When the door shut behind him, Mal scowled at Kat. "What the hell, Kat?"

"What?" she said innocently.

"The interview lasted less than five minutes. We didn't even ask Ronin about his hand-to-hand combat skills or," he scanned his resume, "the fact that he knows kung-fu."

"He knows kung-fu?" Bishop studied his resume. "Damn, he does."

"Who cares?" Kat said. "He's an arrogant asshole and hardly our best candidate."

"Actually, I kind of think he is," Bishop said.

"He's a bird shifter," Kat said. "How tough can he be?"

"Just because you hate birds doesn't mean we shouldn't hire him," Bishop said.

"My hatred for birds has nothing to do with why I don't want him working for us," Kat said.

"No? Then why don't you?" Mal asked.

"Because he butted in line in front of me at the coffee shop this morning, and he's an arrogant asshole who'll end up being more trouble than he's worth. And he called me kitten," she said.

"Kitten?" Bishop laughed, and Kat hissed at him.

"It's not funny, Bishop."

"It's a little funny," Mal said. "I vote we hire him."

"Me too," Bishop said.

"No," Kat said.

Ignoring the way her fingernails lengthened into claws, Mal said, "Two against one, Kat. Sorry."

She hissed again and left the conference room, ignoring her jaguar's happy trills.

CHAPTER 6

Ava stared out the window of her apartment as the sun slowly set. On the street below, she could see the plain grey car that Fenton was sitting in. Garth had brought the cheetah shifter to her apartment around five to introduce him. She raised her hand in a tentative wave, and the cheetah shifter waved back. Her cell buzzed, and she read the text from Fenton.

Everything okay?

Yes. Thanks.

She set her phone down and wandered through her small apartment. Her arms throbbed dully, and she stared at the redness on her skin. She'd gotten lucky. Only a small section on her left arm had blistered. She touched it delicately before sitting on the sofa. She was drained and feeling blue.

She'd called Brody's sister earlier. There was a memorial service for him the day after tomorrow. His sister had steadily cried while they talked and Ava, guilt coursing through her and tears streaming down her cheeks, tried to comfort her as best she could.

She closed her eyes and rubbed delicately at her eyelids.

She'd had terrible nightmares, ones where she was burned alive with Brody, and she had woken Willow up around three by screaming in her sleep.

It frightened Willow badly, and she tried to convince Ava to let her stay with her tonight, but Ava insisted she would be fine. She pressed her lips together to stop them from trembling. Truthfully, she was terrified to go to sleep, but she couldn't let Willow babysit her forever.

Her cell rang, and she studied the unknown number before answering it.

"Hi, Ava. It's Bishop."

"Hello." Butterflies swarmed to life in her stomach.

"How are you?"

"Fine."

"Good. Um, I asked Willow for your number. I just wanted to call and see how you were doing and to, uh, give you my cell number so that if you needed anything, you could call me."

"I'm fine, but thank you," she said.

"Do you need me to bring you anything? Supper or, uh, groceries?"

"No. I'm good."

"Is Fenton there?"

"Yes. He's outside," she said.

"Well, you don't need to worry, okay? Fenton is one of our best, and he'll call me if there's anything suspicious," Bishop said.

"Okay," she said.

"Okay, well, I guess I'd better go. Just call me or text me if you need me. Any time of the day or night."

"Yes, thank you, Bishop."

"You're welcome. Bye, Ava."

"Bye, Bishop."

She ended the call. Her inner voice screamed at her to call Bishop back and ask him to come over. She tossed her phone on the couch beside her. She hated that she was afraid to sleep, hated that she was scared even to leave her apartment, but asking Bishop to come over wasn't a good idea. She would have a bite to eat and then a hot bath. It would help her sleep. She stood and headed toward the kitchen.

BISHOP STARED AT THE CEILING OF HIS BEDROOM. IT WAS close to eleven, and normally he would have been asleep long before now. He needed lots of sleep, all grizzly shifters did, and until tonight he'd never had insomnia. He rubbed Princess's head when she butted it against his arm. She purred and settled on his chest. She closed her eyes, and he felt a moment of bitterness at her ability to fall asleep so easily.

His cell phone buzzed, and he reached for it, nearly knocking the clock off the nightstand. He stared at the number, his heart banging against his ribcage like an overenthusiastic door-to-door salesman. "Ava? Honey, what's wrong?"

"I... nothing." Her low voice sent shivers down his spine. "I'm sorry. It's late, and I shouldn't have called. Goodnight, Bishop."

"Wait!" He sat up in the bed. "I wasn't sleeping."

There was silence on the other end, and he climbed out of the bed when he heard her soft sob. "Honey, tell me what's wrong, please."

"I'm afraid," she said. "I'm afraid to go to sleep, and I'm so tired."

"I'll be right over." He pulled his jeans on as she made a soft hiccupping noise.

"No, I can't ask you to do that, Bishop. I'm sorry. I'm okay, really."

"I'm coming over, Ava," he said. "I'll see you in twenty minutes." He ended the call before she could reply. He yanked his t-shirt over his head and grabbed his truck keys. He made one stop in the kitchen before hurrying out of the house.

He made it to her house in fifteen minutes. Fenton stuck his head out his car window when Bishop strode by him. "Boss? What's wrong?"

"Nothing," Bishop said. "Everything's fine. Has it been quiet?"

"Yup. Nothing so far. Of course, it would help if I knew exactly what type of shifter I was looking for."

"We're not sure. You've got his human description. Just keep an eye out for anything suspicious and text me, okay?"

"You got it. Goodnight, boss."

"Night, Fenton."

He took the elevator up to the seventh floor and walked to her apartment. He knocked and waited patiently. He heard her soft footsteps, and he could smell her embarrassment when she opened the door.

"Hi, Bishop."

"Hi, Ava."

She moved back, and he stepped inside her apartment, staring worriedly at her as he removed his boots. She wore a pale green robe, and her hands fidgeted with the collar. Her face was pale, and she had dark circles under her eyes. Even her hair seemed muted from its usual fiery tone.

"You okay?"

"Yeah, I'm sorry," she said. "I shouldn't have called you."

"I'm glad you did." He followed her into the kitchen. "Sit down, and I'll make you something that will help you sleep."

"What?"

He smiled. "I can't tell you. It's a family secret."

He searched through her cupboards, pulled out a tin of hot chocolate, and set it on the counter. He found a pot and added milk before putting it on the stove. He took a small amber bottle from his pocket and placed it on the counter.

"Hot chocolate?" Ava said with a small smile. "That's your family secret?"

"It's so much more than that." He grinned at her as he took another look through her cupboards and pulled out various bottles from her baking section. She leaned left to peer around him.

"No peeking," he said, "or I'll make you wait in the living room."

She smiled and pulled self-consciously at the edge of her robe as he sat down across from her.

"You have a nice place."

"You've seen the hallway and the kitchen," she said.

"It's nice. I like the kitchen. It's pretty big for an apartment."

"Do you like to cook?"

"I love it. Most grizzlies do. We really like food."

"Yeah, I've noticed. Not to be rude, but Willow says you eat more than anyone she knows."

He patted his flat stomach. "I need to keep up my strength."

She laughed. "Right. It bugs me that you can eat so much and stay in shape."

He shrugged. "I have to be careful, to be honest. Especially in the winter. Grizzlies can gain fifty pounds easily during our hibernation period."

"I thought you didn't hibernate," she said. "At least that's what Willow says."

"Technically, I don't." He stood and stirred the milk. "I usually work a few hours a day during the hibernation period. I go to bed around seven at night and get up about noon, work for a few hours, eat, and go back to bed."

"That sounds really nice," she said. "I love sleeping. Maybe I have some grizzly in me."

Ask her if she wants a little more grizzly in her, his bear whispered.

Can it, you idiot!

"Nah, grizzlies don't have red hair and freckles." He grinned at her as he pulled a mug from the cupboard and stirred the milk again. "Sleep really is the best, though. A cold room with plenty of blankets to burrow under and a firm mattress and soft pillows. I have light-blocking blinds in my bedroom and a white noise machine to drown out any noise. It's my little piece of heaven."

"It sounds really nice," she repeated. She smoothed her hair from her face as he measured out the hot chocolate into the mug before pouring the milk into it. He quickly added the other ingredients to her with his back to her before splashing a healthy dose of liquid from the amber bottle.

He stirred it until the powder was blended in and set it in front of her. "Drink up."

She sipped cautiously at it. "It tastes good. How much whiskey did you add to it?"

"Just a little to take the edge off."

"Did your mom teach you to make this?"

"No. Mal's mom, actually. I guess it's more like their family secret, but I spent a lot of time at their place as a kid."

"Why?" she asked.

"My mom worked a lot, and Mal and I were best friends, so, you know…."

They sat in silence for a while as she sipped at the mug of hot chocolate.

"How are your arms?" He studied them in the bright light of the kitchen.

"They're a little sore but not too bad."

"Do you have something for the pain?"

"Yeah, but I didn't want to take it. They aren't that painful."

He watched as she drank the rest of her hot chocolate. He took the mug and rinsed it before setting it neatly in the sink and glancing at the clock on the wall. It was close to midnight, and Ava rubbed wearily at her forehead.

"Do you want to try to sleep?" he asked.

"Yeah, I guess so," she said. "I'm not usually this big of a baby, Bishop. I just – I had some bad nightmares last night, and, well, I guess they freaked me out more than I thought."

"It's fine, Ava."

"Okay, well, thanks for coming by. I really appreciate it." Her hands trembled, and he reached out and held them in his.

"I'll stay here tonight, Ava."

"I don't have a second bedroom."

"That's fine. I'll sleep on the couch."

"It's really uncomfortable," she said. "I know that grizzlies need a lot of sleep, and you won't fit on my couch."

"I don't mind," he said. "I'd feel better if I stayed, okay?"

"Okay," she said.

She stood, and he tried not to stare at her ass as she left the kitchen. She returned a few minutes later carrying sheets, a pillow, and a blanket.

"Here, I'll make up the couch for you and -"

He shook his head. "Don't worry about it. I can do it. It's late – try to get some sleep."

She hesitated and then smiled tentatively at him as he took the bedding. "Goodnight, Bishop. Thank you."

"You're welcome."

It was two in the morning when she woke him with her screams. He rolled off the couch, a kink in his neck and his left leg asleep and stumbled toward her bedroom. His grizzly roared in confusion, and he soothed it as he limped into her room.

She screamed and thrashed in her bed, and he hurried over and sat down, grasping her shoulders and shaking her lightly. "Ava, honey, wake up. Wake up."

She screamed again. His grizzly growled in dismay at the sound. Bishop pulled her into his arms, rubbing her back roughly and ignoring her flailing limbs. "Wake up, honey. You're okay, wake up."

She woke with a startled gasp and tried to arch her body away from him. He tightened his hold on her and kissed the top of her head. "It's me, honey. It's Bishop. You're safe."

"Bishop?" Her voice was thick with tears.

He kissed the top of her head again. "Yeah, baby. It's me. You're okay."

She threw her arms around him and buried her face in his neck. "I was having a nightmare."

"It's okay. It's over."

"I was burning up, Bishop. I was burning up, and I couldn't…."

She made a gasping moan, and he rubbed her back through her thin nightshirt. "You're safe, baby. You're safe with me."

"Safe with you," she repeated.

"That's right." He shifted her on his lap and continued to rub her back as she trembled against him. It took nearly fifteen minutes for her to stop shaking.

"Better?" he asked when she finally relaxed in his arms.

"Yes, thank you," she said.

He started to ease her back to the bed, and she tightened her hold around his neck.

"Don't leave me." Fear laced her voice.

"I'm not. I'll lie down with you until you fall asleep, okay?" he said.

"Okay." She relaxed her grip and allowed him to place her on the bed. He climbed in beside her, and she plastered her body to his as he pulled up the quilt.

He wrapped his arms around her, and she snuggled into his chest.

"You have a comfortable bed," he said.

She made a slight, choked sound of laughter and stared at the way his calves and feet hung over the end. "It's too small for you. I'm so sorry, Bishop."

"Don't be sorry, honey." He kissed her forehead. "Close your eyes."

"Don't leave me, okay?" she said.

"I won't." He moved onto his side and pulled her closer until every part of their bodies touched and then buried his face in her long hair. She stroked his bare chest with her soft hands for a few minutes before settling against him.

THE INSISTENT BUZZING OF HER PHONE DRAGGED AVA FROM her sleep. She squinted blearily at the phone before picking it up. "Hello?"

She rested her head on the warm chest below her and ran

her fingers through the coarse hair as she closed her eyes again.

"I'm fine, Willow. I was just sleeping," she mumbled.

There was a hard thigh between hers, and she made a contented moan as she rubbed her pelvis against it. The man beneath her made his own sound of contentment. She arched her back when his warm hands skimmed under her nightshirt and squeezed her ass.

"What? No, I'm fine. It's what time?" She pressed her lips against his firm flesh before nipping experimentally at it.

He groaned, his hand tightening on her ass. He pressed his leg against her pussy, rubbing his hair-roughened thigh against her panties.

"Willow, why are you calling me?" She tried to contain her irritation. His warm hands slid inside her panties and kneaded and rubbed her bare ass, and she made a soft moan. "No, I'm fine. I just…"

Ava's eyes popped open. She struggled to sit up as she stared down at Bishop. His eyes were closed, and he bit his bottom lip before sliding his hand between her legs and touching the wet lips of her pussy.

"Bishop!" she gasped.

His eyes flew open, and he stared at her in confusion. "Ava? What's wrong?"

She pulled at his arm as Willow spoke rapidly in her ear.

Ava cleared her throat. "Yes, he's here with me. No, no, nothing's wrong. I just couldn't sleep last night, and Bishop came over and, uh, helped me sleep."

She pushed her way out of his arms and rolled to her side of the bed as she blushed furiously. "No! Not like that, Willow! He just, he made me a drink and then I went to bed."

Bishop sat up and pushed down the covers. He wore just a pair of briefs, and her eyes widened at the sizeable bulge between his legs before she forced herself to look away.

"Dammit!" Bishop suddenly shot to his feet and disappeared out of the room. She heard him fumbling around in the living room, and he cursed again when there was a loud thud.

"Bishop! Are you okay?" Ava glanced at the alarm clock. It was almost noon. She groaned and sat up, holding the covers up around her chest as Willow giggled like a madwoman in her ear.

"Fine." He reappeared in the doorway, his t-shirt on inside out and his hair sticking up everywhere. "I gotta go, Ava. I'm late for work. Can you tell Willow I'm on my way into the office? I broke your chair, I'm sorry. I'll buy you a new one, okay?"

"Don't worry about it," she said.

He ran his hands through his thick hair. "I'll, uh, I'll call you later."

He left, and she collapsed on the bed with a harsh sigh.

"Ava? You there, or are you kissing Bishop goodbye?" Willow asked.

"Nothing happened, Willow," she said.

"Oh really? Because there was a lot of moaning and groaning coming through the phone," Willow said. "Did he sex you up last night to help you sleep or what?"

"No," Ava said. "I asked him to come over to keep me company for a while. He volunteered to sleep on the couch, but then I had a nightmare, and he crawled into bed with me because I was afraid. Then you woke us up when you called."

"Mal's been trying to get a hold of Bishop all morning." Willow laughed. "I can't wait to tell him he didn't answer his phone because he was in your bed."

"Don't you dare tell him, Willow," Ava said. "Nothing happened. Do you hear me? Nothing happened."

"Okay, okay. Don't get your panties in a bunch. Wait – you are wearing panties, right? You didn't give them to Bishop as, like, a trophy, did you?"

"I'm wearing underwear!" Ava said. "I swear to God, Willow Blossom Tanner, I'll break your arm if you tell anyone about what you heard."

Willow giggled. "Your secret is safe with me, honey."

"Like hell it is," she said.

"Listen, I've got to go. Are you feeling better?"

"Yes."

She was actually. She had slept well last night, and she had Bishop to thank for it. She climbed out of bed and went into the bathroom, staring at herself in the mirror before groaning.

"What? What's wrong?" Willow asked.

"Nothing." She stared at the sleep wrinkles on her face and her crazy bedhead. "I look awful in the morning, and today is no exception."

"I'm sure you have a lovely glow happening." Willow laughed.

"Willow," Ava said warningly.

"I have to go, honey. I love you! I'll talk to you later."

Willow ended the call, and Ava set her phone on the vanity before staring at herself in the mirror. "You idiot," she said and reached for her toothbrush.

CHAPTER 7

Bishop rushed into the office. He ignored Willow's sly grin and escaped to his office, shutting the door and collapsing in his chair. He took a deep breath and closed his eyes for a moment. Fuck, he'd been all over Ava. He'd groped her ass when he was supposed to be comforting her. He groaned and dropped his head into his hands.

He'd woken to find Ava sprawled on top of him, that glorious mass of red hair spread over his chest and gleaming like fire in the sun, and then she had nipped him. The feel of her teeth against his flesh, the soft moan she made when he'd gripped her naked ass, had filled him with an undeniable urge to take her.

The door opened, and Mal walked into his office. "What the hell, Bishop?"

"I don't want to hear it, Mal."

"Do you know what time it is?"

"Yes."

"You can't complain about Kat being late after this. You know that, right?"

"Yes," he said.

Mal looked him over. "Are you wearing the same clothes from yesterday?"

Bishop didn't reply, and Mal sat down in the chair across from him. "What were you doing last night? Why are you -"

"Look, Mal, I know what Willow told you, but what she thinks she heard this morning isn't what happened. Ava called me last night because she was afraid, and I went there to keep her company. She was having trouble sleeping, and I offered to stay the night. I started on the couch but then she had a bad nightmare, so I went to her room to comfort her. She didn't want to be left alone, so I stayed in bed with her, and we fell asleep. That's it. Nothing happened, okay?"

"You were with Ava?" Mal said.

"You didn't know that?" Bishop said.

"Nope."

"Willow didn't tell you?"

"Nope."

Willow stuck her head into the office. "Good gravy, Bishop. The first time I'm actually able to keep a secret, you spill the damn beans yourself. Nice work, Chatty Cathy."

Bishop groaned as Willow turned to Mal. "Oh, and don't believe anything he says about nothing happening. I heard moaning, Mal. Moaning."

She ducked out of the room as Bishop growled at her.

"Moaning?" Mal asked.

"Nothing happened," Bishop muttered as he raked his hand through his hair and opened his laptop.

"Sure, it didn't. Listen, we've got a meeting at two with a new client. He owns a restaurant on the south side of the city and is looking for nighttime security. Marika Belfry recommended us, and apparently, they're good friends, so let's try to make a good impression, okay?"

"Fine." Bishop scanned his email, grunting impatiently when Mal leaned forward.

"Go home and shower and change your clothes, Bishop. You've got Ava's scent all over you, and we don't need the client knowing you banged a human this morning."

"I didn't *bang* her!" Bishop snarled.

"Of course, you didn't." Mal grinned and, whistling under his breath, strolled out of his office.

———

AVA OPENED HER DOOR AND SMILED AT THE MAN STANDING IN the hallway. "Hello, Detective Matthews."

"Hello, Ms. Lewis. How are you feeling?"

"Better, thank you."

"Good. Sorry to drop by unannounced, but I wondered if I could take you for that coffee?"

"Oh, um, I'm not sure if I'm up for coffee."

He smiled encouragingly at her. "Have you left your apartment since you were discharged from the hospital?"

She shook her head, and he said, "I understand. I know it's scary, but you can't get much safer than with an officer of the law, right?"

She smiled. "No, I guess I can't."

"I know a great little coffee shop, not two blocks from here."

"Are you talking about The Brewhouse?"

"I am." He smiled again at her, and she flushed slightly.

"I go there for coffee nearly every morning."

"Then you know I'm telling you the truth. What do you say? I promise I won't ask too many questions."

"All right." Ava had a pretty good idea that Bishop would be pissed if she left the safety of her apartment, but she did feel a little stir crazy. And she couldn't put off the detective's questions forever. Better to get it over with on a day where she'd actually had a good night's sleep and could lie effectively, right?

She grabbed her purse and phone and locked the door before following Detective Matthews to the elevator. They rode down in silence, and she nodded her thanks when he held the door open for her. She paused on the threshold, a little anxious despite the bright sunlight.

Detective Matthews held his arm out to her. "You're perfectly safe, Ms. Lewis. I promise."

"Thanks." She took his arm, and they headed toward the coffee shop.

Garth climbed out of the car and walked toward them. "Everything okay, Ms. Lewis?"

"Yes, it's fine. Garth, this is Detective Matthews. He's investigating Brody's death. Detective Matthews, this is Garth. He works for the security company that Willow mentioned."

"Nice to meet you."

"You as well," Garth said. "You sure you're okay, Ms. Lewis?"

"Yes. We're just going a couple of blocks to the coffee shop. I won't be long."

"I'll come with you." Garth turned to lock the car.

"It's fine, Garth. Really," Ava said.

The bull shifter frowned at her. "Bishop and Mal said not to let you out of my sight."

"I'm with a police officer. I won't be in any danger."

"I don't think -"

"It's fine, Garth," she repeated. "I'll text you if there are any problems."

Garth didn't look happy about it but climbed back into the

car. Ava and Detective Matthews walked in silence to the coffee shop. He bought her a coffee, and they found a quiet seat in the back. She sipped at the steaming liquid as he stared thoughtfully at her.

"So, um, have you made any progress on finding Mr. Chambers, Detective Matthews?" she asked.

"No. And please, call me Bren." He scrolled through a screen on his phone. "Sean Chambers died in 1987 of a brain aneurism."

"I'm sorry?"

He showed her a picture of a white-haired man standing on a dock and holding a fishing pole in one hand. "This man? Is Sean Chambers."

She studied the phone. "That's impossible. He looks nothing like Mr. Chambers."

"Your Sean Chambers, or rather the man who's claiming to be him, stole his identity."

"What? Seriously?"

"We have a death certificate for Sean Chambers, and I've spoken to his widow and two of his children," Bren said.

"It's not possible that they just have the same name?" She hesitated. "I guess that's kind of a stupid question, huh? You would have checked that out."

"Not a stupid question, Ms. Lewis."

"Call me Ava," she said.

"Ava," he said with a cute smile. He sipped at his coffee. "The Mr. Chambers that kept showing up in the ER is using the same social security number as this Mr. Chambers. We found some paperwork at his apartment that clued us into the fact that he works at the sawmill. His employer verified the social security number. He hasn't, however, seen Mr. Chambers since the night Brody died and you were injured."

Ava stared down at her hands. They were trembling again,

and she clenched them tightly together. "So, you still don't know where he is."

"No, but," he reached out and touched her hand, "we'll find him, Ava. I promise you."

"How?" she said. "If he's using a dead man's identity, how will you find him?"

"Sooner or later, he'll slip up. He'll use his credit card, or he'll...."

"He'll come after me again," Ava said.

"Maybe," he said cautiously. "But probably not. He'll assume that you're under police protection. I don't suppose you've changed your mind about police protection?"

"No, I have the shifters watching out for me, remember?"

"They do seem rather good at their job." He grinned at her. "I'm used to people trusting me because I work for the police department, but I don't think Garth trusts me."

She smiled a little. "He's just doing his job."

"I'm glad. We need to keep you safe, Ava." His smile made her flush.

"Do you know a lot of shifters?" he asked.

"No, not really. I've met most of them in the last six months because of Willow's job with the security company. Before that, I only knew a couple of nurses and a doctor that works at the hospital," she said.

"I don't know that many myself," Bren said. "My father is Senator Matthews."

Ava's eyes widened. "Your father is Senator Matthews?"

"I'm nothing like my father," he said.

"That's good," she said bluntly. "Sorry, that didn't come out the right way."

He laughed. "It's fine. I know exactly the kind of man my father is. So, do you have any family here in the city?"

She nodded. "My parents and my younger sister. They're

on a safari in Africa at the moment. It was a graduation present for my sister. She just graduated from the university with a degree in social sciences."

"Do they know what happened?"

She shook her head. "They're kind of unreachable at the moment. They left ten days ago and won't be back for another six weeks."

She took another sip of coffee. "What about you? Do you have any siblings?"

He nodded, his face lighting up. "I have a younger brother, Tyler. He's still in high school."

"That's a big age difference."

"It is," he agreed. "Tyler wasn't exactly planned."

"What about your mom?"

"She left when Tyler was just a kid. She stayed in touch for a couple of years, but then she remarried and traveled a lot with her new husband."

"That must be difficult."

"It's difficult on Tyler. My dad isn't exactly the father of the year. Ty spends a lot of time at my place." He checked his watch and smiled at her. "As much as I'm enjoying this, I have a meeting I need to be at soon. Can we chat about what happened the night Brody died?"

Ava's stomach dropped, but she forced herself to smile at him. "Sure."

***

"HEY, BOSS." GARTH WAVED AT HIM, AND BISHOP SLOWED TO a stop. He'd just finished their meeting with the new client and decided on impulse to stop by Ava's place on his way back to the office. He just wanted to check on her and confirm she was okay. He wasn't going to ask her if she wanted to finish what they started this morning, he told himself.

"Hello, Garth. How's it been?"

"Quiet."

"Good. I'll talk to you later."

"She's not at home," Garth called after him.

Bishop froze and turned around. "What do you mean?"

"She went to the coffee shop."

Bishop reached through the window and grabbed Garth by the collar of his shirt. "You were to stay with her at all times, Garth!"

"She wouldn't let me," the bull shifter said. "She said the coffee shop was only a couple of blocks away, and she's with a detective. She's perfectly safe."

"You'd better hope she is," Bishop said. "What direction did they go?"

"That way." Garth pointed down the street, and Bishop bared his teeth at him before letting go of the shifter and storming away.

His heart pounded, and his grizzly snarled with jealousy.

She belongs to us! Find her! Find her right now!

I'm working on it. Just stay calm.

He was nearly running, and he forced himself to slow down as he caught sight of the coffee shop.

Ava's not ours, he reminded himself and his grizzly. *She can have coffee with another guy if she wants. Just keep your cool, for Christ's sake.*

He entered the coffee shop, scanning the area anxiously. His grizzly roared with anger when he caught sight of Ava. A dark-haired man sat across from her, and Bishop could smell Ava's anxiety and nervousness.

He's upsetting her! His grizzly raged at him. *Are you going to allow that?*

No, he was not. He ignored the nervous looks from the other coffee shop customers and stomped toward them, the floor shaking lightly with every step.

"I know this is difficult, Ava." The man reached out and touched her hand. Bishop had to stop himself from throwing the man across the room. "I'm sorry, but I -"

Ava looked over the man's shoulder. "Bishop? What are you doing here?"

"You're upsetting her," Bishop growled as the man turned around.

The detective stood. "This is a private conversation."

Bishop couldn't smell any fear radiating from the human, and a ripple of respect went through him. He tamped it down. He didn't want to respect this man, not when he could smell his interest in Ava seeping out of every pore.

"Not anymore," Bishop grunted. "You're upsetting her, and I'm taking her home."

"I'm fine, Bishop," Ava said as Bishop took her arm and tugged her to her feet. He held her hand tightly.

"I'll walk you home, Ava."

Ignoring Bishop, the detective smiled at Ava. "Do you want to leave, Ava?"

Ava studied Bishop. "Yes, I think that's best."

"No problem. I wasn't quite finished, though, so maybe we could have dinner in a few days? What do you say?" the detective said.

Bishop glared at him. "She has plans with me."

The detective grinned at him. "You don't even know what night."

"She's busy, I said."

"Bishop, stop it," Ava said sharply. "You don't get to speak for me."

He gritted his teeth but shut his mouth.

Ava smiled apologetically at the detective. "I really don't think I can be of any more help, Bren. I still don't remember anything."

"That's fine. Maybe in a few more days, you'll remember. I'll give you a call. I know a great little Italian place downtown. You'll love it."

"I'll talk to you later," Ava said.

Bren held his hand out to Bishop. "It was nice to meet you, Mr...."

"King. Bishop King," Bishop said with a brief shake of Bren's hand.

"Bren Matthews."

"Bishop owns the security company," Ava said. "It's why he's so protective. It's his job."

"Right," Bren said. He watched silently as Bishop put his arm around Ava's waist and tugged her toward the door.

"Bye, Bren," Ava called over her shoulder.

"Bye, Ava."

Bishop hustled Ava out the door, trying not to growl again at the human.

"That was rude of you, Bishop," Ava said as he hurried her toward her apartment.

"He upset you. I could smell it," he said.

"He was asking questions about the night Brody died. Yeah, it upset me, but Bren was just doing his job," Ava replied.

"Bren? Since when did you get on a first-name basis with him?" Bishop scowled at her. "How well do you know this guy?"

"I barely know him."

"He touched you."

She yanked her hand free of his. "The caveman thing is getting old, Bishop."

"I'm trying to protect you."

"No, you're trying to keep away the competition," she said.

"I don't want to fight, Ava. I came over to apologize for this morning," he said.

"You don't have anything to apologize for. I started it. I should be apologizing to you." Colour rose in her cheeks, and she waved briefly at Garth as they climbed the steps in front of her apartment building.

"No, you shouldn't be," he said.

"Thank you for last night, Bishop. It really helped."

"I'm glad," he said. "I could come up now if you'd like. I'll make you dinner."

She hesitated before shaking her head. "I don't think that's a good idea. Besides, I can't take up all of your free time, and I think I'll sleep much better tonight."

"Will you?" he said.

"Yes. I'm not as afraid." She wouldn't look him in the eye.

She was lying, he could smell her fear radiating from her, but he just said, "Call me if you need anything, okay?"

"I will. Have a good night, Bishop."

"You too."

He waited until she was in the elevator before heading toward his truck. He stopped next to Garth's car. "Sorry about earlier, Garth. I was being a real dick."

"You were," Garth agreed. "But I get it, man. I'll talk to you later."

"Thanks." He walked slowly to his truck and climbed in, and drove away, feeling like he was making a mistake.

CHAPTER 8

"Okay, so let's see if I have this straight." Willow followed Mal down the sidewalk toward his house. "Heath is the one about to take the bar exam, and Ellet is studying to be a doctor?"

Mal shook his head. "Heath is studying for the bar exam, but Ellet is studying to be a vet."

"Good gravy, Mal. I've met your entire family how many times now, and I still can't remember who does what."

He laughed. "You were close. Besides, you're doing well. They're my siblings, and half the time, I don't even know who's doing what."

He opened the door and ushered her inside. "Who called you earlier?"

"Ava," Willow said. "She said she was fine, that she just wanted to chat, but she sounded off. I'm wondering if I should go over there."

"It's almost eleven," he pointed out.

"Yeah, she's probably sleeping or having sex with Bishop."

He grinned at her as he flicked on the living room light. "Bishop says they're not having sex."

"Ava says the same thing, but I'm not sure I believe those crazy kids." She bent and peered under the couch. "Hi, kittens! How are my sweet babies?"

They hissed at her, and she straightened. "Are they doing better? Are they coming out from under the couch more?"

"How would I know?" He shrugged. "I feed them, and I change their stupid litter box, and that's it. I told you, I hate cats."

She poked him lightly in the chest. "You have to give them love too, Mal. That's part of being a responsible cat owner."

"I don't want to be a cat owner, remember?" He caught her hand and kissed the palm of it. "Are you staying the night?"

"Yes."

He grinned happily. "That was easy."

"Did you just call me easy?" She gave him a mock scowl, and he bent and pressed a kiss against her collarbone.

"I just meant that usually, I have to be a bit more persuasive in my attempt to get you to sleep here."

She smiled at him and ran her fingers through his hair. "I like being with you, and I like being here. You know that, right, honey?"

"I do."

"Good." She pressed a kiss against his mouth. "I need to use the loo. I'll be right back."

He waited until she'd disappeared down the hallway before sitting cross-legged on the floor. He made a kissing noise and smiled when the two kittens raced out from under the couch. They climbed eagerly into his lap, meowing and purring loudly as they butted their tiny heads against his hands.

"How are my babies?" he crooned. He picked up the larger one and rubbed his nose against her forehead. "Is my Dolly girl happy to see me? She's getting so big, yes she is."

The kitten licked at his face with her scratchy tongue, and he winced when the smaller kitten climbed the front of his shirt. Mal plucked him off the fabric and held him up to his face.

"Don't be jealous, Johnny. You know Daddy loves you just as much as he loves your sister." He kissed the kitten's belly as Johnny dug his claws into his scalp and bit at his thick hair. "Ouch! Be nice to Daddy, Johnny."

"Daddy?"

Willow's voice made him stiffen, and he nearly dropped the kittens as he stared up at his mate. She stood in the doorway with a look of amusement on her face. He set the kittens down and cleared his throat.

"I thought you were in the bathroom."

"I was." She walked toward him, and the kittens arched their backs and hissed like snakes before streaking back under the couch. "You must have lost track of time."

Before he could stand, she dropped into his lap and put her arms around him. "Hate the cats, huh?"

He blushed. "You can't tell anyone you saw me doing that, Willow."

She grinned and stroked his hair. "Of course, I won't. I can't let a couple of tiny kittens destroy the Big Bad Wolf's reputation, can I?"

His blush deepened, and she kissed his neck. "Is this the wrong time to tell you how fucking hot you looked cuddling those kittens?"

"Really?"

"Really, really."

"So, all those years I was single, I could have been using kittens to lure the ladies?" he asked. "So many wasted opportunities."

"Cram it, you." She whacked him lightly on the back. "Now, speaking of opportunities - why doesn't Daddy take his girl to the bedroom?"

Horror washed over him. "Please don't call me Daddy in the bedroom. I'll never get another erection again."

Willow burst into wild giggles. "Oh God, Mal. It's so easy to freak you out."

"Willow," he growled warningly, and she giggled again.

"I'm not going to start calling you 'Daddy' while we're having sex."

"Swear it," he said. "Swear you won't ever call me Daddy, Willow."

She snorted laughter as he climbed to his feet. "I swear, Mal. You're kind of a prude, though. You know that, right?"

"Prude?" He tossed her over his shoulder and slapped her on the ass as she giggled. "You're going to regret that, Willow Blossom Tanner."

SHE CALLED HIM JUST BEFORE ELEVEN, AND BISHOP snatched up his phone as a weight lifted from his chest. "Ava? Are you okay?"

There was silence, and he said, "Do you need me to come over? Are you having trouble sleeping?"

"Yeah," she said. "I'm sorry, Bishop."

"Don't be. I'll be right over."

Fifteen minutes later, he parked his truck on the street and waved to Fenton. He rode the elevator to her floor and knocked on her apartment door. Ava opened it and said, "I'm sorry."

"I told you, you don't need to apologize." He shrugged out of his jacket and left his boots in the hallway before following her into the kitchen. "Do you want me to make you a hot chocolate?"

"No, that's okay."

"Did you eat tonight?"

"I wasn't very hungry," she said.

"You need to eat," he said. "Sit down, and I'll make you an omelet."

She sat down, and he rummaged through her fridge. Tonight, she wore a pair of yoga pants and a thin t-shirt, and his grizzly growled happily at the way her breasts pushed against the material.

"I feel like such an idiot," she said. "I thought I was fine, but then it got dark, and I kept thinking about how I really should go to bed, and the more I thought about it, the more anxious I got."

She cleared her throat. "I called Willow around eight, but she and Mal were at his parents' place. She offered to leave and come over, but I said no. I didn't tell her I couldn't sleep and was afraid, just said I felt like chatting. I tried reading for a while, but it didn't help."

"I'm glad you called me, Ava," Bishop said.

BISHOP SEEMED COMPLETELY AT EASE IN HER KITCHEN. Working quickly and efficiently, he chopped vegetables and sautéed them before adding eggs to the pan. A few minutes later, he slid the omelet onto a plate and set it down in front of her.

"It smells delicious." She smiled at him as he made a second omelet.

"Eat up," he said as he flipped the omelet in the pan.

She took a bite. "Oh my God, this is so good."

"I'm glad you like it." He slid the second omelet onto a plate and sat down beside her. He sprinkled it liberally with hot sauce and then dug in as Ava took another bite.

"Did you not eat supper?" she asked.

"I did," he said, "but I'm hungry again."

"How many times a day do you eat?"

"I don't know, six or seven times maybe? I try to make at least three of the meals just vegetables. They're good for you and fill you up without adding a lot of extra calories," he said.

She grinned a little. "It seems weird to hear a grizzly shifter talk about eating vegetables."

He laughed. "I eat lots of meat too, but we are omnivores by nature."

"What's your favourite food?"

"Any type of berry."

"Really?"

"Yup. Grizzlies can't resist berries. They're so sweet, so delicious." His voice had deepened with pleasure, and she felt a stirring of lust in her belly in response.

She ignored it and gave him a small smile. "I love strawberries."

"They're my favourite berry." He grinned at her as he finished eating his omelet. "I like them smothered in chocolate."

"Me too," she said.

"Dark chocolate is the best." He licked his lips, and another thread of lust went through her. "There's just something about the bitterness of the chocolate and the sweetness of the berry. Don't you think?"

"Yes," she said. She couldn't stop staring at his mouth.

He inhaled deeply before leaning forward. "Do you know what I want to do, Ava?"

His voice had deepened to a raspy growl, and she shook her head as she continued to stare at his mouth. How would it feel to have his mouth between her legs? To feel that dark beard rubbing against her inner thighs? Against the sensitive lips of her pussy?

"I want to connect the dots with melted chocolate and your freckles."

A flash of heat swept through her, and without thinking, she blurted out, "That sounds sticky."

She blushed furiously when he bellowed laughter. "Yes, I suppose it does."

"Oh my God." She picked up their plates and carried them to the dishwasher. "I am such an idiot."

"You're not." He grinned at her.

"I really am." She glanced at the clock, and Bishop stood up.

"Are you ready to try sleeping?"

"Yes, I think so." She wanted to ask him if he would sleep in the bed with her but, God, how much of a wrong impression would that give him? She needed to suck it up and just be happy that Bishop was even willing to cram his large body onto her couch.

BISHOP STUDIED AVA. SHE LOOKED EXHAUSTED AND SCARED, and although he knew she would say no, he couldn't resist asking. "Do you want me to sleep in the bed with you in case you have a nightmare again?"

The blush that had started to fade reappeared with a

vengeance. Bishop swallowed down his disappointment. He was pushing her for something she didn't want just because he had no self-control. "I'm sorry, Ava, I shouldn't have -"

"Yes," she said. "I want you to. If you don't mind?"

"I don't," he said.

She licked her lips nervously. "Just sleeping, Bishop, okay? I'm sorry, I don't want to give you the wrong impression."

"You're not. Just sleeping, Ava. I promise."

"Thank you."

He followed her to the bedroom and quickly shed his jeans and t-shirt. She disappeared into the bathroom and returned wearing a loose sleep shirt and shorts. He tried not to stare at her breasts as she climbed into the bed and pulled up the covers.

He shut off the light and slid into the bed beside her. It creaked alarmingly, and his side of the bed dipped down until it was nearly touching the floor. He wished he could tug Ava into his arms when she rolled into him with a soft grunt.

"I'm sorry." She scrambled back to her side of the bed. "There's a bit of a tilt to the bed."

He studied how she clutched the side of the bed to keep her body away from his. "Maybe I should sleep on the floor."

"No, that's not necessary. I'm comfortable."

"You're clinging to the bed with a death grip, Ava."

"I don't want to crowd you."

"You won't be."

"Are you sure?"

"Yes." He was almost frantic with his need to feel her warm body against his. He held his breath as she waited a few more minutes.

"Well, if you're sure."

She let go of the bed, and his grizzly made a soft roar of pleasure when her curvy body rested firmly against his.

"Comfortable?" he asked.

"Yes, thanks."

She tucked her arm under her pillow as he shifted again. He was too aware of the feel of her ass against his thigh, and he willed himself not to get an erection as her soft hair brushed against his ribcage.

"I don't remember the bed doing this last night," he said.

"It's not a very good mattress," she said.

He moved slightly. "Maybe I should -"

There was a deafening crack, and Ava shrieked with alarm when the bedframe splintered and the mattress crashed to the floor.

"Shit," Bishop said. "I'm so sorry, Ava. I'll buy you a new bed."

Her entire body shook, and he touched her back in alarm. "Ava, honey, are you okay?"

She raised her head, and he stared at her as she laughed and laughed. She almost got herself under control, then shuddered all over, and the giggles started again. Finally, holding her stomach and her face red, her laughter tapered off into the hiccups. She wiped the tears from her face before twisting around and staring up at Bishop.

"We broke the bed."

"We did," he said. "Although I think it's more like I broke the bed. That's two pieces of furniture I owe you now."

She patted his chest. "It's fine, really. The bed was pretty old."

"You're just saying that to make me feel better," he said glumly before staring down at his stomach. "I knew I needed to lay off the ice cream."

She laughed again. "You're not too heavy, Bishop."

"You do realize that we're lying on the floor, and your bed is in pieces, right?"

"Yeah." She snorted soft laughter again. Unable to resist, he pulled her up against his chest and wrapped one arm around her waist.

She rested her head on his broad chest as her arm crept around his waist. "Thanks, Bishop."

"For breaking your bed?"

She smiled. "No, just for being here and cooking me dinner and for not... not expecting anything from me, I guess."

"You're welcome," he said as he stroked her back through her shirt.

"Goodnight, Bishop." She snuggled into him, and he kissed the top of her head.

"Goodnight, Ava."

SHE SPRAWLED ACROSS HIM LIKE HE WAS HER MATTRESS. HE studied her face and her hair in the morning light as desire flooded through him. He loved the way she slept, all four limbs askew with no thought to his personal space. Her long red hair was everywhere, wrapped around his throat, brushing against his arms and his chest, and he touched a few of the soft strands with his rough hands.

He stared at the freckles on her upper arm and traced them lightly. What he wouldn't give to strip her naked and kiss every single one of her freckles. She stirred in his arms and made a soft sigh of contentment before stretching. It pushed her full breasts against him, and he groaned as she moved until she was straddling his thigh and rubbing herself against him like a cat.

"Ava," he said hoarsely. "Wake up, honey."

He needed to get out of her bed before he did the very thing he promised her he wouldn't.

She blinked sleepily. God, she was adorable in the morning, and she gave him a warm smile that made his cock stiffen. It pressed against her stomach, and she made the sweetest little moan before bending her head to his chest.

He inhaled sharply when she licked a warm path across his collarbone, and he tightened his hands around her hips. Jesus, a grizzly only had so much self-control, and the woman on top of him was warm and curvy, and her desire for him rolled off her in waves.

She kissed his thick neck, and, with a harsh groan, he pulled her body over him until she was straddling his hips. His cock pushed against her warm center, and she moaned with need as he gripped the back of her neck and tugged up her head.

Ava stared at Bishop. She wasn't sure what was happening. Bishop gave her a look of pure hunger, and her stomach tightened as lust rippled through her. "Bishop? What time is it?"

She tried to turn her head to look at the clock, and Bishop made a low growl and tightened his grip around her neck. "Look at me, Ava, only at me."

She stared obediently at him, and he groaned before pulling her face toward his. He pressed his mouth against hers, and she gasped when he thrust his tongue between her lips. He kissed her hard, coaxing her mouth to open wider with little nips of his teeth and soft strokes of his tongue. She melted against him, kissing him back eagerly as one warm hand cupped her breast through her shirt.

His thumb found her nipple, and he worried it into an aching hardness as he kissed her. She gasped into his mouth when he pinched it lightly and made a moan of dismay when he broke their kiss and pushed her into a sitting position above him.

"Bishop? What's wrong?"

"Take off your shirt," he said.

She hesitated, and he squeezed her thighs and rubbed his cock against her. She moaned, and a satisfied grin crossed his face.

"Take it off, Ava," he repeated.

She pulled off her shirt and covered her breasts with her arms, feeling a little self-conscious in the bright light. He growled in disapproval and pulled her arms away, holding them against her hips as he stared hungrily at her breasts.

"Bishop -"

"These are mine, Ava." He lifted both breasts, cupping and kneading them roughly as his fingers pulled at her stiff nipples.

She moaned and arched her back, and he gave her a fierce grin. "Say it. Say they're mine."

"They're yours," she said.

"Good girl," he said. He flipped her onto her back, pushed her thighs apart, and settled his body between them. He rubbed his cock against her as he lowered his mouth to her breasts.

"Mine," he repeated before sucking her nipple into his mouth.

Ava moaned, her hands clutching at Bishop's thick hair as he sucked on her throbbing nipple. There was an ache that radiated from her belly down between her legs, and she rubbed herself restlessly against the grizzly shifter as he switched to her left nipple. He bit it lightly, and she gasped and arched her back as he soothed the sting with his warm tongue.

"Oh please, Bishop." She tried to wiggle her hand between their bodies, and with a soft growl, he took both of her wrists and yanked them above her head. He stared down at her as she pulled at his hand.

"Let me go," she said with an embarrassing lack of conviction.

He shook his head and grinned at her. His eyes glowed brightly, and she stared at them in fascination as he tightened his grip on her wrists. "No, Ava. You're mine, and I won't be denied any longer. You're not leaving this bed until I've fucked you. Do you understand?"

She stared wide-eyed at him, and he grinned again before sliding his hand into her shorts and panties. She tried to close her legs, but his hips blocked them, and she couldn't stop him when he slid one thick finger inside of her.

"Your pussy is so fucking tight, Ava," he said. "I can't wait to watch my cock sliding into it."

"Bishop," she moaned as he slid another finger into her.

"Yes, honey?" He pumped his fingers slowly in and out.

"Please."

"I love listening to you beg." He bent his head and licked a path from freckle to freckle across her chest. "I love your freckles, I love your soft skin, and I love your red hair. It's going to look so pretty wrapped around my hand while I fuck you on your hands and knees."

She made another breathless, pleading moan, and he sucked on her nipple as his fingers moved in and out of her at a slow, unhurried pace. "Have you been fucked on your hands and knees before, Ava?"

She shook her head, and his grin widened. "The next time we fuck, it's going to be in my bed. I'll put you on your knees and tie your hands to the headboard. When you're completely helpless, I'll spread your legs, wrap my hand in your beautiful hair, and fuck you from behind. I won't stop until you're screaming my name as you come, Ava."

"Oh my God!" Her hips bucked against him.

"Do you like that idea?" he said teasingly as he licked the freckles on her shoulder.

"Yes!" she cried out. "Yes!"

"Good." He pulled his fingers free of her warmth, and she made a cry of dismay. He sucked his fingers as she watched.

"You taste so sweet, Ava. Sweeter than the sweetest berry."

"Please touch me, Bishop," she pleaded.

"I am touching you." He stroked the full curve of her belly, stopping to trace a circle around her belly button as she wriggled beneath him.

"Not there," she begged.

"Where should I touch you?" He kissed her again, his tongue sliding against hers.

"You know where!" she gasped out when he released her mouth.

"Tell me."

"Bishop!" She pouted at him.

"Tell me."

"My pussy!" she nearly shouted. "Please, touch my pussy!"

"Whatever you say, beautiful." He slid his hand down and rubbed her clit.

Her reaction was hot and immediate. She made a loud noise of pleasure and arched her body beneath his, her arms straining against him as she twisted and turned beneath his skilled fingers.

"When did you come last?" he whispered into her ear.

"I – I don't remember," she gasped.

"You do. Tell me." He sucked on her earlobe.

"I – a few weeks ago," she said.

"Who were you with?" His voice sounded tense.

She refused to answer, and he tugged on her clit. She rewarded him with another loud cry of need.

"Tell me, Ava."

"No one! I was by myself!"

"You were touching yourself?" He smiled with satisfaction when she nodded. "What were you thinking about?"

"That's – that's none of your business," she gasped out and then moaned when he nipped her neck.

"Answer me," he said, "or I'll stop touching you."

She scowled at him, and he grinned at her before licking her throat. "Tell me what you were thinking about, sweet Ava, and I'll let you come."

He rubbed her clit with the rough pads of his fingers. She cried out before moaning, "You! I was thinking of you."

"Good," he growled and rubbed her clit with hard strokes as he bent his head and sucked her nipple into his mouth. She arched against him and came against his fingers. He continued to touch her as she writhed and squirmed beneath him.

"Stop! I can't… please stop," she cried.

He moved his hand up and stroked the curve of her stomach again. "Did that feel good, Ava?"

"Yes, so good," she moaned.

"Are you ready to be fucked?"

She nodded, and he released her hands before yanking her shorts and panties down her legs. He growled happily when she was naked and studied the pattern of freckles on her thighs as he straightened. He knelt between her legs, and she stared up at him as he pushed his briefs down to his knees and freed his cock.

"Bishop, it's, uh, it's too big." She had seen his dick when he saved her life at the farmhouse. He had been partially erect, and she'd thought it was large then but now, seeing it fully erect she felt a thin trickle of fear.

He stroked his cock and smiled at her. "It isn't, Ava."

"Bullshit," she muttered and scowled at him when he laughed.

"I'll go slowly. I won't hurt you, I promise."

"How bad are you going to feel when you split me in two?"

He laughed again. "It's not that big, honey."

"Says you." She sat up, and his breath caught when she curled her hand around his hard length. She stroked him back and forth hesitantly as he moaned encouragingly and arched his hips into her hand. Her grip tightened, and she stroked hard, watching his face as he bit at his lip and groaned.

"I want to taste you," she said. His cock jerked in her hand, and precum spilled from the tip as she gave him a nervous look. "Is that – is that okay?"

"Jesus, yes, it's okay," he groaned. "Please, Ava."

She continued to hesitate, and he wound his hand through her long hair and tugged her toward his cock. She parted her lips, and he watched his cock disappear into her mouth. She sucked gently, her hand grasping him at the base, and he groaned again.

"Harder, honey."

He gripped her hair as she sucked harder. She slid her tongue back and forth over the tip, and his hips jerked.

"Do you like this, Bishop?" She stared up at him, and he touched her mouth before he nodded.

"Fuck yes, Ava. Don't stop."

She took the head of him into her mouth and sucked hard, running her tongue over the sensitive ridge as he panted loudly and wound his other hand into her hair. He stroked the soft tresses before urging her head forward. She took more of his cock into her mouth, making a low noise of surprise when the head of him bumped against the back of her throat. He moved back and petted her long hair.

"Sorry, honey."

She stared up at him, and he stroked her face as she sucked again. He started to pull away, and she clutched at his naked ass and squeezed it as she sucked at his cock.

"Fuck!" he whispered harshly. "Baby, I'm going to come. You have to stop. Please, baby, stop just for a minute."

"Time to wake up, sleepy-head!" Willow's voice filled the bedroom, and Ava's eyes widened in horror as she jerked her head back.

"I brought you coffee and – holy shit!" Willow stood in the doorway of the bedroom holding two coffees.

"I – I am so sorry!" she squeaked before fleeing the bedroom.

Ava scrambled away from Bishop and grabbed her clothes as Bishop yanked his underwear over his cock. "Ava –"

"Oh my God," she said. "You have to leave. I'm sorry, Bishop. I shouldn't have – we shouldn't have done that."

"It's fine, baby." He pulled up his jeans and quickly buttoned them. "It's fine."

"It's fine?" She scowled at him as she pulled on her underwear and shorts. "Willow just saw me giving you a blowjob! What is fine about this situation?"

He stared at her. "I... shit, I've got nothing."

She threw his shirt at him. "You need to go. Please, Bishop."

He nodded and muttered another apology before nearly running from her bedroom.

CHAPTER 9

"Ava?" Willow poked her head into the bedroom. Ava stood in the middle of the room staring at her broken bed, and Willow handed her a coffee.

"Thanks, Willow."

"I'm so sorry," Willow said sincerely. "Are you going to take back my spare key privilege?"

Ava sipped at the coffee. "No."

"I didn't mean to interrupt. I tried texting you and decided to come over when there was no answer. I thought you were still sleeping."

"It's okay. Really."

Willow studied the broken bed. "Sex with Bishop seems… enthusiastic."

"I didn't have sex with him."

"Honey, the bed's broken."

"He broke it last night just lying in bed with me."

"Oh." Willow was silent for a few minutes. "I feel even worse now."

"Why?" Ava still couldn't look at her.

"Well, obviously, I'm the reason you're not banging Bishop's brains out at this very moment. I interrupted a beautiful moment."

Ava groaned and slapped her forehead. "I have never been so humiliated in my life."

"What? Why?" Willow rubbed her back. "It's no big deal."

"No big deal? You saw us, I mean, you saw me giving him a… oh fuck…." Ava slapped herself again.

"Stop that." Willow pulled her hand away. "I didn't see anything, Ava, honestly. Bishop is so large that you were completely hidden. The only thing I saw was your hands and legs, and his ass – he has a great ass, by the way – so you seriously have nothing to be embarrassed about."

"I didn't mean to do that," Ava said. "I couldn't sleep, and I was afraid, so I asked Bishop to come over. He makes me feel safe, you know? And I know it's dumb, and I know all he wants is sex but now that he's made me…."

Willow grinned at her. "Tell me you finally took him up on his offer and rode his face!"

Ava blushed furiously. "No! I told you – I'm not going to do that. But he does have very talented hands."

"Nice. Give me all the details."

"No way, Willow."

"Well, you're no fun at all," Willow pouted. "At least tell me if he's gigantic. I mean, he must be, yeah? The man is over seven feet tall. There's no way his penis isn't as thick as my arm."

"Oh my God, Willow! You saw it at the farmhouse, remember?" Ava said.

"Honestly, I wasn't paying attention to Bishop's naked body. Mal was naked too, and I found him delightfully distracting."

Ava didn't reply, and Willow grinned at her. "Don't

pretend you don't know how big it is. You were up close and personal with it not half an hour ago."

"You're not going to let this drop, are you?"

"Nope. C'mon, honey, just tell me. You know you're dying to," Willow wheedled.

"Fine! Yes, he's huge, okay?"

"How huge?" Willow held her hands out. "Like this huge?"

"Bigger."

She pulled her hands a little farther apart, and Ava shook her head. Willow, her eyes widening, moved them a couple more inches. Ava reached out and nudged them open another inch.

"You're exaggerating." Willow looked at the space between her hands.

"I'm not."

"Good gravy," Willow breathed. "He'll split you in two, Ava."

"That's what I said," Ava said. "He said he would go slowly."

Willow glanced down at her hands again. "You're not exaggerating?"

Ava shook her head, and Willow blew out her breath. "I'm not sure whether to congratulate you or give you my condolences."

"Nothing happened, Willow."

"Obviously not. Pretty sure you wouldn't be able to walk for a few days afterward if you'd slept with him."

"Okay, now you're just being ridiculous. I've seen Mal's dick, remember? He's plenty big."

"That he is," Willow said. "But he's not circus freak big."

"Bishop isn't either!" Ava scowled at her. "And don't you dare tell him I told you any of this."

"I won't," Willow said cheerfully. "Besides, he'll be so embarrassed after this morning that he'll probably never speak to me again. I've scarred your sweet, innocent bear for life."

"He's not that innocent." Ava picked up a piece of the bed frame.

"Oh, do tell." Willow clapped her hands together.

"I – he just has a naughty side, that's all," Ava said.

"How naughty?" Willow asked. "Details, girl – it's all in the details."

"He says naughty things."

"Does he make you call him Daddy?" Willow asked, and Ava burst into laughter.

"No! He does not make me call him Daddy. Why would you think that?"

Willow shrugged. "No reason, and hey – no judgment, remember that."

Ava's mouth dropped open. "Oh my God, you call Mal 'Daddy' during sex, don't you?"

"Nope." Willow grinned at her. "But he had the same look that's on your face when the topic came up. He also said he'd never get another erection in his life if I called him 'Daddy'. Who knew my boyfriend and my best friend were both so close-minded?"

Ava laughed again, and Willow wiggled her eyebrows. "Don't change the subject. What did Bishop say?"

"You have to promise not to tell Mal."

"Cross my heart, hope to die," Willow said.

"He's, well, he's a bit on the dominant side, I guess you'd say, and he kept saying that I was his, that my body belonged to him, and he wouldn't be denied any longer. He said I wasn't leaving the bed until he had, um, fucked me."

"Whew." Willow fanned her hand in front of her face.

"He is naughty."

"The worst part is that I liked it. I mean, really liked it. I hate when he acts all caveman – do you know he practically dragged me away from my coffee with Bren, I mean, Detective Matthews? I was ready to punch him for it, I really was, and less than twenty-four hours later, he's in my bed, and he's all, 'you're my woman, and I'm going to tie you to the bed and fuck you until you're screaming my name,' and I'm not only fine with it, it's making me so hot I can barely think straight."

She took a deep breath and stared at Willow. "What's wrong with me, Will?"

"Nothing," Willow said. "You can be independent and strong and still like being told what to do in the bedroom."

"I guess, but I never realized I was that type of person and honestly, I'm still not sure that I really am or if I just lose my damn mind whenever I'm around Bishop. There's something about him that makes me, well...."

"Horny as hell?" Willow said.

"Yeah."

"You haven't had a lot of experience, Ava," Willow said, "and the guys you have been with didn't strike me as particularly dominant. Maybe you just needed Bishop to show you what you like."

"Maybe," Ava said.

"Look on the bright side," Willow said, "at least now I know what to get you for your birthday."

"What do you mean?"

"Handcuffs! Just think of the look on Bishop's face when you bring handcuffs into the bedroom."

"Do not buy me handcuffs, Willow!"

"Fine, I'll buy Bishop handcuffs for his birthday."

"Willow!"

"I'm teasing – mostly." Willow laughed. "So, you had coffee with Detective Matthews?"

"I did. He wanted to go over what happened again that night. I told him I still didn't remember."

"Was that all you talked about?"

"No, we talked a bit about our families."

"Did you?" Willow said thoughtfully.

"He's not interested," Ava said. "He was just being friendly."

"You always say that, and you're always wrong," Willow said.

"It doesn't matter. I'm not interested in him."

Willow stared gravely at her. "Honey, all teasing aside about sleeping with Bishop, I know you probably don't want to hear this, but he's repeatedly said that he isn't looking for a relationship. He's a great guy, and I know you're attracted to him, but I don't think it would hurt to get to know the detective a little better."

"People change their minds all the time, Will. Maybe Bishop will realize he's interested in more than sex," Ava said.

"Maybe," Willow said hesitantly, "but I wouldn't count on it, honey. It isn't in a grizzly shifter's nature to fall in love, remember?"

"I remember," Ava said.

"I'm sorry." Willow squeezed her hand.

"Don't be. I needed to be reminded of that. Sex with Bishop would be a big mistake. A really fun mistake, but still a mistake."

"Do you want to come over to my place tonight? We can ask Ginger to come by, and we'll have a girl's night. You can sleep over and avoid the temptation to call Bishop for a really fun mistake."

Ava shook her head. "I have an evening shift at the hospital."

"You're going back already?"

"Yes. It's been a few days, and I need to get back into my normal routine. I can't hide in my apartment forever, Willow."

"I know. But at least let Fenton drive you to the hospital."

"I don't want to inconvenience him," Ava said.

"It's his job, Ava."

"You need to ask Mal and Bishop and Kat how much this is costing them. I want to pay them for it," Ava said.

"Don't be silly. All three said they would do this free of charge. Besides, you wouldn't be able to afford it."

"That's not -"

"Nope, not another word about it, Ava." Willow studied the broken bed. "So, you want me to take you bed shopping during my lunch hour or what?"

KAT STARED AT THE BURNT-OUT CEILING LIGHT IN THEIR small supply room and sighed irritably. "Hey, Willow? Do you know where the light bulbs are?"

There was no reply, and she stuck her head out and glanced at reception. Willow was on the phone, and Kat stifled a laugh when Willow gave her a weary look of resignation.

"Yes, Mr. Larkley, I understand. No, I'm certain that there are no invisible bugs coating the mall. Well, yes, I can ask Davis to check for them during his rounds tonight, but if they're invisible, how is he going to see them?"

Kat ducked back into the supply room. Room was probably the wrong description, large closet was more apt. She stood on her tiptoes and reached for the light before giving up. The ceilings were high in their building, and she'd never reach it. She grabbed the stepladder from behind the door and quickly unfolded it before climbing nimbly up the steps.

"There you are," she said as she stared at the box of light bulbs tucked at the back of the shelf next to her. She reached for the light and turned the cap that connected the glass shade, frowning when it didn't budge.

"Oh, for the love of Pete!" she snapped and then grinned. She, as well as Bishop and Mal, had picked up more than their fair share of Willow's sayings. She grasped the cap again and twisted it, grunting softly with the effort.

It didn't move at all, and she was just about to say, 'fuck it' and steal Bishop's stapler from his office when a deep voice spoke behind her. "Need some help?"

She jerked, the ladder tilted alarmingly, and Ronin grabbed it with both hands, steadying it as she glared down at him. "Are you trying to kill me?"

He grinned. "Don't cats always land on their feet?"

"Ha, ha," she said sourly. "I've never heard that one before."

He laughed, and her eyes widened when he suddenly climbed up the ladder. He stood on the step below hers, his body pressing against hers intimately, and she swallowed the purr that immediately tried to bust free of her throat.

"What are you doing?"

"Helping," he said.

"This isn't helping." She scowled at him.

"Sure, it is." He reached up to unscrew the cap.

Kat bit her bottom lip and stared at the wall. Every part of her cat begged her to rub up against Ronin, and she fought tooth and nail against it.

Stop it! He's a bird!

Yes, and such a pretty bird.

She hissed under her breath, and Ronin turned his head toward her. His warm breath washed over her as he gave her a wicked grin, his dimple deepening. "Everything okay, Ms. Frost?"

"Fine," she said.

He unscrewed the cap and carefully pulled the glass away from the ceiling. "Light bulb?"

"There." She pointed to the shelf beside them and ignored the way his crotch brushed against her ass as he leaned over and grabbed the box. He handed it to her, and she opened it and pulled a light bulb free as he unscrewed the burnt one.

"Be my guest." He grinned at her, and she quickly screwed the light bulb into place as he watched.

He pressed the glass back into place when she was finished and tightened the cap. "Good as new."

She shifted on the ladder, her ass rubbing against him again, and ignored the low groan he made. "Get out of my way."

"Of course." He climbed down the ladder and, knowing he was staring at her ass, she quickly followed him, stumbling in her haste to get back to the ground.

He placed his hands on her hips to prevent her from falling, and before she could stop him, he lifted her from the ladder and set her gently on the ground.

"Aren't cats supposed to be light on their feet?" he teased as his warm hands lingered on her hips.

"Why are you here?" She pushed his hands away.

"I work here, remember?"

"I remember. Why are you in the office?"

"I have some paperwork to fill out. Mr. Burke called me this morning – I'm helping out with the Ms. Lewis protection detail tonight."

She frowned. "You should be doing a shift at the clothing warehouse. We have no idea if you're capable, and there's a real threat to Ms. Lewis' life.'

"Obviously, you think I'm capable, or you wouldn't have hired me."

"Let's make something clear – it wasn't my decision to hire you, Mr. Smith. I was outvoted."

"Ouch," he said with a grin. "Did you not want to hire me because of my tattoos or my butsies habit?"

She shot him a dirty look as she smoothed her shirt down. "Neither."

"Ah, then it must be the gorgeous ass."

Her face turned red, and she growled at him. "You misheard me."

"Did I, though?" He cocked his head at her, and her cat purred happily when his gaze dropped to her mouth. "Have a good day, Ms. Frost."

He turned and walked out of the supply room, and, despite her best intention, she stared at what really was a gorgeous ass clad in tight jeans.

"HEY, KAT."

"Hey, big guy. What's up?" Kat looked up from her computer as Bishop entered her office and dropped into the chair. It groaned under his weight, and she winced. "Bishop, love, don't break my chair again."

"I broke Ava's chair and her bed."

"What?" Kat blinked at him.

"I keep breaking her furniture."

"So, you and Ava are…"

Bishop shook his head. "No, I was just sleeping in the bed with her because she keeps having nightmares."

"Right. Willow mentioned that you were staying with Ava in the evenings."

"What else did she tell you?" Bishop asked.

"Nothing." Kat laughed. "She's being oddly quiet about the whole thing."

"Good," he grunted.

"Is there something I should know?" she asked.

"No."

Kat studied him as he stared moodily out the window of the office. It was after five, and Mal and Willow had already left the office. She'd thought Bishop was gone as well. "What's wrong, Bishop?"

He shrugged. "Nothing."

"Are you going to Ava's tonight?"

"She's working at the hospital. It's her first shift back."

"Well, that's good. It's good for her to get back to her normal routine."

"Yeah." He fidgeted in the chair. "Mal and Willow are out doing their ghost thing tonight."

"What are your plans for tonight?" she asked.

"Nothing. I should probably stop at Leslie's," he said gloomily. "What are you up to?"

She closed her laptop and pulled her purse out of the bottom drawer. "Actually, I was about to ask if you wanted to have dinner and maybe hit Bud's for a drink after."

"Oh, yeah?" He gave her a skeptical look as she slipped on her shoes and stood.

"Yes. I've had a rough day, and I could use a drink. What do you say, big guy? Help a lady out?"

He grinned. "I'd like that, Kat."

CHAPTER 10

"Ava?"

Ava looked up from the nurses' desk and gave Fenton a nervous look. "Hey, is everything okay?"

The cheetah shifter nodded. "Everything's fine. No need to worry. I'm finished my shift, and I wanted to introduce Ronin Smith to you. He's new to the company."

Ava shook Ronin's hand as he said, "Nice to meet you, Ms. Lewis."

"It's nice to meet you as well. Call me Ava."

"As long as you call me Ronin," he said.

"Your shift is over at eleven, right?" Fenton asked.

She nodded, and Fenton checked his watch. "Ronin will be waiting for you at the emergency door when you're ready to leave. If he isn't outside, don't leave the building. Okay?

"Okay," Ava said.

"Good. I'll see you tomorrow, Ava."

"Bye, Fenton. Ronin, it was nice meeting you. I'll see you in a couple of hours."

"Nice to meet you as well, Ava," Ronin said.

The two men walked away, and Ginger sidled up to her. "Who was that gorgeous specimen of a man?"

"Which one?" Ava asked. "They're both hot."

"The blond one," Ginger said. She pulled her uniform top away from her chest and blew down the top of it. "He's giving me hot flashes."

Ava laughed. "You're twenty-six years old, Ginger. You do not have hot flashes."

"Just tell me who he is," Ginger said. "I'm dying over here, Ava."

"His name is Fenton."

"Fenton," Ginger said dreamily. "Even his name is gorgeous."

"He's a cheetah shifter. He works for Bishop."

"Really?" Ginger said. "I've never met a cheetah shifter before."

"Mrs. Racen was a cheetah shifter."

"She was a hundred and three years old, and she threw up all over me. I'd managed to block the memory but thank you so much for reminding me," Ginger said.

"What about Robbie?" Ava said.

"What about him?" Ginger said with a weird look.

"Are you two still dating? You don't talk much about him anymore."

"We're still dating," Ginger said. "He's been busy at his new job."

"Where's he working now?"

"Burger King."

Before Ava could reply, Ginger groaned. "I know, I know. But at least it's a steady job. He's working nights cleaning the restaurant."

Ava shrugged. "A job is a job, Ginger. No one cares what

he does for a living. If he loves you and makes you happy, that's what matters."

"Thanks, Ava. How are you feeling?"

"That's the third time you've asked me that tonight."

"I worry about you." Ginger gave her a brief one-armed hug. "Do you want to stay with me tonight after work? Willow texted me and said you were having trouble sleeping."

"Thank you, but I'll be okay. What else has she told you?" Ava asked.

"Nothing. Why? What else is there to tell?" Ginger said.

"Nothing," Ava said.

"Liar." Ginger laughed before walking away.

"KAT, YOU'RE LOOKING AS STUNNING AS EVER. WHEN ARE you going to take me up on my offer of dinner?"

Kat grinned at Mal's brother. "Thanks, Porter, but you know I don't date wolves."

"But big old grizzlies are on the market, huh?" Porter pulled two glasses out from behind the bar as Bishop rolled his eyes.

"Relax, B," Porter said. "I know your heart belongs to a redhead."

"Who told you that?" Bishop scowled at him.

"No one you know," Porter said breezily as he poured scotch into both their glasses.

"I'm going to kill Willow," Bishop muttered. "And nothing is happening between Ava and me."

"How is Ava, by the way?" Porter asked. "Mal told me about the trouble she was having with some stalker."

He smiled at Kat. "I met Ava a month ago. Did Mal tell

you? The four of us went for dinner and a movie. She's a sweetheart and that red hair…gorgeous. Maybe I should stop by her apartment and see if she needs some extra protection."

Bishop snarled and slammed his fist on the bar. "Go anywhere near her, Porter, and I'll tear off your leg."

"Bishop, relax. Porter's teasing you." Kat put her hand on Bishop's arm.

Porter laughed and slapped Bishop on the shoulder. "I'm sorry, B. I couldn't resist."

"You can be such a dick, Porter," Bishop said.

"Yeah, I really can be." Porter agreed cheerfully. "So, what's got you two in here tonight?"

Kat shrugged. "Just finished dinner and thought we'd stop in for a drink. It's been a long day."

"Well, we've got drinks." He poured a little more into Kat's glass as Bishop covered his with his hand and shook his head.

"Hey, are you two coming to the barbecue on Sunday?" Porter asked.

Kat nodded. "Yes, I texted your mom this morning and told her I could make it."

"Good. B? What about you?"

"Yes."

Porter hesitated, and Bishop gave him a curious look. "What?"

"Just to give you a heads up, mom was telling me that she ran into Leslie at the grocery store yesterday."

Bishop groaned. He knew where this was headed.

"She invited her to the barbecue," Porter said. "Sorry, man."

"It's fine," he grunted. "Your mom means well, and, no doubt, Leslie let her know what an awful son I've been lately and how she's completely alone and depressed."

"Yep, it did go a lot like that," Porter said. "And you know Mom – she's way too tender-hearted for her own good. I did try to tell her it was a bad idea, but she wouldn't listen."

Kat glanced at Bishop. "Are Leslie and your mom friends?"

"Sort of," Porter said. "My parents and Bishop's parents were friends before Mal and Bishop were born. Dad said that Mom and Leslie were close but after Bishop's dad left and Leslie went crazy, she and Mom drifted apart. I guess Mom tried to help Leslie, but," he shrugged as Bishop stared into his glass, "it didn't work that well, so she settled for keeping Bishop at our place as much as she could when we were kids."

"That was nice of her." Kat rubbed Bishop's arm.

"You have no idea," Bishop said hoarsely, "Mara saved my life. I love her more than I'll ever love Leslie."

"She loves you too, man." Porter squeezed his shoulder before leaving.

Kat took a sip of scotch. "Maybe Leslie won't show."

"She will," Bishop said. "She won't pass up any opportunity to make me miserable."

"Sorry, big guy."

"Why haven't you ever told me to cut her out of my life, Kat?" Bishop asked. "Everyone else has."

Kat shrugged. "I know a little about overbearing mothers. I love my mom, don't get me wrong, and she's not mean or hurtful like yours is, but she's," she hesitated, "insensitive, I guess is the word. She wants certain things for me and doesn't always consider her words or actions or my feelings on the matter. She thinks I should be married with a few kittens by now and doesn't understand why I'm not. She thinks I'm doing it to hurt her purposely."

Bishop raised his glass. "To difficult mothers."

She clinked her glass against his and drank. "So, are you and Ava a thing now or what?"

"I don't want to talk about it," Bishop said.

"Fair enough." She drained her glass of scotch and smiled her thanks when Porter poured her another.

"WILLOW, IT'S PAST ELEVEN. SHE'S PROBABLY SLEEPING BY now."

"She won't be." Willow balanced the bag on her lap. "She worked until eleven, remember? She's probably just getting home now."

Mal smiled at her. "And you think she's going to want company?"

"I know she will. She won't admit it, but this thing with that Chambers guy has freaked her out. It's my duty as her best friend to provide support and," she lifted the bag, "ice cream."

He flicked on his signal light and turned toward Ava's apartment. "Are you sure you don't need me to stay with you?"

"I'm sure," Willow said. "It's hard to have a girls' night with a guy there. I kind of feel like I've abandoned her lately and want to give her some one-on-one time, you know?"

"I do."

"Besides, I know you need some serious cuddle time with your babies. It must be so difficult to hide your mama instincts with the kittens when I'm there." She grinned at him.

He growled playfully. "Watch it, or I'll teach the kittens to bite your toes."

She laughed. "Your own little furry pack of kitten

minions. How delightful."

He grinned and took her hand, squeezing it firmly as he drove toward Ava's.

"I WAS FINE TO DRIVE, BISHOP," KAT SAID AS HE DROVE down the quiet street.

"Better safe than sorry," he said.

"Well, thanks for giving me a ride home."

"You're welcome. Call me tomorrow, and I'll give you a ride to Bud's to pick up your car," he said.

She squinted at the street sign. "This isn't the way to my house."

She glanced at Bishop, a little amused to see the red rising in his cheeks just above his dark beard. He cleared his throat and said, "I thought I would swing by Ava's place, just to make sure that new guy got her home safe."

"I was surprised that Mal assigned him to Ava," Kat said. "We don't know anything about him."

"No, you don't know anything about him," Bishop said. "After we offered him the job, Mal and I took him for dinner – the dinner you declined in our email request – and got to know him better."

"And?" she said.

"And what?"

"Well, what's he like?"

"As an employee or a person?" He raised his eyebrow at her.

"Employee, obviously," she said impatiently.

"Obviously." He grinned. "He's got some pretty good skills. He's a black belt, and he took home a few championships in some shooting competitions."

"Good for him."

Bishop laughed. "Honestly, I'm not sure why he even wants to work with us. With his skill set, he could do much better."

"That's not a very nice thing to say about our company, Bishop."

He shrugged. "We've got a good company, Kat, and we've got good people who work for us. All I'm saying is that I'm shocked he's not a cop anymore."

"What kind of bird is he?"

"I don't know. The topic never came up. We didn't talk about personal stuff," Bishop said.

"Don't you think it's weird that he wouldn't tell us? Or that he didn't share any personal information with you and Mal?" Kat said.

"I think you've been hanging out with Willow too much. Not everyone lives their life as an open book like she does." Bishop laughed.

"Yeah, maybe," she said. She stared out the window at the dark streets as Bishop drove toward Ava's.

"THANK YOU, RONIN. I APPRECIATE THE RIDE HOME." AVA smiled at the bird shifter and reached for the door handle.

"I'll walk you to your apartment." He unclicked his seatbelt and shut off the car.

"You don't have to do that," she said.

"I don't mind." Ronin waited patiently for her as she crossed in front of the car. "Stay right beside me, please."

She nodded. The friendly and affable man from the car was gone, and in its place was a silent and alert hunter. He took her arm and made her wait as he scanned the narrow street. She looked around, a weird little shiver going down her back. It was almost eerily quiet. No cars drove down the street, most of the windows in her apartment building were dark, and the sky was black with clouds. Drops of rain started to fall, and a gust of cold wind blew her long hair around her face. She shivered again.

"It's so dark," she said.

Ronin glanced at the sky. "We're in for one hell of a thunderstorm. Let's go. The sooner you're in your apartment, the better."

"Is something wrong?" she asked.

"I don't think so. Just have a weird feeling."

"Me too," she said.

"Then let's get you safe and sound in your place." He smiled reassuringly at her, and she didn't object when he took her hand. Despite only having just met him, his touch comforted her. She gripped his hand tightly as they crossed the street and started down the sidewalk toward the steps of her apartment building.

Ronin froze at the whisper of sound above them. The hair on the back of Ava's neck prickled as his hand clamped down on hers. They both stared upward as the skies opened and cold rain poured down in a heavy sheet, and the wind became a howling, blustering scream.

"Ronin, something's wrong!" Ava shouted.

The air felt weird as if too much energy crackled within it, and she screamed when a jagged flash of lightning struck an ancient oak tree across the street. The tree toppled to the ground, dragging the power lines with it and the streetlights blinked out, plunging them into darkness.

"Ronin!" Ava shouted as the shifter pulled her closer to him.

"What the fuck?" he shouted. He still stared upward, and

she followed his gaze. A dark shape soared toward them, and they stared transfixed at it as a boom of thunder shook the ground beneath their feet.

"No," Ava moaned. "It's him."

Another flash of lightning filled the sky with bright light, and Ronin's jaw dropped. "It's a fucking dragon."

Her feet rooted to the spot with fear, Ava watched as the dragon flew closer. He was even bigger than she remembered, and she stared wide-eyed at his massive head and body. His wings flapped, cutting through the torrential rain and carrying him easily toward them. His nostrils flared, and his jaw opened wide and terror shot through Ava.

"Ronin! Watch out!"

As flames erupted from the dragon's mouth, Ronin shoved her hard to the left. She flew backward, landing with a harsh thud in the flower bed in front of her building. She screamed piercingly when seconds later, a wall of flame engulfed Ronin. The force of the fire threw his burning body into the large clump of pine trees to the right of her building, and the dragon shrieked in triumph. He took another deep breath and blew flame into the trees, lighting them up in a fiery blaze despite the pouring rain.

She scrambled to her feet, her head ringing and her skin nearly roasting in the heat of the flames. The dragon hissed at her, and she held up her hands.

"Mr. Chambers, please. Don't do this," she said.

He stepped toward her, the ground trembling beneath his massive feet, and hissed again before drawing a deep breath. She studied his golden eyes and the red scales that covered his body as he drew closer.

He snorted, and a small burst of flame erupted from his nostrils. "You're mine."

The gargled voice was barely recognizable as human. Ava

stared petrified at the massive white teeth when he grinned at her.

"My bride," the dragon said.

"No," she said, "I'm not yours. You have to stop this, Mr. Chambers. I can't be with you. I can't be your bride."

He hissed with fury, and she backed away as more flame erupted from its nostrils.

"I can't," she repeated.

He took a deep breath, and she cringed, waiting for the fire to consume her. A roar of rage pierced the darkness. Ava screamed when the giant grizzly leaped onto the dragon's back. Bishop tore at the dragon's scales as Chambers roared with surprise and anger. He whipped his tail forward, and Ava screamed again when the end of it caught the grizzly in the side. Bishop was torn from the dragon's back and flung high into the air before landing with a ground-shaking thud in front of the dragon.

"Bishop!" Ava screamed as the dragon drew his breath in. Before he could release his flame, a golden-coloured jaguar leaped at his face with a loud snarl. The dragon howled with agony when the jaguar's sharp claws punctured one golden eye. He shook his head and large drops of blood splattered across the ground. Chambers roared again when the large cat was shaken free. She sailed through the air, landing on her feet with a delicate thud. She turned and hissed at the dragon as Bishop climbed to his feet, and a large grey wolf loped out of the darkness to join the grizzly and the jaguar. The wolf snarled, saliva dripping from his fangs, as the three animals stalked toward the dragon.

Another loud burst of thunder shook the ground as sirens wailed in the distance. Blood pouring from his eye, the dragon hissed angrily. His remaining eye turned to Ava, and she shuddered at the fury in it before the massive beast crouched and flew upward into the night sky with a loud flapping of wings.

Ava sank to her butt. Her legs trembled so badly they could no longer support her, and she stared numbly at the grizzly as he ran toward her. He shifted to the familiar bulk of Bishop and knelt in front of her.

"Ava? Honey, are you hurt? Are you hurt?" He cupped her face and stared frantically at her as Willow dropped to her knees beside her.

"Ava? Oh my God, are you okay?"

"She's not saying anything," Bishop said with fear in his voice. "Ava, are you burned?" His hands ran along her arms and down her sides.

"I – I'm fine," she said. "Not hurt."

"Thank God." He sat down and pulled her into his lap, stroking her wet hair and kissing her face as she stared up at him.

Still in his wolf form, Mal joined them and shifted before taking Willow's hand. "You okay?"

"Fine. I stayed in the car like you said," Willow said shakily.

"Good." He kissed her mouth as the jaguar ran by them.

"Where's Kat going?" Willow asked.

"Probably to get some clothes," Mal said.

"Are you okay?" Willow asked as she examined him. "No burns?"

"No, honey, I'm fine."

"Thank God." She threw her arms around him and hugged him hard. "Hey, Mal?" Her voice was muffled against his throat.

"Yeah?"

"I know I've never seen a darthen lizard before, but I'm pretty fucking sure that was a dragon."

He nodded. "It was."

Bishop cupped Ava's face. "I'm sorry I didn't believe you, baby. I'm so sorry."

She didn't reply, ignoring the worried look he gave her as Kat reappeared wearing one of Bishop's shirts. "Everyone okay?"

"Yeah," Willow said.

"Where's Ronin?" Kat asked.

Ava stared blankly at her, and Kat touched her arm. "Ava? Where's Ronin?"

"Dead," she said woodenly. "Mr. Chambers burned him up. He shoved me out of the way, and then his body was – was burning."

"Fuck," Mal muttered as Kat's face paled.

"Are you sure?" Kat said.

Ava pointed toward the burning clump of trees. "His body is in there."

———

KAT STARED AT THE BURNING CLUMP OF TREES THAT AVA pointed to. Ronin couldn't be dead. He couldn't be. Her jaguar yowled in misery, and her sorrow intensified Kat's own. Kat started toward the trees, ignoring Mal when he said, "Don't, Kat. The fire's too hot – there's no way he survived."

She walked closer to the burning trees. The heat was immense despite the cold rain pouring down, and she threw her arm over her face as she took a few steps closer. It felt like her lungs were starting to sear, and she held her breath, squinting into the flames before finally moving back.

She released her breath in a harsh rush and slammed her fist against her wet thigh. "Fuck!"

She pushed her hair away from her face and stared in

disbelief at the burning trees. Her stomach roiled, and she shivered despite the heat. She'd known the bird shifter for less than a week, but the thought that Ronin was dead and she would never hear his voice again made her want to scream and vomit at the same time.

"Don't suppose you have any marshmallows, Kitten?"

The familiar voice speaking in her ear made her whirl around. A naked and dripping wet Ronin stood behind her. He grinned. "I could go for some smores right now."

Her cat purred and trilled with delight. Kat threw her arms around Ronin and hugged him hard.

"Wow." His warm breath tickled her ear. "That's quite the greeting, Kitten."

His hands stroked her back through the wet material of Bishop's t-shirt, and she shivered in his arms before forcing herself to let him go and step back. "You're not dead."

"Nope."

"But – but Ava saw you die. She said flames engulfed you."

"Nah, just a few singed tail feathers." He grinned again.

"That's impossible." She ran her hands over his broad shoulders and down his arms before touching the reddish-coloured hair on his chest. She studied the tattoos that covered his upper body. "There's no way you can be standing here without a mark on you."

He shrugged. "I got lucky. I managed to fly out of the way before the flames hit me."

"She said she saw your body burning." Kat frowned as she touched the hard ridges of his abs. Her fingers floated over his narrow hips, and he inhaled sharply.

"Unless you want to start something right here, Kitten, you need to stop with the touching and the stroking," he muttered.

"What?" She gave him a startled look before dropping her gaze to his rapidly hardening dick. "Oh my God."

She forced herself to look away from the all-too-delicious sight. "Are you kidding me?"

"Hey, you started it." He shrugged. "I can't help it if seeing me naked makes your kitty purr."

"I – it doesn't…" She took a deep breath and stepped back. "Seeing you naked does not make my kitty purr."

"Whatever you say." He gave her a sexy little grin that did indeed make her kitty purr. His gaze dropped over her body, and she cursed and pulled Bishop's wet shirt away from her breasts.

"Stop being a pervert," she said.

"Oh, I'm the pervert now." He chuckled. "You were about to grab my dick in front of everyone, and I'm the perverted one."

"I wouldn't grab your dick if – if you were the last shifter on earth!" Feeling incredibly foolish, she turned and stormed back to the others as Ronin followed her.

"BISHOP, WE NEED TO GET AVA OUT OF HERE," MAL SAID. No neighbours had ventured outside yet, but plenty of faces peered out the windows, and the sirens were growing steadily louder.

"I know," Bishop said.

"She and Willow can stay with me tonight," Mal said.

"No," Bishop said. "I'm taking her back to my place."

Willow took Ava's hand. "No, Bishop. Not tonight."

Bishop snarled under his breath. "She's staying with me."

"Bishop, she doesn't need -"

"I want to, Willow," Ava said. "I want to stay with

Bishop."

"Are you sure, honey?" Willow asked. "I know you're afraid, but -"

"I want to stay with Bishop," Ava repeated.

Willow smoothed Ava's hair away from her face. "Okay, honey. You can call me though if you change your mind, okay?"

She nodded. "Yes. Will you help me up, Bishop?"

He pressed a kiss against her mouth before helping her to her feet.

She swayed on her feet, and he steadied her. "Maybe you should go to the hospital, honey."

"No, I..." Her face paled, and she pointed behind him. Bishop looked over his shoulder to see Kat and Ronin approaching them.

"You okay, Ava?" Ronin asked.

"You – you're dead. I saw it," she said as she clung to Bishop's waist.

Ronin glanced at the others. "No. I flew away."

"You didn't," she said. "I know you didn't."

"You're mistaken." He smiled at her. "It happened pretty fast, and it was scary."

"I know what I saw," she said.

"We need to leave," Mal said. "Bishop, get Ava out of here."

"Mal, can you give me a ride home?" Kat asked.

"Yes. Everyone get moving. Ronin, take your car and go home. Don't speak to anyone about what you saw, all right? I'll call you in the morning and explain everything," Mal said.

Ronin nodded, and Mal blew his breath out before staring at the downed power lines and the burning trees. "Let's get the fuck out of here."

CHAPTER 11

"Your place is nice," Ava said as Bishop ushered her into the house. He shut the door behind them, drowning out the sound of the rain and the thunder.

He studied her carefully. She was pale, and her eyes had an odd vacant look to them that made him nervous.

"Honey, are you okay?" he asked.

"Yes."

She was dripping wet and shivering, and he led her up the stairs to his bedroom. "Let's get you warmed up."

"Sure," she said.

Princess met them at the top of the stairs, purring and weaving around both their legs, and a faint smile crossed Ava's face. "You have a cat. What's its name?"

"Princess," he said.

She squatted and petted the cat gently. Princess rubbed up against her wet leg before sneezing and then sauntering down the hall.

"She's sweet," Ava said.

"C'mon, honey, you can have a hot shower, and then I'll make you something to eat."

She followed him into his bedroom. She blinked in surprise when he flicked on the light, and she saw his bed.

"That's the biggest bed I've ever seen," she said.

She touched the quilt on the bed as Bishop stared at her worriedly.

"How big is it?" she asked.

"It's eight feet long and six feet wide. I had it custom made."

"I suppose you would have to. No chance of breaking this one, huh?" Her odd laugh had a jagged note of hysteria to it.

"Ava?" He touched her arm, and she burst into loud sobs. She tried to turn away, and he pulled her into his embrace, stroking her back through her wet clothing as she clung to him.

"I'm sorry, I'm so sorry," she repeatedly sobbed.

"Shh, you have nothing to be sorry about, baby." He cupped her head, and she buried her face in his chest. He had pulled on a pair of jeans back at her apartment but hadn't bothered with a shirt, and her tears mixed with the rainwater on his skin.

"Shh, it's okay, baby. You're safe. I'll never let him hurt you. I promise," he said.

"I was so scared," she said. "I thought I was going to die."

"You're all right," he said.

"Thanks to you." She lifted her head to stare at him, and he wiped the tears from her face with his thumbs. "Why were you at my apartment?"

"Kat and I went for dinner and drinks, and I swung by to make sure you had gotten home okay after work."

"Thank God," she said. "You and Kat... you saved my life tonight."

She hugged him fiercely, and he kissed the top of her

head as she shook against him. "Why were Mal and Willow there?"

"I don't know," he said.

Her eyes were puffy and red from crying, but the vacant look in them had disappeared. He breathed a sigh of relief as she stared up at him. "Thank you, Bishop. Thank you so much. I'll never be able to repay you for what you did tonight."

"Stop, baby. You don't have to repay me." He stroked her wet hair away from her face. "You're freezing. Have a shower while I make us something to eat. Okay?"

She nodded, and he led her into his bathroom. He brought her clean towels and one of his t-shirts and kissed her lightly before leaving her to her shower. He headed downstairs to the kitchen and pulled out the leftover soup in the fridge. As it heated, he called Mal.

"Bishop?" Mal answered on the first ring. "Everything okay?"

"Yeah. We're at my place. You and Willow get home okay?"

"We did. We dropped off Kat at her place and then headed straight home."

"Fuck," Bishop groaned. "I completely forgot about Kat. I'll have to apologize."

"She understands, Bishop. Don't worry about it."

"Yeah." He paused. "It was a fucking dragon, Mal."

"I know."

"I didn't believe her. She tried to tell us, and I didn't believe her. She almost died tonight because I decided she couldn't possibly have seen a dragon."

"This isn't your fault, Bishop."

"It is. If I hadn't shown up tonight...."

"It's not your fault," Mal repeated. "Why were you and Kat there?"

"We went for dinner and drinks after work. I was driving Kat home, and I wanted to check that Ava made it home," Bishop said. "Why were you there?"

"Willow knew Ava wasn't sleeping well and decided she would surprise her with a girls' night."

"She almost died tonight," Bishop repeated. His whole body shuddered, and his grizzly whimpered as a wave of fear swept over both of them. He'd almost lost Ava.

"She's okay," Mal said. "But you need to talk to Kaida."

"I know." Bishop stirred the soup as Princess wandered into the kitchen and leaped onto the table. She watched as he poured water into two glasses and took two bowls from the cupboard. "I'll call Kaida tomorrow and see if she can stop at the office."

"What about Ava?"

"I'm not letting her out of my sight," Bishop said. "She can come to the office with me tomorrow."

"Don't come in until later," Mal said.

"I can't. I have a conference call at ten with Mr. Beckham and a meeting at eleven-thirty with -"

"Kat and I will cover for you," Mal said. "Take the morning off, and we'll see you and Ava in the afternoon."

"Thanks, Mal."

"You're welcome. Keep her safe, buddy."

"I will. Goodnight."

Bishop tucked his phone into his back pocket and stared out the kitchen window. The rain continued to pour down, and when a deafening clap of thunder shook the windows, Princess hissed and leaped from the table before disappearing into the living room.

He cocked his head and listened. The shower was still

running, and he rubbed a hand through his hair as he stared out the window again. Ava had nearly died. When he had turned onto her street and seen the massive body of the dragon standing over her, he'd almost lost his mind with rage. For the first time since he'd reached puberty, he lost control over his grizzly. It had roared to the front, pushing past his human side as easily as a ragdoll, and gone after the beast that threatened his mate.

Mate.

He closed his eyes and took a deep breath. It was useless to deny that his grizzly thought of Ava as his mate. Grizzlies weren't meant to mate for life. He'd watched his mother be destroyed by her love for a man who, despite his love for her, couldn't ignore his true nature. It was stupid, hell, downright dangerous to indulge his grizzly's obsession with Ava as his mate, but he didn't know how to stop it.

What his grizzly felt for Ava now would fade over time, just like his father's love for his mother had faded. He wouldn't hurt Ava like that. He wouldn't.

She almost died tonight, his inner voice whispered. *You need to tell her that you love her.*

He'd been afraid, terrified in fact, that he was about to watch Ava die. The thought of her death filled him with a cold kind of terror that he had never experienced before. He gripped the counter tightly as more shudders wracked his body.

Keep it together, asshole. She needs you.

He heard the faint sound of the shower turning off, and he quickly put the soup and water on a tray and started up the stairs.

Ava wiped away the steam from the bathroom mirror and stared at her reflection. She was too pale, making her freckles more noticeable than usual. She had a headache but considering that she'd almost been burned to a crisp not an hour earlier, a headache was a small price to pay.

Before opening the medicine cabinet, she took a deep breath, rubbing her forehead. She took two Advil from the bottle in the cabinet then studied the dark green box beside it. She took it out of the cabinet, colour returning to her cheeks when she realized it was exactly what she thought it was.

The box of condoms had a picture of a grizzly on it, and she swallowed down the weirdly hysterical laughter that bubbled up in her chest as she read the back of the box. Apparently, grizzly shifters had their own line of condoms.

Obviously, you idiot. Do you think Bishop could fit a regular condom on his dick?

An image of Bishop trying to roll a standard-sized condom onto his giant penis flooded through her. This time it was impossible to stop the hysterical giggling. She clutched the box of condoms as she snorted and snickered, and tears dripped down her cheeks.

There was a knock on the bathroom door, and Bishop's worried voice drifted through it. "Ava? Honey, are you okay?"

"Fine," she said, her voice weird and strangled sounding. "Be out in a minute."

She took three deep and even breaths, waiting for the giggles to dry up, before slipping into Bishop's shirt and smoothing back her wet hair. She studied the box of condoms sitting next to the sink as Bishop knocked again.

"Honey?"

"I'm fine," she said distractedly as she continued to stare at the condoms.

Do it, Ava. You want him, and he wants you. Stop denying yourself what you want. You could have died tonight, and you would never have known what it was like to be with him. For once, take control of your life and take what you deserve. No regrets - even if it's just for tonight.

"No regrets," she whispered and, holding the box of condoms in her hand, opened the bathroom door.

"I have some soup here for you," Bishop said.

"I'm not hungry."

"You need to eat, baby." He started toward the dresser, where the food tray sat on top of it.

She grabbed his arm as he walked by her and tugged him to a stop. "No, Bishop."

"Ava," he gave her a helpless look, "please."

She shook her head. "I don't need food."

"What do you need?" he said.

She leaned forward and placed a soft kiss against his broad chest. "You. I need you, Bishop."

"Honey," he groaned as she pressed her mouth against his chest for a second time and tasted him with her tongue, "this isn't a good idea. You need to rest after what happened."

"No," she said. "I need you."

He continued to hesitate, and she took his hand and squeezed it tightly. "Do you want me to beg, Bishop? Is that what you need?"

"No, Ava."

"Good." She tugged him toward the bed, and he watched as she set the box of condoms on the nightstand.

She reached for the button on his jeans, and he stroked her arms as she unbuttoned and unzipped them. She wiggled her hand into his pants and grasped his cock, stroking it firmly as he groaned. It hardened under her touch, and she rubbed her thumb over the tip, smiling at the look of lust on his face.

"Will you give me what I need, Bishop?" she asked.

"Yes." He leaned down and kissed her.

She opened her mouth, touching his tongue delicately with her own as her hand stroked and caressed. He moaned into her mouth and deepened the kiss, pushing his tongue into her mouth with a rough force that brought a bite of lust to her belly.

"I want you so much, Ava," he murmured.

"I want you too," she breathed.

He threaded his hand through her long, damp hair and tugged until her head tilted back. He kissed her throat, running his tongue across the soft skin, and she moaned and tightened her grip on his cock.

"God. You make me want to come in my pants like a damn teenager," he groaned.

She laughed, and he smiled at her as she pushed his jeans down his legs. He stepped out of them, and she raised her arms so he could lift her shirt over her head.

He dropped it to the floor and stared at her naked body. "You're so beautiful, Ava."

"You're beautiful too." She traced one trembling hand over his chest as he cupped one breast and squeezed lightly.

She bit her bottom lip as he dipped his head and traced the pattern of freckles on her upper chest with his tongue before sucking on her nipple. She buried her hands in his hair and gripped tightly as he sucked.

"That feels so good, Bishop," she moaned.

"Open your legs, Ava," he said.

She spread her legs and then gasped when he traced the soft red curls at the top of her mound before sliding his hand between her legs. He rubbed her pussy, growling happily.

"You're so wet for me, baby." He kissed her again. She clutched at his broad shoulders as he slid his finger deep inside of her. He used his thumb to rub at her clit, and she moaned as pleasure speared through her belly.

"Mine, Ava," he said against her mouth.

A shudder of need went through her, and she nodded. "Yes, yours."

He kissed her again, and she rubbed herself against him as he stroked her pussy roughly.

"Please, Bishop. I want to come," she pleaded when he pulled his hand away.

"Soon, baby," he promised.

He backed her toward the bed and quickly pulled the covers down before pushing her onto her back. He settled on his side next to her and ran the tip of his finger between her breasts. He circled a small cluster of freckles on the curve of her right breast before leaning down and kissing it.

"I want to kiss every freckle on your gorgeous body, Ava."

"Oh my God," she moaned. "Bishop, I can't wait – not tonight. Please."

"Are you sure?" He licked another of her freckles.

"Yes," she said, allowing the frustration into her voice. "I need you to – to fuck me."

She blushed at her words, and he nuzzled her breast. "Say it again, Ava."

"Fuck me, Bishop," she said as her flush deepened.

"Again."

"Fuck me." This time, knowing she needed to drive him crazy too, she reached down and rubbed his cock with long, sure strokes.

He groaned before cupping her pussy possessively. "I'll

fuck you, Ava, but first, I'm going to watch your sweet face as you come for me."

She released her breath in a drawn-out hiss as his fingers found her clit and rubbed. "Only me, Ava. From this moment on, you come for me and only for me. Do you understand?"

His fingers slowed, and he grazed her swollen clit with the pad of one large finger. "Do you, Ava?"

Her hands clenched in the bedsheets as he brought her closer and closer to her orgasm. "Yes! Only you."

He growled again and rubbed hard at her clit.

Her chest heaving and her pelvis arching uncontrollably, Ava stared wide-eyed at the ceiling as Bishop sucked on her earlobe before tracing the shell of her ear with his warm tongue. Her entire body was on fire, every nerve ending singing with the need for release. She writhed and twisted against Bishop's hand as he drove her higher and higher until, with a hoarse cry, her body arched, and her orgasm swept through her.

She shook and shuddered against Bishop's solid body as he stroked the wet lips of her pussy and nuzzled her neck.

"You look so pretty when you come, Ava," he said before sucking on one hard nipple. "Your nipples are so tight, and look how wet your pussy is."

He raised his hand, and another tingle of lust went through her when she saw the wetness on his fingers. She was so wet she could feel moisture sliding down her thighs, and she supposed she should have been embarrassed. Instead, she felt only a driving need to have Bishop between her legs, to feel his hard cock sliding into her oh-so-wet pussy.

"Please, Bishop. I need you. Fuck me," she whispered into his ear before biting his earlobe.

He sucked in his breath, his hand tightening around her breast before he abruptly rolled away from her and sat up.

She heard him fumbling with the box and smiled when he cursed under his breath before tearing open the foil. She loved how much he wanted her.

CALM DOWN. YOU'LL FRIGHTEN HER.

Bishop took a deep breath as he rolled the condom onto his dick. He turned to face Ava, and she stared at his cock as he stroked her thigh. "Don't be frightened, baby. I won't hurt you. I promise."

"I know. I'm not afraid, honey."

"Do you want to be on top?" he asked. He tried to conceal his need for her to be under him, his need to feel her curvy body cushioning his and those long legs wrapped around his waist as he entered her. It would be understandable with their size difference if she didn't want him on top of her. But, holy hell, did he want that.

"No. I trust you," Ava said.

Her words and how she smiled at him made him feel weak with his lust for her. What he wouldn't do for this woman. He knelt between her legs, and Ava spread her thighs as far as she could to accommodate his large body.

"Relax, baby, all right?" He stroked the curve of her hip. "I'll move slowly."

"I'm ready for you," she said with that same look of trust. "Don't make me wait any longer."

He reached between them and guided his cock to her warm entrance. As the head of his cock pressed against her, she smiled and ran her hands over his chest. "Make me yours, Bishop."

He groaned harshly and pushed the head of his cock into

her wet warmth. She released her breath in a low moan, and he stopped.

"Okay?" he asked.

"Yes. Don't stop."

He pushed again, sliding more of his cock into her wet warmth, and forced himself to withdraw as her walls squeezed him tightly.

"I'm good, honey," she said with a touch of frustration. "Please."

"I know," he said. He slowly slid deeper into her, every muscle straining against the urge to just slam into her tight pussy, to make her feel every thick inch as he fucked her.

He withdrew slightly and thrust in again, repeating the motion until, with another harsh groan, he sunk his entire length into her. He stopped, staring at her sweet face as she bit at her lip and her thighs pressed against his hips.

She was helpless beneath him, impaled on his thick cock, and the thought sent a stab of lust through his body. She belonged to him now, and he would cover every inch of her soft body with his scent until every shifter who came near her knew she was his.

"You're mine, Ava," he growled. "Mine."

"Yes." She cupped his face and pressed a gentle kiss against his mouth. "Now fuck me, Bishop."

He kissed her again, sliding his tongue into her mouth as he withdrew and pushed into her. She moaned and lifted her legs, wrapping them around his waist and squeezing as he plunged in and out of her.

"Harder, honey," she whispered against his mouth. "I need it harder."

"Fuck, Ava," he muttered as her words sent a jolt of pleasure straight to his dick. "You're going to make me come if you keep talking like that."

She grinned at him and nipped his thick neck. "I can handle everything you have to give me."

He thrust roughly back and forth, his control wavering when she made a soft cooing noise and stroked his broad back. "That feels so good, honey."

"Oh God, Ava," he moaned. "You're so fucking tight."

Her pussy gripped him wetly, and she arched her hips, meeting each of his thrusts as he propped himself above her and stared at her sweet face.

He slid in and out of her, and when she closed her eyes, he made a low growl. "Open your eyes, baby. Look at me as I fuck you."

Her eyelids fluttered open, and he stared into her clear, green eyes as he thrust harder. "Can you come this way?"

"Not usually," she panted, "but you're so damn thick that I think maybe...." She shuddered with pleasure. "Keep going, Bishop. Make me come with your cock."

He jerked, his pelvis slapping against hers and then made another harsh groan. Ava dropped her legs, bracing her feet against the bed, and wrapped her arms around his broad shoulders as his pace quickened and his eyes began to glow. His balls were tightening, and he didn't think he could hold off his orgasm.

"Ava, baby, I'm going to come. I can't wait much longer."

"Yes," she moaned, "I want you to come, honey."

He groaned, and his steady rhythm grew ragged as her cheeks flushed and she stared wide-eyed at him. "Bishop, oh, Bishop, I -"

Her body stiffened beneath him, and her pussy gripped him tightly as she came. The extra pressure and the flood of warm wetness pushed him over the edge. He threw his head back and roared as he came deep inside of her.

Shuddering all over, he collapsed against her, and she made a soft 'oof' before pushing at his shoulders.

"Bishop, can't breathe!" she gasped.

He rolled off of her and stared up at the ceiling, his heart thudding heavily and his entire body shaking.

She leaned over him and touched his chest. "Bishop? Are you okay?"

"Hell, yes," he muttered.

She reached down and slid the condom off of him. She disposed of it in the wastebasket before curling against him and resting her head on his chest.

"Thank you, honey." He stroked her long red hair as she sighed contently.

"You're welcome. Thanks for giving me the best orgasm of my life."

"My pleasure." He grinned at her, and she patted his chest.

"Stop looking so smug, Bishop."

He laughed and held her closer. "Do you want to eat now?"

"No." She yawned and kissed his chest. "Sleep now, eat later."

He kissed her forehead and rubbed her back. "Goodnight, Ava."

"Night, Bishop."

CHAPTER 12

She woke before he did. She was curled up on her side with his heavy body tucked against hers. One large arm wrapped around her, and his hand cupped her breast possessively. His bed was incredibly comfortable, and although she suspected it was morning, the blinds did a fantastic job of blocking the light.

She remained snuggled against him for a while longer, listening to the deep rhythm of his breathing and studying the hand that cupped her breast. Eventually, the need to pee had her sliding out from under his arm. She used the bathroom quickly and made her way down to the kitchen.

It was just after seven, and she opened a few cupboards until she found the coffee supplies. As the coffee brewed, she peeked her head into the living room and smiled at the over-sized couch and chair that dominated the room. Every piece of furniture in his house was built for his size, and she smiled a little as the calico cat jumped down from the couch and rubbed against her legs.

"Hello, Princess." She picked up the large cat and petted her head as she purred and bumped her face against hers.

"You're a good girl." She set her down and returned to the kitchen. Her stomach growled, and she opened the fridge.

"Good grief," she said, "he wasn't kidding about loving berries."

She studied the various packages of berries that were packed into the fridge before placing a few of the plastic containers on the counter. She popped some bread into the toaster, poured two cups of coffee, grabbed the small milk container and the ceramic bowl of sugar, and piled everything on a tray she found in a lower cupboard. She buttered the toast and added it to the tray before heading upstairs.

As she climbed the last stair, Bishop came stumbling out of the bedroom, his face panicked. "Ava! Ava, where are you?"

"Right here," she said as he stared blankly at her.

"Jesus, don't do that to me, honey." He rubbed his chest as she moved past him and into the bedroom.

"Sorry," she said. "I made us breakfast."

"You didn't have to do that."

"It isn't much." She set the tray down next to the tray of soup before adding milk and sugar to her coffee. "What do you take in your coffee?"

"Lots of milk and sugar." He moved behind her, put one thick arm around her waist, and kissed her neck as she added milk and sugar to his coffee.

"Here, let's eat in bed." He took the tray, and she climbed onto the bed and sat cross-legged as he placed the tray between them.

He held out a piece of toast to her, and she shook her head. "I just want berries."

He frowned but ate the toast silently as she bit into a strawberry. He watched her eat, and she gave him a self-conscious look.

"What?"

"What – what?" he said.

"You're staring at me."

"Just thinking about how your nipples would taste with berry juice on them."

"Bishop!" She blushed, and he grinned at her.

"Sorry."

"Eat your breakfast and be good," she chided gently.

"Yes, ma'am." He grabbed the container of blackberries and tipped it to his mouth. He growled happily at the tart taste, and he ate all of them before setting down the container and reaching for the raspberries.

Ava tried not to grin as he looked at the empty container and then at her. "I'm sorry, that was rude. I should have offered you some blackberries."

She smiled at him. "It's fine, Bishop."

"I like berries," he said.

"I know you do." She sipped at her coffee and took a handful of raspberries when he held the container out to her.

"How do you feel this morning?" He tossed some blueberries into his mouth and finished off the last of the toast as she ate more strawberries.

"Better." She smiled faintly at him. "But still afraid."

"I won't let him hurt you, Ava. I promise," he said.

"I know." She stared into her coffee mug and didn't protest when Bishop gently tugged it away.

"Eat the rest of the strawberries, honey."

———

BISHOP BUSIED HIMSELF WITH CLEARING THE TRAY FROM THE bed as Ava ate the last two strawberries. She sat cross-legged with his shirt pulled down over her knees. He sat next to her and rested his forehead against hers.

"What time are you going to work?" she asked.

"Not until this afternoon, and you're coming with me," he said.

"I have to call work," she said. "I need to let them know that I won't be in for a few days."

"Later," he said. He nuzzled her neck, and she shivered as his hand slipped under her shirt.

He stroked her thigh, and she cupped his face. "What happens now, Bishop?"

Tell her she is our mate, his grizzly growled. *Tell her she belongs to us.*

He couldn't tell her that, but he didn't want her thinking last night had just been the proverbial roll in the hay for him.

"Ava, I -"

"We can't fight a dragon," she said worriedly. "He's too big and too strong, and he breathes fire for God's sake."

He breathed a sigh of relief that it wasn't them she was talking about. "It'll be okay, baby."

"No, it won't." She scowled at him. "Don't say that when it isn't true, Bishop."

He kissed her forehead as his big hand stroked her bare thigh. "I'll text Kaida and ask her to come by the office today. If there's a rogue dragon in the city, he'll probably belong to her clan, and the elders will need to know about him. They'll stop him."

"Are you sure?"

"Yes. Dragons have strict rules about revealing themselves to humans. The clan elders will punish him."

"Punish him? How?"

He cleared his throat and stared uneasily at her. His time with Kaida had given him insight into the world of the dragons that very few shifters would ever gain. Kaida had trusted him with her clan's secrets, and he would not break that trust, not even for Ava.

"Bishop? Do you know?" she asked.

"I'm not certain what they'll do to him."

He wasn't completely lying. Kaida had always been vague with the details, but he did know that it was enough to frighten her. Considering that she was the toughest woman he knew, the punishment had to be incredibly bad.

"How do you know Kaida?"

"We met when we were young," he said briefly. "Are you still hungry, Ava? I can bring you more to eat."

She shook her head. "No, I'm good."

"You're not eating enough."

"I am," she said absently.

She suddenly pressed her lips against his. "Thank you, Bishop. You saved my life last night, and I don't know how to tell you how thankful I am."

He inhaled deeply, smelling the sweet scent of his mate and tasting her on his lips. "You don't have to thank me. I'm sorry I didn't believe you."

"It was kind of a dick move," she said with a small smile.

"I should have believed you." He cupped her face and kissed her. She tasted like strawberries, and he deepened the kiss as he trailed his hand up her thigh under her shirt and then cupped her pussy.

"Bishop," she gasped as she grabbed his wrist through her shirt. "Wh-what are you doing?"

"What does it look like I'm doing?" He nipped her jaw and rubbed her clit as her fingers squeezed his wrist.

"I – I thought last night was just a one-time thing," she said.

"Did you? How strange. There's still so much I want to do to you," he said.

"Like what?" Her voice was hoarse, and she moaned when he slid his finger into her pussy.

"I haven't taken you on your hands and knees yet," he said. "I haven't tasted the sweetness of your pussy. Would you like me to do both of those things to you?"

"Oh my God," she muttered, "I can't think straight when you're – you're…."

"Rubbing your pussy?" he asked with a slight grin.

She nodded, and her head fell back as he rubbed her clit. "That feels so good, Bishop."

"My tongue will feel better." He moved his hand away, smiling at her moan of dismay, before pulling his shirt from her body. He admired her heavy breasts and the smooth curve of her belly before lying on his back on the bed. "In fact, I know just how you can thank me for last night, Ava."

"Bishop, I can't." She gave him a wary look, and he took her hand.

"Yes, you can, honey."

"I'm too heavy – I'll suffocate you. Do you suddenly have a death wish?" She scowled at him as her cheeks flushed.

"It would be a hell of a way to die." He grinned and then sat up when she didn't return his smile.

He cupped her face again and said solemnly, "Ava, I promise not to suffocate while you're riding my face."

A high-pitched and nervous giggle spilled from her lips, and he stroked her cheek. "Just try it, baby. If you don't like it, I'll stop."

"Why do you want this, Bishop?" she asked.

"Because more than anything, I want to be surrounded by

your scent and your taste and to have the warmth of your body all around me as I taste you for the first time."

"I don't want to hurt you," she said.

"You won't." He put his hands around her waist and lifted her easily into his lap. "The benefits of being with a bear shifter, Ava. We're unbelievably strong and tough."

He lifted her again, his muscles barely straining, before setting her back in his lap.

A small smile crossed her face. "Now you're just showing off."

"Maybe just a little." He licked her bottom lip. "Let me taste you, Ava."

She continued to hesitate, and he smiled at her. "If you don't want to do this, honey, we won't. Okay?"

She took a deep breath. "I do want to try it, Bishop. I'm just, uh, nervous."

"If you want me to stop, just tell me," he breathed into her ear before sucking lightly on the lobe.

She nodded, and he laid on his back as she straddled his hips. He put his warm hands around her waist and urged her forward. She eased over him until her knees rested on the bed on either side of his head.

"You're so beautiful, Ava," he said.

"Thank you," she said.

He rubbed her inner thighs and stared at her pussy. "Your pussy is beautiful too."

She blushed as he traced the soft red curls. "I need to taste you, Ava. Right now."

She took a deep breath and allowed him to tug her down. He kissed her lightly, and she moaned, her hands clenching into fists when his beard rubbed against her pussy lips. "Oh, God."

He licked a slow path across her pussy lips, and she moaned again, her pelvis already arching against his mouth.

"You taste so sweet, baby." His voice was muffled, and he stroked her thighs. "As sweet as honey."

"Oh please," she whispered when she felt his hot breath. "Oh, please."

"I'm going to eat your sweet pussy until you're screaming my name, Ava." He clamped his hands down on her thighs, and she was helpless to stop him from pulling her down onto his face. He swept his tongue over her throbbing clit, and she cried out, her back arching and her hands holding tightly to his wrists.

She seemed to forget her nervousness and worry and ground herself against his face to his delight. He growled happily, his hands squeezing her thighs even tighter, and thrust his tongue into her tight entrance.

"Oh my God!" she cried out when he rubbed his beard against her wet lips and licked her clit repeatedly.

"Oh!" she shouted, her hips grinding against his face as she grew closer to her orgasm.

He sucked firmly on her clit before growling again, and the vibration sent her over the edge. She screamed his name, her hips thrusting and her body shaking as her orgasm swept through her. Her thighs shaking wildly, she pushed herself away from him and fell onto her back on his wide bed. She stared at the ceiling, taking breath after shuddering breath as her body twitched uncontrollably.

Bishop rested one warm hand on her trembling stomach. "Okay, honey?"

She nodded and then touched his wet beard. "I'm sorry."

"Never say sorry for that," he said.

She stared up at the ceiling again. "Are you okay?"

"Yes, why?"

"I lost control, and I was, you know…."

"Riding my face?" He grinned at her soft blush. He gave her a few more minutes, and when her breathing slowed, he nuzzled her breast and placed a gentle kiss on one hard nipple.

"Break time is over." He flipped her to her stomach, grinning at her surprised squeak, and rubbed her beautiful ass before pushing between her thighs and rising to his knees.

"On your hands and knees, honey." He slapped her ass lightly, and she jerked before moving to her knees.

"Bishop, I'm not going to come again," she warned him as she twisted around to look at him. "That last one was intense, and I -"

He reached around her and cupped her breasts, tugging roughly on her nipples as he lifted her to her knees and pressed her back against his hard chest. She gasped and arched her back, pushing her ass against his rock-hard erection as he bit her shoulder lightly.

"You'll come again for me, Ava," he whispered into her ear.

"Bishop," she moaned, "I -"

"Say it, Ava. Say you're going to come for me." He cupped her throat with one hand and rubbed and kneaded her full breasts with the other.

"I'm going to come for you, Bishop," she said, and he grinned in hard satisfaction.

"That's my good girl." He released her and pushed on her back. "Hands and knees, baby."

She bent over, resting her hands on the bed as he reached for a condom. He rolled it on and then tugged on her thighs. "Spread your legs wider."

She widened them obediently, and he studied her pink

pussy for so long that she made a soft sound of embarrass-ment. "Bishop, are you -"

"Hush, Ava." He stroked her ass before dipping his hand between her thighs and rubbing her pussy. "This is mine, isn't it?"

"Yes," she said, and he made a low rumble of approval.

He guided his dick into her, watching her pussy lips slide down over his cock, and his balls tightening at the way she moaned. He moved slowly, giving her plenty of time to adjust to his thickness as she wiggled against him.

"Bishop, more." She turned her head to pout at him, and he held her hips and pushed himself in to the hilt. She made a startled gasp, and he smoothed his hand over her lower back.

"Is that better, baby?"

"Yes," she moaned.

"Such a greedy little pussy," he said.

"You're so thick," she moaned again as she moved rest-lessly under him.

He rubbed her ass and waited for her to adjust to him. He had never been with a human woman who could take all of him, and having his entire cock sheathed completely in her wet, tight heat drove him insane with need. He muttered a curse when her pussy suddenly tightened around him.

"Fuck! Baby, stop that." He squeezed her full hips.

"You don't like it?" she asked sweetly before squeezing him again.

"Ava," he warned, "be a good girl or else."

"Or else what?" She stared over her shoulder at him and grinned cheekily.

For the first time since he'd met her, shy, sweet Ava had disappeared, leaving a vixen with flame coloured hair in her place. His grizzly growled his approval. Ava thrust her hips back and forth, taking her pleasure from his cock. He let his head fall back and groaned with pleasure as she rocked back and forth on her knees, sliding his cock in and out of her.

He let her control the pace, keeping his body perfectly still and holding her hips loosely as he watched her pussy suck hungrily at his dick. She moaned with every stroke, and with a small grin, he reached down and gathered her hair in one large fist. He pulled on it before pressing his other hand in the small of her back.

He bent over her and pressed a kiss between her shoulder blades before forcing her head to the side. He nuzzled her ear and licked the sensitive spot behind it. She shivered and cried out, and he captured her mouth with his, sliding his tongue deep into her mouth as his cock throbbed within her.

"My turn, Ava," he whispered against her lips.

He straightened and tightened his hold on her hair while his other hand gripped her hip. He pulled on her hair, forcing her to arch her back, and then smoothed his hand over her ass.

"Bishop, please," she moaned.

He grinned at the pleading in her voice and slowly thrust back and forth as he reached under her and squeezed her full breast.

AVA STARED AT THE CEILING. BISHOP'S HAND WAS WOUND tightly in her hair, and she was surprised at how much she liked the sensation. In fact, she was shocked at how much she liked everything about this position. Something primal and animalistic about it made her entire body vibrate with lust. She tried to squeeze Bishop's cock again. His thickness made it incredibly difficult, but she loved his reaction. She made a soft grunt when he spanked her three times on the ass. The slaps were harder than the previous ones, creating a stinging pleasure/pain that brought on another almost unbearable surge of need.

She ignored the unexpected lust – nice girls didn't like to be spanked, right? - and tried to turn her head to frown at Bishop. He kept her firmly in place with his hand in her hair, so she tried to wiggle away, a sharp stab of lust sinking into her pelvis when he growled and slid his other hand around her throat, cupping it firmly. "Where do you think you're going?"

"Who said you could spank me?" she asked.

He released his grip on her hair, and disappointment went through her. Right or wrong, she enjoyed Bishop's dominant behaviour, and she assumed being cheeky with him would increase his need to dominate her. She wanted that badly. She wanted him to pull her hair and spank her and push her down on the bed and fuck her like the only thing that mattered was his pleasure, not hers.

Why would he? You can't expect him to just know that about you. Until two minutes ago, you had no idea that you liked this kind of sex, so why would he?

She bit back her moan of disappointment, and then, to her surprise and pleasure, Bishop spanked her again, his hand landing firmly on her ass with hard, even strokes. She moaned happily and squirmed and writhed against him, her pussy clenching helplessly around his thick cock with every slap.

She was on the verge of another orgasm, and there was something both shameful and darkly exciting about that realization. His hand rose and fell steadily, and she screamed his name again as the pleasure burst within her in a fevered pitch of heat and light.

Bishop cursed, his hand tightening almost painfully

around her throat for a moment before he released her and pushed her face down onto the bed. He pumped furiously into her, one large hand pressed into the middle of her back to keep her still, as he thrust wildly back and forth.

She moaned, the sound muffled by the bed, as he made a harsh sound of need and pounded into her. His hand slid between her thighs, and she cried out when he rubbed her clit.

"No! Wait! I can't, not another one, not...."

She stiffened and screamed again, her entire body on fire as a third orgasm, unexpected and nearly painful in its intensity, rushed through her. She writhed helplessly as Bishop howled her name and his entire body shuddered above her.

He collapsed against her, pressing frantic kisses against her back before rolling to his side. She continued to lay on her stomach, her body trembling and little aftershocks of pleasure making her pelvis twitch, as he stood up and disappeared into the bathroom.

He returned a few minutes later, and she jerked when cool liquid touched her ass. "Bishop?"

"Hold still, baby." He rubbed the liquid into her ass cheeks. It eased the burning sensation, and she closed her eyes and relaxed against the bed.

"Better?" he said after a few minutes.

"Yes, thank you." She craned her head to stare at her ass. Bright red handprints covered it.

"I'm sorry," he said.

She twisted onto her side to face him as he coiled a lock of her hair around one finger. There was shame on his face, and she touched his cheek lightly. "What's wrong?"

"I shouldn't have done that without talking to you first," he said. "I'm sorry, Ava. I like to be dominant in bed, and I like to spank, but I don't normally do those things without knowing for sure that -"

"I liked it, Bishop," she said.

He studied her, the shame still visible in his eyes. "Are you sure?"

Embarrassed beyond belief but wanting to take away his shame, she said, "I had an orgasm while being spanked. I'm sure."

His body relaxed, and he smiled at her before reaching behind him. "Drink this."

She took the glass of water and drank eagerly. Her throat was dry, and her body overheated.

"Thank you." She handed him the glass, and he drank the rest of it in two large swallows before setting it on the nightstand. He relaxed on his back, pulling her into his arms. She rested her head on his broad chest as she traced small circles on his chest.

"Bishop?"

"Yeah?"

"Has it ever been like that for you before?"

"No. It was incredible, Ava." His big hands stroked her back before reaching around her to cup her breast and tease her nipple into a tight bud. "I can't get enough of you."

"I don't think I'm up for round three just yet." She rubbed her aching thighs. "As it is, I'm not entirely sure I'll be able to walk later."

He laughed, squeezing her breast and kissing her forehead before pulling up the sheet and quilt around them.

"What time is it?" she asked.

"Nap time."

She snuggled against him. "Your bed is unbelievably comfortable."

"Hmm," he agreed sleepily.

She closed her eyes and drifted.

CHAPTER 13

"Here, honey, I brought you some tea."

Ava smiled at Willow as she entered the board-room and set a mug of tea on the table. She left her spot by the window and sat down at the table. She winced and then blushed when Willow grinned at her.

"You didn't have to make me tea," Ava said. "I already feel completely useless just sitting here. Are you sure there isn't something I can do to help you?"

Willow sat down beside her. "There sure is. Tell me if sex with Bishop was awesome."

"Keep your voice down." Ava glanced at the open door. "And how do you even know that we had sex?"

Willow laughed. "You're walking bowlegged."

"Ha, ha." Ava glared at her. "I am not."

"Okay, maybe not, but you keep wincing every time you sit down." Willow stared at Ava's lap. "He didn't, like, totally ruin things down there, did he?"

"Willow!"

"Hey, it's a legitimate concern." Willow shrugged. "I may or may not have Googled some grizzly shifter, uh, romantic movies on the internet, and wow – if Bishop is as big as some of those actors, I don't get how you're even walking."

Ava's mouth dropped open. "You did not Google grizzly shifter porn, Willow Tanner."

"Of course, I did," Willow said. "Strictly for research purposes, of course."

"Research? What research?"

"Listen, if you're going to be banging a grizzly shifter, it's my duty as your best friend to know what you're dealing with. What if you needed medical care after?"

"Medical care? Willow, you're insane." Ava couldn't help but laugh.

"At the very least, I figured I might have to bring you some ice packs for your poor hooch," Willow said.

"Oh my God," Ava said. "My hooch is *fine*, Willow."

"You should have seen the look on Mal's face when he strolled into the kitchen and caught me watching the shifter porn parody of *Goldilocks and the Three Bears*. You know, I think I might have given him a complex. He denied it, but later that night – wowza - he made my toes curl. Repeatedly," Willow said. "If you know what I mean. And I think you do."

Ava burst into laughter. Willow sat patiently as Ava laughed and wiped at the tears streaming down her face. When she had finally gained control of herself, she reached out and squeezed Willow's hand. "I love you, Will."

"I love you too, Ava. Now, spill your guts. I don't need details unless," Willow grinned at her, "you want to share them, but at least tell me if you had fun."

"It was amazing," Ava said. "I've never been with someone like Bishop. He knows exactly what to say and do to drive me crazy in bed, and I can't seem to get enough of him."

She glanced at the open door before lowering her voice.

"We had sex last night and then this morning after breakfast. Then we napped and had more sex. Then we ate lunch and had another round of sex before showering and coming into the office."

"The man's a machine," Willow said.

Ava blushed. "He makes me feel so pretty. I know that's stupid, but I feel pretty and delicate when I'm around him. He lifts me and acts like it's not even difficult."

"It isn't difficult," Willow said. "You're curvy, Ava, not the Goodyear blimp."

"Yeah, well, remember that time Clint picked me up and put his back out?"

"Clint was an asshole and a fucking liar," Willow said angrily. "He only pretended to put his back out because he thought it would be funny to embarrass you. The best decision you ever made was to stop answering his three a.m. booty calls."

She paused. "Not that there is anything wrong with booty calls, you know I've had my fair share of them, but Clint was bad for you, honey."

"Yeah, I know," Ava said.

"It's all in the past now, though," Willow said. "You're dating a great guy and -"

"Bishop and I aren't dating," Ava said. "This is just another booty call relationship."

"No, it isn't," Willow said. "Ava, what's happening between you and Bishop is -"

"Nothing is happening between us other than sex," Ava said. "Grizzlies don't date or get married or raise a family."

"Well shit," Willow said with a sympathetic look.

"I'm fine with it, Willow. Since when did I ever date anyone anyway? I'm the booty call queen, remember?" Ava said.

"You don't have to be, honey." Willow squeezed Ava's hand. "You deserve more than just being someone's booty call. Why won't you believe that?"

"Maybe because the only thing guys want from me is sex."

"That isn't true. You just need to find a good guy, Ava."

"Bishop's a good guy," Ava said. "Isn't that what you said?"

"Well, yes, but…" Willow looked incredibly uncomfortable.

"So, I found myself a good guy, and all he wants from me is sex," Ava said.

"Do you know that for sure?" Willow asked. "You need to sit down with him and talk about this. He acts like you're more than just a damn booty call."

"I don't want to talk to him about it," Ava said. "I don't want to hear that he's like every other guy in my life, and all he wants is sex. I want to pretend for a little bit that it's more than that."

"Ava, you can't -"

"Enough, please, Willow," Ava said. "A goddamn dragon is stalking me. I can't go back to my apartment or my job, and I feel like every time I turn around, Sean Chambers is going to be there ready to incinerate me."

She rubbed at her forehead. "When I'm in Bishop's bed, I forget about all of it, and I need to forget for a while. Why shouldn't I take what he's offering me? Why do I need to have him tell me what I already know? If we have that conversation, what's happening will end, and I need him right now. If I want to pretend that he wants more than to give me a bit of happiness before a rogue dragon kills me, why can't I? Besides, after last night and this morning, he's probably done with me anyway. He wanted sex, and I gave it to him, and I know I swore I was done with men who wanted just sex, but I don't regret it, Willow. I don't regret it at all."

Her voice rose, and Willow put her arm around her and hugged her. "I'm sorry, honey. I shouldn't have said that. You do whatever you need to, okay? I just want you to be happy, and if crazy, hot sex with Bishop makes you happy, then have at it."

"Thanks, Will."

Willow kissed her smooth cheek. "And you're not going to die. We'll figure out a way to fix this."

"I know," Ava said and tried to sound like she meant it as Garth and Fenton stuck their heads into the boardroom.

"Ava?"

"Hi, guys," Ava said. "How are you?"

"We're good," Garth said. "The boss had us go over to your place."

"What for?"

"Just to check things out," Fenton said. "There were reporters everywhere."

Ava groaned as Willow patted her shoulder. "It's been all over the news."

"Shit."

"The good news is – no one knows you're involved. Apparently, your neighbours didn't see you. I guess the dragon distracted them."

Ava groaned again as Willow continued. "Only, they're not saying it's a dragon."

"What do you mean?"

Willow shrugged. "None of the witnesses have said it's a dragon. A few of them said they saw something big with large wings flying away, but that's it. Not one of them even knew how the fire started. They just said they saw the flames."

"How did they miss a damn dragon?" Ava said.

Garth shrugged. "Humans see what they want to see. No one believes in dragons. Hell, until this morning, I thought they were extinct, and I can guarantee you that most of the shifter world thinks that too. Even if they did see it, it's doubtful they would have thought it was a dragon."

Fenton grunted dismissively. "Humans. Even years after the paranormal world revealed themselves, they still don't have a clue what's beyond their noses." He hesitated and glanced at Willow and Ava. "No offense."

"It was pretty dark," Willow said, "and Mal hustled us all out of there really fast. We were probably gone before most of them even figured out anything was going on other than a fire caused by lightning."

"Anyway," Garth disappeared for a moment and returned with a blue suitcase, "we went into your apartment and grabbed some extra clothes and some toiletries for you."

The bull shifter's face turned pink, "I tried not to, uh, really look at your, uh, unmentionables, and I wasn't sure what exactly you wanted, so I just mostly grabbed jeans and t-shirts."

Ava stood and hurried across the room. The shade of pink on Garth's face deepened when she hugged first him and then Fenton. "Thank you so much – both of you."

"It was Bishop's idea," Fenton said as Ronin stuck his head into the boardroom.

"Hi, Ava. Can I talk to you alone for a minute?"

She nodded, and Willow and the others left. Ronin shut the door behind them and sat down, smiling at her. "How are you feeling?"

"Okay. How are you?"

"I'm good."

"You look good for a man who burned to death last night," she said.

He leaned forward. "Ava, you're mistaken. I flew away."

"No, you didn't," she said, "and you know that I know you didn't. It's why you're here."

He drummed his fingers restlessly on the table. "I know we don't know each other well, but I need to ask you for a favour. Will you tell the others that you were mistaken? That you were confused and scared, and you're not entirely sure what you saw?"

She studied him before nodding. "Yes, I can do that."

A look of relief crossed his face. "Thank you."

"What are you?" she asked.

"I'm just a bird." He reached out and took her hand. "I wouldn't ask you to lie for me if it wasn't vital. I promise you."

"I believe you."

The door opened, and Bishop stepped into the room. A thunderous look crossed his face when he saw Ronin holding Ava's hand. "What are you doing?"

"Just making sure she's doing okay after last night," Ronin said with an easy grin.

"You don't need to touch her to find out if she's okay," Bishop said.

Ronin let go of her hand and stood. "I think it's probably best if I go."

"Yes, it is." Bishop glared at him, and Ronin dropped a wink at Ava before leaving.

Bishop flushed at the look on her face. "What?"

"He saved my life last night, Bishop."

"That doesn't give him the right just to touch you when-ever he wants," he said.

Ava rolled her eyes as Bishop sat down beside her. "How are you?"

"Fine. I feel useless and in the way."

"You're not," he said before stroking her hair.

"Thanks for asking Fenton and Garth to grab some of my stuff."

"You're welcome." He smiled at her. "I figured you would be more comfortable in your clothes than mine."

He studied her. She wore one of his shirts and her scrub pants, and he rubbed one thigh. "Not that you don't look incredibly sexy in my shirt."

A rush of heat went through her, and she licked her lips before smoothing down his shirt. "Yes, because wearing a shirt that's eight times too big is a sexy look."

He grinned and leaned forward to nuzzle her neck. "You smell so good, Ava."

He cupped her breast through her shirt and stroked his thumb over her nipple, growling with satisfaction when it hardened through her bra.

"Bishop," she pushed his hand away. "we're at your office."

"We are," he agreed, "and all I can think about is bending you over my desk and fucking you."

Another flash of heat went through her, and she moaned softly. "You're being a very bad bear."

He laughed and nipped at her neck. "It's your fault. How am I supposed to work when I can smell your scent throughout the entire office? I can't wait to have you back in my bed where you belong."

"I – am I staying with you again tonight?" she asked.

He frowned at her. "Of course, you are. Where else would you stay?"

"I can stay with Willow."

"No."

"Bishop, I won't be offended if you don't want me staying another night. I'm not under any illusions that -"

"Bishop? Kaida is here." Mal stood in the doorway of the boardroom. "Sorry, I didn't mean to interrupt."

"It's fine," Ava said. Clasping her hands together, she followed Bishop and Mal out of the boardroom.

The woman standing in the reception was stunning. She was tall, Ava wouldn't be surprised if she were over six feet, and she had perfect breasts and a small waist with full hips. Her long dark hair fell to her waist, and streaks of dark blue wove throughout it.

Dismay went through Ava when Bishop hugged Kaida warmly. She returned his hug and smiled at him.

"Bishop," her voice was low and ridiculously sexy, "it's so good to see you again."

"It's good to see you too, Kaida." Genuine happiness infused Bishop's voice, and Ava swallowed down the ugly jealousy welling up inside of her.

"Gram says hello," Kaida said.

"How is she?"

"You know Gram. She's as feisty as ever." Kaida laughed.

Willow appeared next to Ava. "Good gravy," she said in a low voice, "that woman is seriously sexy."

"I know," Ava said.

"How does Bishop know her?"

"He was vague with the details."

"Uh oh."

"Yeah," Ava said. "What do you think the odds are that they've slept together?"

"The way she's looking at him? I'd say pretty high," Willow said. "Sorry, honey."

Kaida laughed again at something Bishop said, and

Willow said, "Yowza – that voice. She's like a damn sex goddess - I think *I* want to sleep with her."

"You're not helping, Willow," Ava said.

Willow patted her arm. "You have nothing to worry about, honey. Bishop's totally obsessed with you."

They watched as Mal greeted Kaida with a light kiss on the cheek. "Hello, Kaida."

"Hello, Mal. You're looking well."

"Thanks, so are you."

Kaida glanced at Ava and Willow, and Bishop cleared his throat. "Kaida, this is Willow, our receptionist, and this is Ava."

"Hello! I love your hair." Willow held her hand out, and Kaida shook it.

"Thank you," Kaida said before turning to Ava.

Ava shook her hand. "It's nice to meet you."

"You as well."

There was a moment of awkward silence, and Bishop cleared his throat again. "You're probably wondering why I asked you to come to the office."

"A little," Kaida said.

"We have a problem, and we're hoping you can help," Bishop said. "Come into the boardroom, and we'll explain."

CHAPTER 14

"We have a problem with a dragon," Bishop said.

Kaida glanced at Ava. "Dragons do not exist, Bishop."

"She knows, Kaida," Bishop said. "She's being hunted by one. He has revealed himself to her twice."

"A dragon revealing himself to humans," Kaida said.

Bishop nodded, and Kaida leaned forward to stare intently at Ava. Her eyes were golden with small flecks of blue, and Ava was oddly fascinated by them. "It was not a dragon you saw, human."

"I know what it was," Ava said. "I'm not an idiot."

She knew she was being oversensitive and ridiculous. What did she care if Bishop had chosen to sit next to Kaida instead of her? He was obviously very fond of the shifter, and besides, it wasn't any of her business what their relationship was. Just because she had sex a few times with Bishop didn't mean she had the right to tell him what or *who* he could do.

She made herself smile at the gorgeous shifter. "He was a dragon."

"It is impossible," Kaida said gently, "Dragons do not -"

"I saw him too, Kaida," Bishop said. "And so did Mal and Kat."

Kaida stiffened before turning toward Bishop and Mal. "A dragon who would reveal himself to humans is a dragon who has gone mad."

"He wants Ava. He said she was his bride and that she belongs to him," Bishop said.

"Fuck," Kaida said before rubbing her forehead.

"Don't take this the wrong way, Kaida, but is there a dragon in your clan who has...."

Kaida smiled grimly at him. "Gone mad? No."

"You're certain?"

"I am. He must be from another clan." She rubbed her forehead again. "I need to speak to Cadmus. The elders need to be told immediately."

She leaned forward and studied Ava. "There was only one? No other dragon was with him?"

"I don't think so," Ava said. "I work at the hospital, and he's been showing up for the last couple of months with various fake injuries. I just thought he was a hypochondriac or lonely."

"He killed a human, Kaida," Bishop said.

Kaida's eyes widened. "What?"

"The first night he attacked Ava, she had a friend with her. This Chambers guy thought they were dating, and he killed Brody – burned him to a crisp."

"This just gets worse and worse," Kaida groaned. "What did you say his name was?"

"Sean Chambers," Ava said, "But the detective assigned to the case said that he'd assumed a dead man's identity."

"Kaida," Bishop said, "have you ever seen this type of behaviour before?"

"Not personally. Most dragons would never reveal themselves to a human, let alone want to mate with one. Dragons remained hidden for a reason, Bishop."

Kaida squeezed Bishop's hand, and Ava bit back her urge to smack the woman.

"He must have been banished from his clan. It's the only explanation for his behaviour. I will speak with Cadmus and the elders, and they will contact the other clans to see who has been banished."

"Thank you, Kaida," Bishop said gratefully. "I appreciate your -"

There was a soft knock on the door, and Willow stuck her head into the room. "Sorry. Ava, do you have a moment, please?"

With a final look at Bishop and Kaida, Ava left the room, closing the boardroom door behind her.

"Willow, what's wrong?"

"Nothing," Willow said, "Detective Matthews is here to see you."

"What?" Ava blinked in surprise as Detective Matthews stood from his chair.

"Hello, Ava."

"Hi, Bren," Ava said. "How did you know I was here?"

"Lucky guess," he replied with a small grin.

"Detective, why don't you and Ava meet in Bishop's office." Willow took Ava's arm and tugged her into Bishop's office, smiling brightly at Bren when he followed them.

"I APPRECIATE YOUR HELP," BISHOP SAID TO KAIDA. "HOW will you explain that you know about him to the elders?"

"They know we're friends, Bishop," Kaida said. "They just don't know that -"

She hesitated and glanced at Mal. He stood and walked to the door. "I'll give you two a minute."

Kaida waited until the door closed behind them and then stroked Bishop's thick hair. "You look good, my friend."

"You do too." Bishop smiled at her.

Kaida linked their fingers together. "I have missed you."

"I've missed you as well. It has been too long since we've talked."

"Yes," Kaida nodded, "but it's for the best. Drago was beginning to suspect we were more than friends, and if he had gone to the elders with his suspicions, there would have been trouble."

"Is he still determined to make you his mate?"

Kaida sighed irritably. "Yes. It becomes more difficult with each day to avoid his advances."

"I can talk to him," Bishop said.

Kaida burst into laughter. "Oh, I have missed you, my ferocious bear."

She cupped his face and pressed her lips against his cheek. "You are brave, Bishop, one of the bravest shifters I have ever known, but you are no match for a dragon. Stay away from Drago. I can handle him."

"It's been over a year, Kaida. We can renew our friendship without Drago growing suspicious, especially since -"

He stopped abruptly as Kaida gave him a small grin. "Especially since you are so taken with the redheaded human?"

"I don't... I'm not -"

"Hush, my bear," Kaida said. "There is no point in denying it. I can smell her scent all over you, and you never were very good at hiding your emotions."

Bishop snorted. "I'm excellent at it – just not with you."

Kaida laughed. "She seems very sweet."

"She's sweet and kind and so smart," Bishop said. "She's tough too. She doesn't think she is, but she has this amazing inner strength." He paused, "Just, um, don't make her angry. She has a bit of a temper."

"It sounds like she is a good mate for you, my friend," Kaida said.

"She is," Bishop said. "She isn't afraid to call me on my bullshit, and she doesn't -"

He stopped, his face reddening, and said, "She's not my mate, Kaida."

"Is she not?" Kaida asked.

"No."

"Because she refuses to be your mate or because you haven't told her she is?"

"I can't tell her that," Bishop said. "I've only known her a few months, and it would freak her out if I claimed her as my mate. Besides, I don't mate for life, remember?"

Kaida retook his hand. "I remember. But you are not your father, Bishop."

"Why does everyone keep saying that? We don't know that I'm not like him. I could be exactly like him. I could hurt Ava the way he hurt Leslie, and I can't do that to her. I can't, Kaida," Bishop said.

"I know," Kaida said. "But you're so afraid of becoming your father that you aren't living your life. You are not like other grizzlies, my bear. You are unique, and you are not meant to wander this earth alone."

He shook his head in disagreement, and she frowned at him and cupped his face again. "I'm right, Bishop. You're meant to be a husband and a father, and if this woman is your mate, then you must tell her."

"It's not that easy," Bishop said.

"Love never is, my bear," Kaida said.

"What did you mean when you said the only explanation for his behaviour was his banishment?" Bishop changed the subject abruptly, and Kaida squeezed his hand a final time before sitting back in her chair.

"Many years ago, when my kind decided to stay hidden from the humans, the elders from each clan met and agreed that any dragon who disobeyed and revealed themselves to the humans would be banished from their clan. They would be cast out and abandoned by their loved ones and the other members of the clan. If they try to stay, other members of the clan will drive them away repeatedly using their flame."

Bishop frowned. "How does banishing help if they've revealed themselves to a human? Wouldn't they just join the humans and put the dragons in even more danger?"

Kaida shook her head. "A dragon without a clan goes mad very quickly, Bishop."

"What do you mean?"

"We can't exist without our clan. Madness sets in, and a banished dragon usually kills themselves within days of being banished."

"You're kidding me," Bishop said.

"I am not," Kaida said.

"If they're going to die anyway, why do you not just kill them?" Bishop asked. "What you're doing is brutal and barbaric."

"Yes, it is," she said. "But the threat of being banished, of knowing that you will go mad and die alone, is usually effective in stopping our kind from revealing their true natures."

"But," Bishop said, "then you've got dragons like this Chambers going around killing humans and trying to take one as his mate. You've put your kind in more danger."

"Until today, I had only ever heard of one dragon revealing herself to a human and being caught."

"So, there are dragons who reveal themselves to humans without being banished?"

Kaida nodded. "I am sure of it. There is a rumour that in Eastern Europe, a human male mated with a dragon and lives with her clan. I suspect that there are more humans and shifters who know about dragons than the clan elders would be," she paused, "comfortable with. Some have been revealed intentionally and some accidentally – like I've been with your mate and her friend."

"I'm sorry," Bishop said.

"It couldn't be helped, my bear," Kaida said.

"What happened to the dragon who was caught?"

"Her clan banished her, and within a day or two, she went mad and killed herself."

"So, are you saying that Sean Chambers will eventually just kill himself?"

"Yes," Kaida said, but he could hear the doubt in her voice. "I imagine that he revealed himself to Ava and his clan found out. He's been banished, and now he's gone mad. How long was it in between attacks?"

"Nearly a week."

"In a few days, your dragon problem should solve itself," Kaida said.

"Do you believe that?" Bishop asked.

Kaida paused and then said, "No, I do not. If he were banished after revealing himself to your mate the first time, then he would not have revealed himself again. The separation from his clan would have been all he could think about. He should have killed himself a day or two after being banished."

"Don't take this the wrong way, Kaida, but dragons are fucked up," Bishop said.

"I believe the banishment is wrong," Kaida said, "and it is my hope that soon our elders will realize that banishment is not the answer. There are already a few that are beginning to see the danger in it."

"Cadmus?" Bishop asked.

A soft smile crossed her face. "Yes, Cadmus is one of them."

The door opened and Willow, holding a tray with two cups and a teapot, entered the room. "I thought you might like some tea." She set the tray down. "Do dragons drink tea? I could make coffee."

Kaida smiled at her. "Dragons love tea."

"Excellent!" Willow sat down and poured a cup of tea as Bishop stiffened and inhaled in the direction of the open door.

He stood up so quickly he knocked his chair over. Kaida stared at him as Willow said, "Bishop, calm down."

"Where is he?" Bishop snarled.

"He's talking with Ava in your office. Just give them a few minutes," Willow said. "If you go in there all grizzlified and beat up the detective, Ava's going to be pissed at you. Besides, you'll have to pay me extra for blood splatter clean up."

Bishop snarled and stormed toward the door. "You should have told me he was here, Willow. I don't want him alone with her."

He stalked out of the room as Willow said, "So, Kaida, do you believe in ghosts?"

Ava sat down in Bishop's office, giving Bren a hesitant smile when he sat down beside her as Willow left the office and closed the door.

"How are you, Ava?" Bren asked.

"I'm good."

"Are you?"

"Yes," she lied. "How did you know I was here?"

"I did a bit of research on Bishop King and found out the name of his security firm. After what happened at your apartment last night, I figured you would be either at his home or his office."

Ava didn't reply, and Bren smiled at her. "You know because it's his job to be protective of you."

She blushed and stared at her hands that twisted nervously in her lap.

Bren reached out and put his hand over hers, stilling them. "Why don't you tell me what happened last night, Ava?"

"I don't know. I wasn't there," she said.

A brief look of surprise crossed his face. "You weren't there?"

"No. I was at work."

Bren nodded. "Yes, but according to your co-worker, Ginger, you only worked until eleven. The fire at your apartment building happened closer to midnight."

"You talked to Ginger?"

"I did. You weren't answering your cell phone."

She groaned inwardly. After a quick text to Ginger last night to tell her she was okay, she had put her cell phone on silent and hadn't looked at it since. She'd meant to check it, but a certain grizzly had a way of making her forget everything but him.

"I'm sorry," she said, "it's been a little crazy the last couple of days."

"Understandable," Bren said. "So, you weren't at your apartment building at all last night?"

"No."

"That's odd," he said, "because your neighbour, Mrs. Billings, swears that around eleven-thirty, she saw you and a guy walking toward your building, holding hands. She was just going to bed, she said, and she remembered it clearly because she didn't know you were dating someone, and according to her, she knows everything about her neighbours."

Ava flushed nervously, "Oh, well, I mean, I did go home briefly just to grab some clothes and stuff. Ronin, he works for the security firm, drove me home from the hospital and walked me up to my apartment. I grabbed some stuff, and then we left."

"So, you were at your apartment last night?"

"Uh, well, yeah, but only briefly."

"Briefly, right." Bren pulled his phone out of his pocket and scanned it. "So, after your brief stop at your apartment, where did you go next?"

"Ronin drove me to, uh, Bishop's house."

"Did you spend the night there?"

"Yes."

"And came into the office with him this morning?"

"Um, just after lunch. Bishop and Mal thought that with everything going on, I shouldn't stay at my apartment anymore and to, um, take a few more days off from work."

"Right. So, how long were you at your apartment last night?" Bren asked.

"I'm not sure exactly, but I know it wasn't very long. Just long enough to grab some clothes."

Bren didn't reply, and feeling desperate, Ava gave him a large, false smile. "So, uh, what do you think happened last night? Was it just a lightning strike or…"

"Why don't you tell me, Ava," Bren said.

"I don't know. I wasn't there when it happened."

Bren stared quietly at her. His light blue eyes seemed to pierce right through her, and she willed herself not to squirm under his gaze.

"Why are you lying to me, Ava?"

"I'm not," she said.

"I want to help you. You know that, right?"

She nodded as Bren leaned closer. "I'm very good at what I do, Ava. I'm going to find out who killed Brody and tried to kill you. I promise you that."

"I know," she said.

"But it would go a lot smoother if you told me the truth about last night. Did Sean Chambers show up at your apartment?"

"Bren, I -"

The door flew open, and Bishop stalked into the room. He growled at the detective, his entire body swelling. "Get away from her."

"Mr. King, it's nice to see you again," Bren said.

"I said get away from her." Bishop glared at him as his eyes glowed.

"Stop it, Bishop," Ava said sharply.

"I was just speaking with Ava about last night, and we're not quite done yet. If you could give us a few more minutes, I'd appreciate it."

"I'm not leaving her alone with you," Bishop said.

"Bishop, enough. Give us some privacy, please," Ava said. "I'll talk -"

"Shush, Ava," Bishop said as he glared at Bren. "If you want to speak to Ava, Detective, then you can ask me to -"

He flinched back when her face burning hot, Ava jumped up and stood in front of him. She glared up at him as her hands curled into fists. "Oh, you did *not* just shush me, Bishop King."

"Ava, honey, calm down." Bishop raised his hands and gave her a placating smile. "I didn't mean -"

"*Shush*, Bishop," she said. "I've told you repeatedly that you do not get to speak for me. Do you remember any of those conversations?"

"Yes," Bishop said. "I apologize, I shouldn't have -"

"I'm a grown woman, and I'll talk to who I want when I want. Are we clear?"

Bishop scowled. "He's interested in more than just a -"

"It's a yes or no answer, Bishop."

"Yes," he snapped. "We're clear."

"Thank you." Ava turned to Bren, "Bren, there's a coffee shop not far from here. Why don't we finish our conversation there?"

Bishop's face reddened, and he growled under his breath. Ava gave him a cool look. "Is there a problem?"

"It's dangerous for you to be out in public."

"I'm perfectly safe with the detective," Ava said. "I'll have him walk me back to the office when we're done."

She glanced behind her at Bren. "Would you mind walking me back to the office, Bren?"

"Not at all."

"I'll just go with you," Bishop said. "I'm sure the detective is very busy, and I -"

"It's not a problem," Bren said. "I'll walk her back."

Bishop made a noise of frustration as Ava brushed past him and stood in the doorway. "Ready, Detective?"

"Yes." Bren nodded to Bishop. "It was good to see you again, Mr. King."

Bishop glared at him before giving Ava a wounded look. Her stomach clenched, but she ignored it and stared steadily at him. "I'll see you later, Bishop."

"SERIOUSLY," KAT SAID, "SOMEONE HAS TO GO IN THERE AND tell him to calm the hell down."

"Not it," Mal said immediately.

Willow rolled her eyes. "What happened to my big, brave wolf?"

"He's smart enough to know when to stay away from an angry grizzly."

"Oh, for the love of Pete!" Kat said before marching to Bishop's office. She yanked open the door and stepped inside, glaring at Bishop, who muttered angrily to himself as he stomped back and forth.

"Bishop, get it together." She folded her arms across her chest and stared pointedly at him.

He snarled at her, and she hissed loudly in return as Ronin ducked into the room and stood next to her. "Need some help, Kitten?"

"Stop calling me Kitten," she said through gritted teeth, "or I'll fire your ass. Are we clear?"

"Perfectly clear, Ms. Frost," he said cheerfully before eyeing the still-pacing angry grizzly.

"You should go. I've got this," she said.

He just shrugged, and she stared at him in exasperation before turning her gaze to Bishop. "Enough, big guy. She's perfectly safe with the detective."

He bared his large canines at her. "You know that isn't

true, Kat. If that damn dragon shows up, that idiot detective won't be able to do a thing to save her."

"You can't try to control her, Bishop." Willow popped into the room. "Ava won't like that."

"I'm not trying to control her. I'm trying to keep her safe." He glanced at his watch. "That idiot has ten more minutes, and then I'm going to find them."

"It's only been half an hour," Willow said. "You'll piss her off if you show up there all caveman-like."

Bishop slowed to a stop and stared uncertainly at Willow. She nodded solemnly. "Do you want her so angry with you that she won't have anything to do with you?"

Bishop paused, and Willow took a step back when he turned and slammed both his fists onto the top of his desk. There was a loud crack, and the desk broke in two. His laptop and phone slid to the floor with loud thumps, folders full of paper went flying, and his coffee mug shattered on the floor, spraying cold coffee across the tile.

Ronin had stepped in front of Kat, and she tapped him on the back of his shoulder. "What are you doing?"

He turned and grinned at her. "Just protecting you from the angry bear, Ms. Frost."

She snorted, "You're a bird. What are you going to do? Peck him to death?"

"Ouch. You're a mean little pussy cat, aren't you?"

"I'm more than capable of protecting myself, thanks," she said coolly. "Besides, Bishop would never hurt me."

"Feel better, buddy?" Mal had joined them in the office, and he stared at the mess as Willow put her arm around his waist.

"I'm not cleaning that up," she announced.

"Cleaning what up?" Ava stuck her head into the office. "What the hell happened?"

She pushed past Willow and Mal and stared worriedly at Bishop. "Bishop? Are you hurt?"

He shook his head before bending and picking up the larger pieces of the coffee mug. Ava stared in confusion at Willow, who shrugged before bending and gathering up the papers.

"Thanks, Will," Bishop said.

"You're welcome, honey," Willow said.

CHAPTER 15

Ava followed Bishop into his house. The air was thick with tension and, as she slipped off her shoes and watched Bishop carry her suitcase upstairs, she wished that she had gone to Willow's place instead. She'd gone home with Bishop because she wanted to fuck him again, but there was so much tension and anger between them that sex was the last thing that would happen tonight.

Liar. You went to Bishop's because you're in love with him and you hate being apart from him.

Not true. I'm not in love with him. I'm just really attracted to him.

Her inner self snorted as Bishop clumped down the stairs and gave her an angry look. "Come into the kitchen."

He turned and disappeared into the kitchen. Ava felt her own flare of anger at both his demand and dismissive behaviour. She struggled to control it, taking a few deep breaths, before walking slowly to the kitchen.

"What's your problem, Bishop?" she asked.

He pulled a pot from the cupboard and slammed it down on the counter. "What's my problem? You're the one who's deliberately putting yourself in danger, and you're wondering what my problem is."

"I did not put myself in danger," she said. "I was safe with the detective."

"What did you talk about?" he asked.

Her temper flared, and she glared at him as her hands clenched into fists. "Not that it's any of your business, but we talked about last night, and I continued to lie about not being there when it happened."

"Is that it?" he asked with a hint of disbelief.

"We talked about some personal stuff."

"What?"

"None of your business, Bishop," she said.

He growled, and she stalked forward and poked him in the chest. "Just because I fucked you doesn't give you the right to question me about my private conversations with other people."

"That detective wants in your pants, Ava," Bishop snarled.

"So, what if he does? Kaida wants in yours, and you don't see me freaking out about it!" Ava shouted.

Bishop's mouth dropped open. "Kaida doesn't want in my pants."

"Please!" Ava said. "Tell me you aren't that damn naïve, Bishop. That dragon was all over you like a horny little tart, and you weren't pushing her away!"

"We're friends, Ava. Good friends and -"

"But did I say anything? Did I break a desk? No! I remained perfectly calm!" She couldn't stop shouting. "Because I am a calm and rational human being who doesn't need to overreact with irrational jealousy when some hot-as-hell dragoness with a 'come fuck me' voice starts kissing what belongs to me!"

Bishop stared wide-eyed at her as she turned and punched the wall.

"Fuck!" Pain lanced through her hand. She massaged it as Bishop reached for her.

"Don't!" she warned before pacing back and forth.

"Kaida wasn't kissing me," he said cautiously as she glared at him.

"She kissed you on the cheek," Ava said.

"We're just friends."

"But you've slept with her."

"Yes, but it was a long time ago," he said. "We're just friends now, Ava. I swear it."

He took a step back when Ava stomped toward him and pushed him in the chest. "Sit down, Bishop."

He sat in the chair, and Ava straddled him and gripped his head in her hands. "You drive me crazy, Bishop King. You make me so angry I can barely think straight."

He inhaled deeply, a small grin crossing his face. "That isn't anger you're feeling, Ava."

Her nostrils flared, and she kissed him hard on the mouth. "Just because I want to fuck you doesn't mean I'm not angry with you, Bishop. Do you hear me?"

"Yes." He cupped her neck and kissed her, thrusting his tongue into her mouth until she moaned and pulled away.

"Your jealousy is ridiculous." She yanked his shirt over his head, and he quickly returned the favour before unfastening her bra.

"So is yours." He pulled her bra off and cupped her breasts, kneading them roughly before dipping his head and sucking on one nipple.

She arched her back, her fingers digging into his broad shoulders as he sucked greedily at her nipples.

"I haven't slept with the detective. There's no point to

your jealousy," she gasped out as his hands slipped into her scrub pants and gripped her ass.

"He wants to sleep with you." Bishop nipped her neck, and she squeaked softly at the sharp pain.

"He wants between your legs," his hand gripped her long red hair, and he pulled until her head was back and he could kiss her throat, "and you need to tell him that your pussy belongs to me."

He nipped her again, and she twitched before shoving her hands between their bodies and gripping his cock through his pants. "Fine. I'll tell him as soon as you tell Kaida that your cock belongs to me."

He groaned harshly as she clawed open his pants and stuck her hand into his briefs. Her hand closed around him and stroked firmly. With a low roar, he ripped her scrub pants apart. She bit him hard on the shoulder as he pulled the tattered remains of her pants from her body.

He flinched and pulled her head back with a sharp tug of her hair. "You bit me."

She smiled sweetly at him and rubbed his cock. "I'm sorry, it was an accident."

He stared suspiciously at her, and she melted against him, rubbing her bare breasts against his chest until he released his hold on her hair. She kissed his chest, licking at him with her tongue as he moaned and lifted his head so she could place warm kisses against his throat.

He roared again when she bit him a second time, and she cried out when he slapped her hard on the ass.

"Be a good girl," he warned her. She sucked on his bottom lip, and he moaned before wrapping his fingers around her panties and tearing them away.

"Stop ruining my clothes!" she scolded him before pinching his flat nipple.

He flinched and spanked her again. She squealed and arched her back as he reached between her legs and cupped her pussy. She was soaking wet, and he slid two fingers into her as she moaned and tugged his cock free from his underwear.

"Condom," she said when he rubbed his dick against her.

"Pocket," he groaned.

She wiggled her hand into his pocket and pulled out the foil package. At her look, he grinned wickedly at her. "I told you – I wanted to fuck you against my desk at the office."

"Too bad you broke it in a fit of jealousy." She ripped open the package. She smoothed the condom over his cock, and he made a harsh groan when her fingers lingered.

"I'm going to come all over your fucking hands if you don't stop that," he said.

"Don't you dare, Bishop King." She squeezed the base of him, secretly delighted by the look of naked desire on his face and gave him a warning look. "I want to fuck you despite your ridiculous behaviour."

"My ridiculous behaviour?" He cupped her breast and kneaded it roughly. "Who left the safety of the office just because they didn't like being told what to do?"

"I'm not going to ask, 'how high' when you say 'jump', Bishop," she said as she rubbed her pussy against his erection. "You don't get to tell me what to do, understand?"

He wrapped his arm around her waist and lifted her before guiding his cock to her wet opening.

"Except in bed," he said as she moaned and tried to wiggle free of his tight grip and slide down his thick cock. "In my bed, you'll do exactly what I tell you to do. Isn't that right?"

"Bishop, please," she said pleadingly. She was suddenly

frantic for his cock, needed to feel him thrusting inside of her, and she pulled at the arm around her.

"Say it, Ava." He tightened his grip around her. "Tell me what I need to hear."

"Yes," she said as she slid her hands into his hair and stared into his eyes. "I'll do what you want in bed, Bishop."

A pulse of pleasure went straight to her clit at the look of desire on his face. It was so strong it made her shudder uncontrollably, and she cried out when he lowered her onto his cock. Her breath hissed out between her teeth as he stretched her. He waited patiently, stroking her nipple lightly with his thumb as she slowly sank down until his entire cock was seated within her.

Ava bit at her bottom lip. She felt full and stretched to the brim, and she moved experimentally on top of him as Bishop's breath hissed out. "Fuck, you feel so good, baby."

She smiled at him and braced her feet on the floor before moving up and down slowly. Bishop groaned, and she licked at his mouth before switching to a rocking motion. It put a delicious pressure on her clit, and she rocked faster as Bishop grinned at her.

"Does that feel good, baby?" He rubbed her back as she gripped his shoulders in a fierce grip.

She rocked harder, her breath coming in harsh pants, and he watched as she stiffened and voiced a loud cry as she came all over him. She collapsed against him, and he gripped her hair and pulled her head back until she stared at him.

"Ride me, Ava," he demanded, and she bounced obediently on his cock, her feet braced against the floor as he thrust into her. The chair creaked loudly, and she stared at him in alarm.

"Bishop, the chair. It's going to -"

He cut her off with a hard, demanding kiss that made her

toes curl. She forgot her worry and rode him hard as his fingers dug into her waist, and he bit at her upper chest and neck with rough nips.

He made a low, harsh groan, and she stared down into his face as she pushed herself up and down. He began to lose his steady rhythm, and a look of desperate need crossed his face before he thrust one final time, and he came deep inside of her. Her eyes widened at the surge of wetness, and she quickly hopped off his lap.

"Shit," she said.

He studied the broken condom and muttered his own curse before rolling it off and throwing it in the garbage. She picked his shirt up from the floor and slipped into it, her face pale. He gave her a worried look as she left the kitchen and went to the bathroom.

When she returned, he was wearing his jeans, pulling vegetables from the fridge, and setting them next to the cutting board on the counter.

"I thought I would make stir fry for supper," he said.

"That sounds good. I can help." She took the knife he handed her and chopped the vegetables as he put a pot of rice on to cook.

They worked in silence for a while before Bishop cleared his throat. "I'm negative for STIs, Ava. I get tested regularly, and I, uh, haven't been with anyone but you since the last time I was tested. I can show you my medical records."

"I'm negative too," she said. "I haven't been tested in a while, but I haven't had sex in a while either, so…."

Bishop reached out and squeezed her hand. "I'm sorry."

"It's not your fault the condom broke." She squeezed back before cutting up a red pepper.

He brought the wok out and set it on the stove before adding oil. "I guess angry sex wasn't a good idea."

A faint smile crossed her face. "Is that what it's called? Angry sex?"

"I didn't hurt you, did I?" he suddenly asked before scanning her body. "Are you -"

"I'm fine," she said. "I, um, like angry sex."

He grinned at her. "I liked it too. Although, I don't like fighting with you, and I -"

"I'm not on the pill," she said.

He stared at her, and she flushed. "I'm sorry. I just – I thought you should know. The pill messes with my hormones, and I wasn't in a relationship, so I went off of it."

There was an odd combination of panic and satisfaction on his face, and she cleared her throat. "I really am sorry."

BISHOP STARED AT AVA. HIS GRIZZLY RUMBLED WITH delight, and he tried to ignore it as Ava mumbled another apology.

A cub! Our mate carries our cub! His grizzly crowed triumphantly.

Shut up! You don't know that!

His heart raced with adrenaline and panic and, he hated to admit it, excitement.

Tell her she is our mate! His grizzly demanded.

His gaze dropped to Ava's belly, and another surge of excitement went through him as he pictured her belly swelling as his cub grew inside of her. He had a brief fantasy of coming home every night to Ava's sweetness and warmth, of a life spent raising their cubs together and growing old in her arms before a vision of his mother swept across him. He took a deep breath as his mother turned into Ava. He imagined Ava's sweet face turning harsh with bitterness, her warmth turning to ice, and he shuddered all over as she touched his arm.

"Bishop? Please say something." She was close to tears, and he pushed his fears aside and gathered her into his arms.

"It'll be fine, Ava." He kissed the top of her head and stroked her long hair as she took a shuddering breath.

"What if I'm – I mean, I'm probably not - but what if...."

He kissed her head again. "We'll worry about that if it happens, okay?"

She stared up at him. "I won't ask you to be something you're not, Bishop. I need you to know that. If I am pregnant, I'll raise the baby by myself. I won't ask you for anything."

He held her tightly before repeating, "Everything will be fine, Ava."

"WILL YOU TELL ME ABOUT KAIDA?"

Ava stared up at him, and Bishop stroked her bare back with the tips of his fingers. After dinner, Ava had wanted to go to bed, and he hadn't argued, just followed her to his bedroom. Things were a bit awkward until Ava had kissed him and pressed her warm body against his.

"Are you sure?" he'd groaned.

She nodded immediately before sinking to her knees in front of him and unbuttoning his jeans. As her mouth slid over his cock, sucking it into an aching hardness, he groaned and threaded his hands through her hair. The worry and doubt disappeared, and he'd spent the last three hours coaxing orgasms from her willing body and listening to her soft cries of desire and delight before finding his release.

Princess jumped onto the bed and butted her head against Ava's back before climbing up and spreading her large body across Ava's hip and onto Bishop's stomach. She purred loudly as Ava rubbed her throat and kneaded her sharp claws into his flesh. He winced and tugged lightly at her paws. She meowed angrily and bit his fingers before flouncing off the bed.

"She has a temper," Ava said.

"It's why I like her," he said, and she snorted as he squeezed her bare ass.

"Will you tell me how you met Kaida?" she repeated.

She rested her head on his chest as he stared up at the ceiling. "I was fourteen, and it was summer holidays. Mal's family was gone on holiday. They'd left for the Grand Canyon nearly three days before, and I was lonely and bored. Normally Mara would have convinced Leslie to let her take me with them, but she refused this time."

"Leslie?"

"My mom," he said.

"Oh. Why didn't she want you to go?"

"She said she would miss me too much."

Ava studied him. Could she tell he was lying? He had an idea that she could. That she could see through him as easily as a pane of glass.

"That makes sense," Ava finally said.

Bishop breathed a sigh of relief. He hated lying to Ava, it made him feel awful, but he couldn't tell her that Leslie had refused to let him go because she had wanted to hurt him. "Anyway, Leslie was at work and -"

"Why do you call her Leslie and not mom?" Ava asked.

"Oh, uh, she hates being called mom. Says it makes her feel old."

Another careful look from Ava suggested she knew he was lying. But she only said, "Go on."

"I rode my bike out to Parsons Woods on the north side of

the city and followed the river for a while. I decided to explore deeper in the woods, and that's when I got caught in the bear trap."

She sat up and stared at him in horror. "Oh, Bishop, you didn't."

"I did." He tugged her arm, urging her to lie down again, and after a moment, she did, nestling her head against his chest.

"I was in my bear form, and the trap caught me by the right leg. The pain was so bad that I shifted to my human form and passed out. I woke up to Kaida crouched over me. I didn't know who she was. In fact, in my pain and my fear, I thought she was the hunter, and I lashed out at her."

He closed his eyes, smiling a little at the memory. "She was only a teenager herself and not quite in control of her dragon. She shifted and nearly roasted me alive."

"Oh my God," Ava said quietly.

"Once we both calmed down and realized that neither of us wanted to hurt the other, she pried open the trap and took me to her clan."

"She pried open the trap?"

"Kaida is incredibly strong, even as a teenager," he said. "I was nearly unconscious from blood loss and -"

"Your body didn't start to heal itself?" she asked.

"It was starting to, but the trap had nearly taken my leg off, and as a teenager, my healing abilities were not as strong as they are now."

"Jesus," she whispered.

"Kaida half-carried and half-dragged me home to her Gram. Gram's the healer of her clan, and she put some kind of poultice on it – it burned like hell – and bandaged me up. I spent the next three days at Gram's and Kaida's until my leg fully healed."

"Three days?" Ava blinked at him. "Wasn't your mom worried? She didn't come looking for you?"

He cleared his throat. "Uh, she was worried, but she was also working two jobs at the time, and she was, um, pretty busy. You know."

Ava gave him an odd look. "Bishop -"

"Anyway," he hurried on, "Kaida and I became pretty good friends after that. I had to face the clan elders, but after speaking with me, Cadmus decided to let me live."

"Let you live?" Ava said.

Bishop nodded. "Dragons are serious about staying hidden, Ava."

"You were only a child."

"I was a teenager."

"Kaida should never have taken you back to her clan. What if they'd decided to kill you?" She sat up again with anger on her face. "What she did was -"

"She saved my life," Bishop said quietly. "I would have died in that trap if Kaida hadn't freed me, Ava. And I would have died trying to get home after she released me. She did what she had to."

"But if her clan had -"

"They didn't."

She stared at him in frustration, and he tugged her head down and gave her a slow and thorough kiss. "Kaida's clan are not the terrible people you believe them to be."

She didn't reply, and he sat up as she tugged the sheet around her and sat cross-legged beside him. "When did you and Kaida become lovers?"

"Not until our late twenties."

She was quiet, and he took her hand and squeezed it. "Our time together was brief, Ava."

"Why?"

He shrugged. "A few different reasons. I think it was more of an experiment for both of us, and there is another in her clan who desires Kaida for himself. He began to suspect that we were more than friends, and if he had discovered the truth, it would have caused trouble."

"Why is that?"

"Dragons aren't fond of the idea of mating with anyone other than a dragon."

"Racists," she muttered, and he smiled at her.

"No. They just desire to remain hidden."

"So, you aren't together because of her clan." He could hear the worry in her voice and smell it on her scent.

"We aren't together because neither of us wanted a relationship and because our tastes in bed aren't compatible. I like control, and so does she. Even if Drago had not grown suspicious, we would have ended it. We're better as friends," he said.

She stared steadily at him. "Do you love her?"

"I love her because she saved my life and has been a good friend for many years, but I'm not in love with her." He paused. "What about the detective?"

"He asked me out, and I said no," Ava said briefly.

"I told you he was interested in you," he said.

"I'm not interested in him." She smiled tentatively at him. "Thank you for telling me about Kaida."

He leaned forward and rested his forehead against hers. "It is in the past, Ava. And it was only sex."

"Right," she said.

He could smell her sorrow, and he kissed the tip of her nose. "Why are you sad? I promise there is nothing beyond friendship with Kaida."

"I know." She smiled at him. "I'm pretty tired. Let's get some sleep."

CHAPTER 16

"Ava, you don't need to do the filing," Willow said as she squatted next to Ava.

Ava sat cross-legged on the floor and surrounded by a large pile of papers. She shrugged as she sorted through them. "I don't mind. I hate just sitting around and doing nothing."

"Has Bishop heard from Kaida yet?" Willow asked.

"No, I don't think so," Ava handed her a piece of paper. "Is this a corporate contract or a personal one?"

Willow scanned the paper. "Personal. Is everything okay between you and Bishop?"

"Yes."

"Yes?"

"Yes."

Willow waited patiently, and Ava glanced around the empty reception area. "The condom broke last night while we were having angry sex."

"Shit, you're not on the pill," Willow said.

"Yeah."

"What are you doing to do?"

"If I'm pregnant, raise the baby by myself. I already told Bishop I wouldn't ask him for anything."

"What did he say?"

"He just said everything would be fine," Ava said.

"You won't be pregnant, Ava," Willow said reassuringly.

"I know."

Willow cocked her head at her. "Do you want to be?"

"What? No, of course not," Ava said.

"You sure?"

"Yes."

"Okay." Willow leaned closer. "Although, I never took you for a girl who would have angry sex."

Ava's mouth twitched. "It's good to try new things."

Willow laughed. "Indeed, it is."

The bell over the door jingled, and Willow bounced to her feet. "Ginger! What are you doing here?"

"Just came to check on Ava." Ginger looked over the desk and twitched in surprise at Ava sitting on the floor. "Hey, honey."

"Hi, Ginger. How are you?"

"Good. How are you?"

"Okay. How is it at the hospital?"

"Fine. We miss you." Ginger leaned against the desk. "Mr. Chambers was spotted at the hospital last night."

"What?" Ava jumped to her feet.

"You're sure?" Willow said.

"I'm sure. After my shift, I was leaving the hospital, and I saw him just, like, lurking in the shadows. He stared right at me, and then he started toward me." Ginger shivered as the boardroom door opened, and Fenton and Garth came out into reception. They stood silently behind her as Ginger smoothed her dark hair back from her face.

"Did he say anything to you?" Ava asked.

"I turned and ran back into the hospital before he could and then called 9-1-1. The cops took their sweet time in getting there. In fact, I called Detective Matthews after I called 9-1-1, and he got there first. They searched the hospital grounds, but he was gone."

She shivered again as Willow glanced at Ava. "We need to talk to Mal and Bishop about this. And I think we should have someone from the firm keep an eye on Ginger as well. This Chambers guy knows that you two are friends, right?"

"Yes. He came to the ER often enough to know," Ava said. "I'm sorry, Ginger."

"It's okay," Ginger said. "Although I don't think I need protection or anything like that."

"It's better to be on the safe side," Willow said.

"Maybe," Ginger sighed before suddenly brightening. "Hey, do you think you could get that gorgeous cheetah shifter to watch over me? I'd be a lot happier about it if I get to stare at his tight ass while he -"

"Ginger," Willow said in a high-pitched voice as she stared pointedly at her, "you're gonna want to shut it, sweetie."

Ginger stiffened. "Please tell me he isn't standing behind me."

"I wish I could, honey."

Ginger closed her eyes as a dark flush crossed her face. Sighing, she turned and smiled at the two men standing behind her. "Hey, I'm Ginger."

"Fenton." The cheetah shifter gave her hand a brief shake before disappearing into Kat's office.

"I'm Garth." The bull shifter grinned at her and took her hand in his large one. "You know, cheetah shifters aren't everything they're cracked up to be. Sure, they're one of the fastest animals on earth, but they're fast at *everything*, sweetheart. Now bull shifters, they know that slow and steady is the way to go."

Ginger's blush brightened as Willow rolled her eyes. "Keep it in your pants, Garth."

Garth winked at Ginger before following Fenton into Kat's office. Ginger buried her face in her hands.

"I'm an idiot."

"But a super cute one." Willow kissed her forehead. "I'll talk to Mal about sending you home with some shifter protection. In the meantime, why don't you hang out here with Ava? It's safer."

"BISHOP, YOU DIDN'T HAVE TO EMPTY A DRAWER," AVA SAID.

"I don't mind," he said. "It's easier than living out of a suitcase. I cleared a spot in the bathroom vanity for your girl things too."

"Girl things?" she said.

"You know," he waved vaguely, "perfume, and makeup, and stuff."

She laughed. "Thanks, Bishop."

"You're welcome."

Bishop left the bedroom, and she placed her clothes in the drawer before moving her toiletries to the bathroom. She'd been staying with Bishop for two days now, and it was a bit ridiculous how much she enjoyed living with him.

She gripped the bathroom sink, staring at herself in the mirror. She was getting entirely too used to sleeping in Bishop's bed, and she needed to remember what this was before she started picturing a more permanent living arrangement.

The doorbell rang, and adrenaline pumped through her

veins. She hurried out of the bathroom and bedroom and stood uncertainly at the top of the stairs. "Bishop?"

"Stay there, Ava." Bishop's body was already starting to swell, and she waited anxiously as he peered through the peephole.

"It's fine," he said before opening the door and smiling at the dragon shifter. "Hey, Kaida."

"Hello, Bishop. Is this a bad time?"

"No, come in."

Kaida stepped into the house. She was followed by two men, both wearing long dark robes. The first man had long white hair with streaks of orange that flowed down his back. He clasped Bishop's hand and smiled. "Hello, old friend."

"It is good to see you again, Cadmus," Bishop said.

"You as well. We have missed your presence in the clan."

Cadmus turned to the man beside him. "Do you remember Ryul? He is an elder now."

"Hello, Ryul," Bishop said.

Ryul nodded. His hair was grey and shorter than Cadmus's, but it had the same streaks of orange woven through it.

Cadmus peered past Bishop at Ava, who had joined them in the hallway. "Hello, human."

"Hello," Ava said.

"Cadmus, Ryul, this is Ava. She's the one being stalked by the dragon," Bishop said.

"We are sorry to meet you under such circumstances, human," Cadmus said.

Ava smiled tentatively at him as Bishop led the three dragon shifters into the living room.

"Do you want tea or coffee?" Bishop asked.

Kaida shook her head and sat down on the couch with Cadmus and Ryul. "We cannot stay long, Bishop."

"Sit down, Ava." Bishop urged her into the chair before standing next to her. "What have you discovered?"

Kaida glanced at Cadmus, who nodded to her. "The dragon who revealed himself to Ava is very dangerous. He was banished from his clan nearly two months ago."

"That's impossible," Bishop said. "You told me he would go mad."

"Oh, he has gone mad," Cadmus said. "There were issues with him before his clan banished him. Some clan members believed him to be on the cusp of madness before his banishment. They believed that the banishment would finish him."

"What do you mean finish him?" Ava frowned.

Cadmus turned his gaze toward her. "Our species cannot survive without our clan. If we are banished and cast out from our clan, we go mad and kill ourselves."

Ava stared at him in horror. "You banish your – your family and friends knowing that they'll die? What is wrong with you?"

"Ava, don't," Bishop said.

"It's fine, bear shifter," Cadmus said. "It is a horrific punishment. The human is right to question it."

"Cadmus, do not speak that way in front of the other species," Ryul said sharply. "They are beneath us, and what we do with our kind is none of their concern. You do not need to agree with them, nor do you -"

"Hold your tongue, Ryul, or I will rip it from your mouth," Cadmus said.

Ava shrank back in her chair as light glowed beneath Cadmus's robe. He was breathing heavily as he glared at Ryul, and she reached out and grasped Bishop's hand. He squeezed it reassuringly.

Ryul stared at the floor between his feet and muttered an

apology. After a moment, Cadmus sat back on the couch and smiled benignly at Ava and Bishop. "Where were we?"

"Banishment, Cadmus," Kaida prompted gently.

"Right. When one of our kind is banished, they go mad and kill themselves."

"So, I don't have to worry?" Ava said slowly. "He's going to kill himself."

"There is something terribly wrong, Ava. He should have killed himself only a few days after he was banished. It has been two months, and not only is he still alive, but he integrated himself with the human community. He took on a human's identity, found employment with them, and has lived in this city for nearly a month and a half. Never before has a dragon survived so long after banishment," Kaida said.

The hope building in Ava's chest deflated, and she sat back in the chair, blinking back the tears. There was no way in hell she would cry in front of the dragons.

"Ava, are you okay?" Bishop asked.

"Just fine," she said. "Go on."

She wasn't fine. She felt sick to her stomach, and she wanted to climb into Bishop's giant bed, pull the covers over her head, and forget that any of this was happening. Panic built inside her, but she swallowed it down grimly.

"We do not know how he has survived so long," Cadmus said.

"He is an anomaly," Ryul said dismissively.

"Perhaps, perhaps not," Cadmus said. He stared at Ava again. "We don't know why he's fixated on you, but we will find him and stop him."

"You mean kill him," Ava said.

"Yes," Cadmus said gravely.

"Why was he banished in the first place?"

Kaida cleared her throat, "He killed another of our kind."

"Seriously?" Bishop stared at her in disbelief.

"Yes," Kaida said. "He became obsessed with the mate of another in his clan. When she rejected him, he killed her mate."

"Oh my God," Ava whispered. She couldn't stop trembling. She rubbed compulsively at a large freckle on her wrist as Bishop stared at her in alarm and then placed his hand on her back.

"Members of Larry's clan will be here within a few days. They know his scent, and they'll assist us in finding him. Until then -"

Cadmus was interrupted by Ava's burst of laughter. "Larry? His name is *Larry*?"

"Yes, human." Cadmus blinked in surprise when Ava burst into laughter again. She leaned forward, holding her stomach as her entire body shook with laughter. Cadmus glanced at Kaida, who shrugged.

"Ava? Are you okay?" Bishop squatted next to her. "Honey?"

"Larry. His name is Larry!" Ava howled with laughter and wiped at the tears streaming down her face.

"Yes," Bishop said hesitantly.

Fresh giggles exploded from her mouth at the look of confusion in his eyes. "Seriously, Bishop? There's Kaida and Cadmus and Ryul and then *Larry*."

She bent her head and laughed until her belly hurt, and her face ached. She could feel Bishop's warm hand on her back and knew he was worried about her, but she couldn't stop the laughter. She glanced up. Kaida stared at her with concern, and Ryul stared at her with barely-hidden distaste, but it was Cadmus's look of serenity, as though he regularly witnessed a human laughing hysterically, that made her bark harsh laughter again.

"Larry!" she gasped. "Bishop, tell me you see how funny that is."

"I do, honey," Bishop said.

She giggled and wiped again at the moisture on her face. "You don't. You really don't."

When her giggles finally dried up, Cadmus smiled at her. "You do not need to worry, human. His clan will find him when they arrive."

"Which of you will be helping us until his clan arrives?" Bishop asked.

Ryul frowned at him. "What do you mean?"

"We can't defeat him," Bishop said. "He's almost killed her twice."

"You saved her," Ryul said dismissively.

"It was nothing but luck," Bishop said. "We need a dragon to defeat a dragon."

The three dragons didn't reply, and Bishop cursed under his breath. "Are you really going to stand back and do nothing?"

"It is not our concern. He is not from our clan," Ryul said.

Bishop turned to Kaida and Cadmus. "Kaida, Cadmus – please. Can't you speak with the other elders?"

"We have spoken already, Bishop. Kaida volunteered to stay with your mate, but the elders will not allow it," Cadmus said.

"You're their leader, Cadmus," Bishop said, "Command them to allow it."

"I cannot," Cadmus said. "Not this time, bear shifter."

Ryul stood and shook out his robes. "We've already helped you enough, bear shifter. We are breaking our own rules even discussing this with your human. If other clans were to find out that she knows not only of the existence of dragons but of our ways, our clan would be in grave danger. She is lucky the elders did not call for her death."

"Go anywhere near her, and I'll kill you, dragon," Bishop snarled. He started to swell, and Ava stood hurriedly and put her hand on his arm.

"Stop, Bishop. Please."

He snarled again, and Ava put her arm around his waist and squeezed lightly. "Look at me, Bishop."

He stared at her, and she reached up and stroked his dark beard. "It'll be fine."

Cadmus and Kaida stood, and the old dragon shifter held out his hand. "I am sorry, bear shifter. I will have Kaida inform you when Larry's clan has arrived. It will only be a matter of hours after that until they find him."

"Maybe they should get here a little faster," Bishop grunted.

Cadmus smiled. "We must be careful not to reveal ourselves, Bishop. They can travel only under cover of darkness."

"Yeah," Bishop muttered.

As Cadmus and Ryul left the room, Kaida hesitated and then said in a low voice. "I will come back later tonight after the elders and other clan members have retired to their beds and help protect Ava."

"No," Ava said. "You'll only get yourself banished, Kaida. Bishop will protect me."

"Bishop is strong, but he is no match for a dragon. I'll return and -"

"Ava's right," Bishop said. "I won't have you risk being banished, Kaida."

"I want to help," Kaida said.

"You have," Ava said. "Thank you, Kaida."

The dragoness hesitated a moment longer before nodding

resignedly. They followed her out of the room to where the elders waited by the front door.

"It will all work out, bear shifter," Cadmus said. "Do not worry."

"Goodbye, Cadmus. Goodbye, Kaida." Bishop refused to look at Ryul. Ava squeezed his arm again as Ryul snorted and left the house. Kaida and Cadmus followed him, and Bishop shut the door with a hard bang.

She smiled at him, trying to ignore the panic curdling in her stomach. He pulled her into his arms and kissed her forehead. "I won't let him hurt you, honey. Come with me to the kitchen. You need to eat."

CHAPTER 17

"Willow, are you sure this is a good idea?" Ava asked. "I wasn't invited to the barbecue."

"It's fine. Mara has a firm 'the more, the merrier' rule when it comes to family gatherings." Willow turned in her seat and smiled at her. "Hell, she'll probably ask Fenton to stay too."

"I can't." The cheetah shifter shoulder checked and moved into the next lane. "I'm working tonight."

"Covering Ginger?" Willow asked.

He nodded before asking, "So, is she single?"

Willow grinned at him. "No, she's dating a guy named Robbie."

"I haven't seen him at her apartment," Fenton said.

"He works nights," Willow said.

Ava stared out the car window as Fenton drove them toward Mal's parents' house. It was Sunday afternoon, and Bishop and Mal had been pulled into an emergency meeting with a client for most of the day. Bishop drove her to Mal's house, and she'd stayed with Willow until Fenton arrived to drive them to Mara and Roland's.

"Stop worrying, Ava," Willow said. "Bishop is going to the barbecue, so he would have brought you anyway."

"He didn't mention the barbecue to me," Ava said.

"He probably just forgot."

"Or he didn't want me to go."

"Why wouldn't he?" Willow frowned at her as Fenton pulled into the driveway.

"I don't know," Ava said.

Willow squeezed Fenton's arm and opened the car door. "Thank you, Fenton. It was nice of you to drive us over here."

"You're welcome. Have fun."

Ava and Willow climbed out of the car and waved to Fenton as he drove away. Ava slowly followed Willow toward the front porch. She was feeling nervous and anxious, and she wiped the palms of her hands on her jeans as they climbed the steps. She had a feeling that Mal's family, Mara, in particular, were important to Bishop, and she was worried they wouldn't like her. It was ridiculous to be worried about it, but her feelings of trepidation only grew as Willow reached for the door.

"Willow, wait. Are you sure I should be here?"

Willow stared at her in confusion. "Of course, I am. What's wrong, Ava? You look like you're going to pass out."

The door opened, and a tall and slender dark-haired woman pulled Willow into her embrace. "Willow, honey, I'm so glad you're here. I'm a bit behind, I'm afraid, and I need all the help I can get in the kitchen. Come in and – oh, who's this then?"

"Mara, this is my best friend, Ava Lewis. Ava, this is Mal's mother, Mara Burke."

"It's nice to meet you, Mrs. Burke," Ava said.

Mara swept past Willow and took her gently by the arms, looking her up and down before smiling. "So, you're Bishop's Ava. It's wonderful to meet you finally. Bishop's told me so much about you."

"He has?" Ava asked.

Mara hugged her. "Well, of course, he has. Come in, my love. I'm glad you're joining us today. I hope you don't mind helping out in the kitchen."

"Not at all," Ava stared at Willow in surprise, and the tiny brunette shrugged as they followed Mara into the kitchen.

"WHO ARE YOU TRYING TO CALL?" MAL ASKED AS HE DROVE toward his parents' house.

Bishop set his cell down with a muttered curse. "Garth. He's watching Ava tonight at my place while I'm at the barbecue. He's not answering his phone, and I still need to drive Ava back to my place. If he doesn't show, I won't make the barbecue, Mal. I'm not leaving Ava alone. In fact, I'm only going to stay for a bit. I don't like the idea of -"

"Willow and Ava are already at my parents' place," Mal said.

"What?" Bishop's stomach dropped.

Mal nodded. "Willow texted me earlier and asked if we were coming back before the barbecue. I said probably not and asked Fenton to drive them over to my parent's place. Willow texted me a couple of hours ago to say they were there."

"Fuck." Bishop slammed his hand down on the dashboard.

"Hey! You're paying for any damage." Mal grinned at him.

"Why don't you drive a normal-size car, anyway?" Bishop grumbled as he pulled at the seat belt cutting into his chest. He'd wanted to drive his truck to the client's, but Mal wanted to make a good impression, so they'd taken his car instead.

"What's wrong?" Mal asked as he turned off the highway. "Why don't you want Ava at the barbecue?"

"It's not that I don't want her there. It's just – Leslie is going to be there," Bishop said miserably.

"Well, shit. That's not good," Mal said. "Sorry, buddy. Mom didn't mention it, or I would have told Willow not to bring Ava."

"Maybe she's not there yet," Bishop said. "If she isn't, I'm taking your car and getting Ava the hell out of there, okay?"

"You bet." Mal parked in the driveway as Bishop scanned the cars in the street and breathed a sigh of relief.

"I don't see her car."

"Maybe she won't show."

"She will," Bishop said. "I need to get Ava out of here."

The two of them hurried into the house. Bishop scanned the living room as Mal's youngest sister Becky launched herself at him. He caught her with a loud grunt, and she grinned at him and kissed his cheek.

"Hey, Bishop."

"Hey, rugrat." He ruffled her hair affectionately, and she stuck her tongue out at him before hugging Mal.

"You're late."

"Client meeting. Where's Willow?" Mal asked.

"She's in the kitchen with Mom and Porter and Ava."

Becky squealed when a dark-haired man, he bore a remarkable resemblance to Mal, picked her up and threw her over her shoulder before holding his fist out.

"Hey, Mal. Hey, B."

"Hi, Heath." Bishop fist-bumped Heath's hand. "How's studying for the bar exam going?"

Heath shrugged. "I'll be happy when the damn thing is over."

"Good, that's good," Bishop said distractedly.

Heath gave him an odd look as Bishop followed Mal to the kitchen, the knot of tension tightening in his stomach when he heard Ava's soft laugh. He pushed past Mal and growled softly when he saw Porter standing next to her.

A bright pink apron covering her blouse and jeans, Ava grinned up at the wolf shifter. Bishop walked over and tugged her into his embrace before dropping his mouth onto hers. He kissed her deeply. When he finally released her, she was flushed and breathless.

He smiled smugly at Porter. "Hey, Porter."

Porter laughed and punched him on the shoulder. "Hey, B. How's it going, big guy?"

"Fine."

"Pumpkin! Button! You're here!" Mara stood at the stove, and Willow and Kat leaned against the large island in the center of the kitchen.

Mara crossed the room and hugged Mal before kissing Bishop on the cheek. "Hi, Button. How are you?"

"I'm good, Mara," Bishop said as she affectionately pinched his cheek.

"I've been getting to know your Ava a little better. I'm so glad you invited her to the barbecue. She's lovely," Mara said.

"She is," Bishop said. "But I'm sorry, we need to go."

"What?" Mara frowned at him. "Why?"

Bishop hesitated. "It's not safe for her to be here. She's been having some trouble with a shifter and -"

"Nonsense!" Mara said. "She's in a house full of wolf

shifters – she's perfectly safe. Now, do you want a beer or a soda to drink?"

BISHOP CLEARED HIS THROAT AND STARED AT AVA. Her stomach dropped at the look on his face, but she smiled at Mara and kept her voice from wavering when she said, "Bishop's right, Mara. I probably should go. I would feel terrible if something were to happen to your family."

"Nothing's going to happen. Mal, tell them," Mara said.

"Mom, maybe we should just let them go and -"

"Honey?" Roland stuck his head into the kitchen. "Leslie's here."

Bishop stiffened against her, and Ava bit back her squeak of pain when his fingers pressed painfully into her side.

"We need to go. We need to go right now," he said in a low voice.

She nodded, and he pulled her quickly toward the kitchen's back door. Before he could open it, a rough voice said, "Bishop? You're not going to introduce your lady friend to your mother?"

Looking like he was caught in another bear trap, Bishop turned around.

"Of course. Ava, this is my mother, Leslie. Leslie, this is my friend, Ava."

Ava stared at the woman standing behind them. She was well over six feet, and she had short dark hair and eyes like Bishop's. She sniffed the air, her nose twitching, before staring at Ava. "Your scent is all over her, Bishop. Smells like she's more than a friend."

Bishop turned bright red, and Ava quickly held out her hand. "It's so nice to meet you, Mrs. King."

Bishop's mother shook her hand before dropping it and wiping her hand on her pants. A look of disgust flickered briefly across her face. "How did my son get involved with a human?"

Mara hurried forward. "Leslie, I'm so glad you're here. Why don't you go into the living room and relax with the kids? I'll have Roland bring you a beer."

"Sure." Leslie glanced at Bishop. "You didn't come by last week. I was all alone. What kind of son doesn't visit his own mother?"

"I'm sorry, Leslie," Bishop said, "I was busy, but I should have called to tell you I wasn't going to drop by."

Her gaze settled on Ava. "Yeah, I know what you've been busy doing."

Ava flushed as Mara took Leslie's arm and tugged her toward the living room. "Leslie, come sit down, please."

When they left the room, awkward silence descended. Bishop stared at the floor at his feet, his face still bright red. Ava didn't know if she should say something or leave him be. Willow broke the silence.

"So, that's Bishop's mom," she said. "She seems nice."

Bishop stared at her in disbelief, but both Mal and Kat laughed. After a moment, Porter joined in and grinned at Ava. "C'mon, Ava. Crack a smile – you survived your first encounter with B's mom. That's something to celebrate."

Willow gave Mal an innocent look. "What? I mean it. She seems really nice. We should have her over for tea."

Mal laughed harder, and Ava could feel giggles bubbling up in her chest. She stared at Bishop. His look of misery killed her urge to laugh. She stood on her tiptoes and kissed his broad cheek.

"Don't worry, Bishop."

"I'm sorry, Ava, I -"

"You have nothing to be sorry about," she said before taking his hand and squeezing it. "Come on, let's get out of here."

"It's too late. Now that Leslie has seen us, there will be hell to pay if we leave," he said.

"Then we'll stay. Don't worry. It'll be fine," she said.

"Don't take anything she says personally, okay? She's... well, she's unhappy," Bishop said.

"That's the understatement of the year," Porter said.

Mal punched him on the arm as Bishop flushed again.

"I won't," Ava said. "Now, help us carry the food to the dining room."

AVA STARED AT HERSELF IN THE BATHROOM MIRROR. HER face was pale, and there were dark circles under her eyes. She sighed and washed her hands. She thought dinner would be awkward and uncomfortable, but Mal's family had done an excellent job of dispelling any lingering tension. Porter and Heath, in particular, had kept the mood light, and she felt a moment of envy toward Willow. She was part of a large and welcoming family who, it was apparent to see, loved and accepted her as Mal's mate. On the other hand, Ava was having sex with a bear shifter whose mother openly disliked her.

Not fair, Ava. Willow deserves every bit of the Burke family love. At least you still have your parents and your sister. Willow was alone until she met Mal. Besides, Amos was making plenty of snide remarks about humans during dinner.

That was all very true. Roland had spoken quietly to Amos more than once after a few particularly nasty jabs during dinner. Willow had ignored it, had even continued to be her cheerful self, but Ava knew her better than anyone. Amos's dislike hurt her badly.

"Okay, Ava," she said. "Just a few more hours, and then you'll be in Bishop's bed and forgetting all of your troubles."

Yeah, because that's a super healthy coping mechanism.

She ignored her inner voice and stepped out of the bathroom. Amos staggered down the hallway in front of her, one hand rubbing at his chest, and she hurried after him. "Mr. Burke? What's wrong?"

His face was white and small, deep lines of pain etched around his mouth. He winced, and she slid her arm around his waist when he lurched forward.

"Bedroom," he gasped before pointing to a door just a few feet away. "Pill."

Ava led him into his bedroom and helped him sit on the bed. He continued to rub at his chest as he pointed to the bedside stand. There was a bottle of pills and a blood pressure cuff, and she grabbed the bottle and scanned it before opening it and shaking a pill out.

"Open," she said.

He opened his mouth, and she placed the pill under his tongue. Amos closed his mouth, and she rubbed at his chest.

"Take some slow, deep breaths," she said before reaching for his wrist. She found his pulse and counted out the beats as he closed his eyes and breathed slowly. After nearly five minutes, he relaxed a little and opened his eyes.

"Better?" she asked.

"Ayuh," he muttered. He frowned when she reached for the blood pressure cuff. "What are you doing?"

He tried to pull his arm away as Ava pushed up his shirt sleeve. "I'm a nurse, Mr. Burke. Hold still, please," she said.

She took his blood pressure as he sat silently on the bed.

She smiled at him. "110 over 70, that's good."

She sat next to him on the bed and gave him a sympathetic look when he rubbed at his forehead. "Do you have a headache now?"

"Yeah, a little."

"The side effects of nitroglycerine, I'm afraid." She patted his arm. "How long have you had angina?"

"A couple of years," he said.

"You know, you shouldn't wait until the pain is that bad to take a pill," she said. "It's better if you take it as soon as you start feeling chest pain."

"I know," he said irritably. "It snuck up on me. I must have overeaten at dinner."

She pressed her hand against his forehead, and to her surprise, the old wolf shifter didn't jerk away. "Are you sure it's just from the heavy meal?"

"Yes."

"Okay." She smiled at him.

"Ain't ya gonna ask why my healing powers don't help?"

"I work in a hospital, Mr. Burke. I've seen plenty of injured shifters, and I know that after a certain age, healing powers start to fade."

They sat silently for nearly five minutes before he gave her a side glance. "You're quiet for a human."

"How many humans do you know?"

He shrugged. "Just you and that flakey little girl my grandson is hell bent on marrying. She never shuts up, always running at the mouth."

"When Willow's nervous, she talks a lot," Ava said. "And she's not flakey. She's brilliant. Just because she's a little… perky, doesn't mean she's a flake."

Amos scowled at her. "What the hell does she have to be nervous about?"

"Really?" Ava said.

Amos flushed a little and looked down at the floor. "She's making a fool out of my grandson by not marrying him. He claimed her months ago and they still ain't married. In my day, when a wolf bit a woman, she married him the next day."

"They're not married yet because they're worried about you." Ava decided that was only a partial lie.

"What the hell you talking about, human?" Amos snarled.

"One - my name is Ava, not human, and two – you know exactly what I'm talking about, Mr. Burke. You're mean to Willow, you say horrible things about humans in front of her, and she's worried that if she marries Mal, you'll start mistreating him as well."

Amos gaped at her. "I would never do that. I love my grandson."

"Then you should be happy for him. No matter who he chooses to love," Ava said. "Willow loves Mal, and she would never do anything to hurt him. You need to be happy for him and give Willow a chance. You're making a fool of yourself by treating her so terribly because of your hatred toward humans."

"I have my reasons for hating them," he said sullenly.

Sympathy rushed through her. "Yes, I know, and I'm more sorry than I can say for what my kind did to you. But it wasn't Willow who did those horrible things. She's the most open-minded, loving person I know. If you'd just take the time to get to know her instead of being such a crusty old man, you'd see it for yourself. You're being deliberately obtuse to the fact that Willow is a lovely person who is wonderful to your grandson."

He growled at her, and a grey beard sprouted on his face as his eyes lightened to yellow. Despite the way her heart thumped, she made herself stare calmly at him.

After a moment, a small smile crossed his face. "You're brave for a human."

"I'm not brave at all, Mr. Burke. Trust me," she said.

He continued to study her. "Pretty too, even with those freckles. I can see why Bishop wants you as his mate."

"Bishop doesn't want me as his mate," she said.

"Now who's being deliberately obtuse?" he said.

It was her turn to flush, and she cleared her throat. "We should get back downstairs. Are you feeling better, Mr. Burke?"

"Ayuh. And you can call me Amos." He grabbed her arm before she could stand. "Don't you listen to a single word that comes out of Bishop's mother's mouth. That woman is nastier than a nest of riled-up rattlesnakes, and she hates her boy. She'll say and do whatever she can to hurt him."

Ava frowned at him. "Leslie doesn't hate Bishop. He's her child."

"She hates him," he repeated, "and she ain't ever gonna change. Don't listen to anything she says."

"Dad? Are you okay?" Roland appeared in the doorway and hurried into the room. "What's wrong?"

"Nothing," Amos said. "I'm fine."

"He had an angina attack, but he's feeling much better now," Ava patted his arm before standing. "We were just heading back downstairs."

"Do you want to lie down for a while, Dad?" Roland asked as Amos stood.

"No, I don't want to lie down. I told you – I'm fine." Amos scowled in irritation and jerked his arm away from Roland's hand. "And I don't need help walking."

Without looking at either of them, he walked out of the bedroom.

CHAPTER 18

"**B**ishop, sit down! You're making all of us nervous with your pacing," Leslie barked.

Ava sighed inwardly. It was close to nine, and most of Mal's siblings and Kat had left. Mal's grandfather was right, she decided. Leslie was meaner than a nest of rattlesnakes.

She'd spent the entire evening listening as Leslie made dig after dig against Bishop, and Ava's temper was dangerously close to exploding. She tried to rein it in. Bishop was a grown man and didn't need her defending him. Besides, if he wanted to allow his mother to be so nasty, who was she to judge him? It wasn't any of her business, she reminded herself.

She glanced discreetly at her watch. She sat on the couch, sandwiched between Porter and Amos, and she smiled at Amos when he looked her way. He returned her smile grudgingly, and Willow's eyes widened across the room. Ava grinned at her as Willow stared at her like Ava had just parted the Red Sea.

Bishop sat down on one of the kitchen chairs Mal had

brought into the living room. It creaked alarmingly beneath him, and Leslie said, "You need to lose weight, Bishop. There's no excuse for the weight gain when you don't hibernate. You think the redhead will still want you when you're fat and breaking all the furniture in her house?"

Bishop turned red and gave Ava a fleeting, guilty look. Leslie pounced on it immediately. "Let me guess. You've already broken her furniture."

She turned to Ava. "I've lost track of all the furniture he's broken in my house over the years. All because he doesn't know when to step away from the dinner table. I told him time and time again when he was growing up that he'd never find a woman looking the way he does. It's for the best, though."

"I like the way Bishop looks," Ava said. "There isn't anything wrong with enjoying your food."

Leslie looked her up and down. "I suppose you would know. You look like you haven't quite figured out when it's time to step away from the dinner table either."

"Leslie!" Bishop snarled. "Enough! You keep your mouth shut about her."

Leslie's eyes widened in surprise. "Did you just tell your mother to shut up?"

Mara stood up. "Tea. Why don't we all have a nice cup of tea?"

"Is this what happens when you finally find a woman?" Leslie ignored Mara as she leaned forward and glared at Bishop. "You turn on your mother just like that?"

"I'm not turning on anyone, Leslie. But if you don't have anything nice to say, don't say anything at all," Bishop said.

Leslie laughed bitterly. "Now you think you're the parent? I spend the best years of my life raising you, and this is the thanks I get? Choosing some human over your mother?

I suppose I shouldn't be surprised. You're as selfish and cold-hearted as your father."

She waved one beefy hand at Ava. "You should run while you have the chance. Bishop might be saying all the right things now but believe me – in a few years after you've done whatever he wanted, after you've given him a child – he'll leave you for someone younger and thinner."

"Thanks for the tip, Mrs. King." Ava could feel her face reddening, and she couldn't stop her hands from clenching into fists. Her temper was fraying badly, and she clung grimly to her self-control as Amos patted her arm.

"She ain't worth it, Red," he muttered under his breath.

Willow popped up out of her chair. "You know, I think Mara is right. Tea would be great right now. Ava, come to the kitchen and help us make -"

"You don't believe me?" Leslie leaned forward in her chair. "That's because you're a silly human with stars in her eyes. Bear shifters aren't into commitment, and my son is no exception. You think you'll be the one to change his mind, but you won't be."

When Ava didn't reply, Leslie said, "I'm saying these things for your own good, girl. My son is not a good man. I know you think that makes me a bad mother to say that, but you don't know him the way I do. You'll never know him the way I do. He's lazy and simple-minded, just like his father. The only thing he's interested in is food and sex, and once you stop opening your legs for him, he'll kick you to the curb. He'll abandon you just like his father abandoned me. Is that what you want, girl? Do you want to be alone and stuck with a child who's too stupid even to know that -"

"Shut up!" Ava shouted. She shot to her feet and glared at Leslie.

"Oh shit," Willow said in a soft voice. She backed away and ducked behind Mal as Ava stomped toward Leslie.

"You keep your mouth shut about Bishop! Do you hear me, you nasty old woman?" Ava said.

Surprise washed over Leslie's features. "You don't get to speak to me that way, human."

"I'll speak to you however I fucking want!" Ava snarled. "Bishop is the kindest, sweetest man I know, and I won't sit here any longer and listen to you abuse him. He doesn't deserve that. I don't know why you hate your child so much, and, honestly, I don't fucking care. But you'll treat him with the respect he deserves."

She glared at Bishop's mother. Her entire body vibrated with anger, and she didn't give one shit that Leslie could easily tear her apart.

"You know what I think?" Ava said. "I think you're a nasty, bitter old woman who feels so awful about her own life that she can't stand it if her son is happy. I'm not surprised your husband left you or that your son hates you."

"Hates me?" Leslie stared at Bishop in shock. "You told this little bitch that you hate me?"

"Mom, I -"

"No, he didn't, but there isn't a chance in hell that he loves you," Ava said. "You've made sure to destroy any of the love he might have had for you with your insults and your anger and bitterness. No one loves you. No one *likes* you."

"That isn't true," Leslie stood and glared at Ava. "You best be keeping your mouth shut, human."

"Or what?" Ava asked, disdain practically dripping from her tongue. "You going to shut it for me?"

"I'll rip out your tongue, you insolent little bitch!" Leslie shouted. She started forward, her body swelling and her clothes ripping. Bishop threw his arms around her as Mal, Roland, and Porter stepped in front of Ava.

"You're going to die old and alone!" Ava shouted around Roland's broad back. "And you deserve it! Bishop won't have -"

"AVA! ENOUGH!" Bishop roared at her.

She shut her mouth with a snap as Leslie stared up at Bishop. Her lower lip trembled, and tears streaked down her face. "Is that the kind of woman you're in love with now, Bishop? The kind who would say such terrible things to your mother?"

"She didn't mean it, Mom," Bishop said.

"I meant every word!" Ava snapped.

"Ava!" Bishop glared at her.

Her stomach churning, Ava said, "Bishop, you can't -"

"Ava, stop," he said wearily. "You've done enough."

He wrapped his arm around Leslie's waist. "I think it's time to leave, Leslie. I'll drive you home, okay?"

"Thank you, son." Leslie sniffed. "I'm so upset I don't think I could drive."

"Bullshit," Ava muttered.

"Mal, can you give Ava a lift back to my place and stay with her until I get there?" Bishop asked.

"Yes," Mal said as Bishop led Leslie toward the front door.

When the door had closed behind them, there was silence for a moment before Amos stood from the couch. He patted Ava's back gingerly. "I told you to pay no mind to her, Red. Although it was mighty impressive watching you go up against a bear shifter."

He started toward the door. "I'll make the tea." When Willow didn't move, he frowned at her. "Well, c'mon, girl. I'll need some help."

"Uh, okay." Willow stared nervously at Mal.

"I'll give you a hand as well, Grandpa," Mal said.

"We don't need your help, boy," Amos said grouchily. "I'm not going to hurt your woman. C'mon, girl."

"Be right there!" Willow said.

Amos left the room. Willow grabbed Ava's arm and whispered into her ear, "If Mal's grandfather kills me in the kitchen, make sure you get rid of the sex toys in the bottom drawer of my dresser before anyone else finds them. Also - avenge my death."

Ava smiled faintly, and Willow stroked her hair and kissed her cheek. "It'll be okay, honey. You did the right thing in telling off Bishop's mother. She was awful to him, and I would have done the same thing."

MARA SAT DOWN ON THE SIDE OF THE BED AND STARED AT Roland. He put down the book he was reading and took off his glasses, rubbing at the imprints the pads left on his nose.

"Well, it wasn't the worst dinner party we've hosted," he said.

"Are you kidding me?" Mara said as she climbed under the covers and curled up against him. "We had a human and a bear shifter screaming at each other in the middle of our living room."

"True, but remember the barbecue when Porter brought that coyote shifter over as his date? Jessa and the woman nearly destroyed the kitchen when they got into a fight."

Mara laughed. "Oh God, I had forgotten about that. It was Porter's fault. He knew his sister had just had her heart broken by a coyote shifter. What was his name again?"

"I don't remember," Roland said. "Bill, maybe?"

"The things Leslie said tonight, Roland. How could she be so cruel to her child?" Mara asked.

Roland put his arm around her before kissing her forehead. "You need to tell Bishop the truth, honey."

She didn't reply, and he kissed her forehead again. "I know Leslie was your friend, and you want to protect her, but she's not the person you knew before. Bishop deserves to know the truth."

"I know." Mara rested her head against Roland's shoulder. "I know."

"Honey, sit down with me," Mal said.

Willow stopped pacing Bishop's living room and joined Mal on the couch. "He should be home by now."

"He'll be back soon. I'm sure Leslie made him stay with her for a while," Mal said.

Princess jumped into Willow's lap and purred as Willow petted her. They heard the front door open, and relief washed over Willow when Bishop walked into the living room.

"Are you okay, Bishop?" she asked.

"Yes," he said. "Where's Ava?"

"She's upstairs."

"Thanks for bringing her back here. I'll talk to you later," he said.

Willow frowned. "Bishop -"

Mal squeezed Willow's hand, and they watched silently as Bishop trudged up the stairs.

"Come on, honey. Let's go home," Mal said.

"No, we need to wait a few minutes," Willow said.

"Willow, we can't listen in on their private conversation," Mal said.

"We're not. But if it doesn't go well, Ava will leave. I don't want her taking off by herself. Okay?"

Mal nodded, and Willow leaned against him, absentmindedly stroking Princess's soft fur. "I hope I'm wrong, and we hear them having angry sex, Mal."

"Gross," he said with a small smile.

Willow rested her head on his shoulder. "Tell me she'll be okay, Mal."

"She'll be okay, honey."

Sick to his stomach and wishing like hell he'd gotten Ava out of the house before Leslie showed up, Bishop stepped into his bedroom. Ava sat on the bed, and they stared silently at each other for a moment.

"Are you okay?" Bishop asked.

"I'm fine. It wasn't me who was being insulted by my own mother."

Bishop winced. He had hoped Ava's anger would have faded, but she was still furious. "Ava, my mother is a very unhappy woman. I told you that."

"That doesn't give her an excuse to be so cruel to you."

"I'm used to it, and it doesn't bother me. Besides, she can't help it. She's been through a lot."

"Bullshit, Bishop King," she snapped. "Your mother is a terrible person, and I don't know why you're defending her."

Anger rushed through him. "Because she's my mother! You expect me to just abandon her because she is occasionally cruel?"

"Occasionally? Bishop, the things that she said were horrible. No one should be treated that way," Ava said.

"You shouldn't have said anything, Ava," he replied. "You just made it worse."

"I shouldn't have defended you?" Ava stood and crossed her arms over her chest. "Did you expect me just to stand there and keep my mouth shut while someone said such horrible things about you?"

"I expected you to do as I asked!" he shouted. His grizzly snarled at him for shouting at their mate, but Bishop ignored him. "She's my mother, Ava, and while she may not be the nicest person ever, I won't abandon her just because you want me to."

"I'm not asking you to abandon her. All I'm saying is that just because she's your mother, it doesn't give her the right to treat you that way."

He didn't reply, and she walked toward him and cupped his face. "Bishop, honey, what she's doing is abuse, and you don't have to put up with that. You don't have to listen to those horrible things she says or believe them. You're nothing like she says. It's terrible that your father abandoned your mother, but if she treated him the same way she treats you, can you blame him?"

He pulled away from her, sorrow mixing in with the anger. "Stop it. You don't know what she's been through. Can you not have some sympathy for her?"

"No, I can't," she said. "Not when she treats you the way she does. She's toxic to you, Bishop. You don't need her in your life."

"I won't abandon her the way my father did," Bishop said. "If I do, I'll be exactly like him. I can't be that person, Ava."

He could see the anger fade from her face. "She's using

you, honey. She's using your guilt over what your father did to keep you shackled to her and her abuse."

"She's not the monster you think she is," he said hoarsely as a healthy mix of anger and guilt and grief flooded his senses.

"Bishop -"

"Enough. You may be sharing my bed, Ava, but it doesn't give you the right to demand that I choose you over my mother."

She recoiled from him. "That's not what I'm doing, Bishop. I care about you, and I don't want to watch her abuse you."

"She's not abusing me," he shouted again. "Stop saying that!"

"She is, honey. If you would just take a step back and look at it from -"

"Stop it! You're not my girlfriend or my mate, Ava. You don't have the right to tell me how to deal with my mother. What you and I have is sex and nothing more, remember?"

His grizzly snarled in fury at him, and Bishop's immediate and overwhelming regret nearly took his breath away.

Her face paled, and she blinked rapidly. "I remember."

His guts churning like a category five hurricane, he reached for her. "I'm sorry, Ava. I didn't mean it that way. I just meant -"

"I know what you meant," she said and stepped away from him. She grabbed her purse and walked toward the door.

"Where are you going?" he said.

"I'm leaving."

"What? No, it isn't safe. I'm sorry, I shouldn't have -"

"Stop apologizing, Bishop," she said. "I'm not angry with you for being truthful with me. But this isn't going to work between us anymore, even if it is just … a sex thing. I won't watch you be treated horribly by your mother without being allowed to defend you. I can't, I'm sorry."

She left the bedroom, and he hurried after her.

"Ava, wait. It isn't safe for you to be out there alone."

"I won't be. I'll stay with Willow and Mal."

Willow stood at the bottom of the staircase, and she took Ava's hand as Ava glanced at Bishop. "I'll drop by tomorrow when you're at work and pick up my things. Thank you for letting me stay with you for so long, Bishop. I appreciate it."

She walked quickly down the hallway as Bishop joined Mal at the bottom of the stairs and made a harsh noise of frustration. He started after her, and Mal grasped his shoulder. "Give her a couple of days, Bishop."

"Mal, she's in danger," he said.

"We'll keep her safe. I promise you." Mal clapped him on the back, and Bishop sat down on the stairs with a harsh thud as the three of them left. He buried his head in his hands as Princess, meowing softly, weaved around his legs.

BISHOP KNOCKED ON THE FRONT DOOR BEFORE OPENING IT. "Mara? You home?"

Mara stuck her head into the hallway from the kitchen and smiled at Bishop. "Button! What are you doing here?" Her smile faded as she took a closer look at him. "Honey? What's wrong?"

"Nothing. Are you busy? I can come back later," he said.

"Don't be silly. I always have time for you," she said. "I just made some tea."

He followed her into the kitchen, and she poured him a cup of tea before setting a plate of cookies in front of him.

"They're chocolate chip – you're favourite. Have some."

"I'm not hungry," Bishop said.

Mara's eyes widened, and she sat down beside him at the table, taking one of his hands in both of hers. "You're starting to scare me, Bishop. Tell me what's wrong, dearest."

"Ava and I fought. It's been two days, and she still won't talk to me," he said.

"Oh, my poor Button." Mara leaned over and put her arms around him. He buried his face in her neck.

"I was awful to her, Mara."

"She knows you didn't mean it, honey. She cares for you deeply. That's easy to see."

"Not anymore," Bishop said as he sat back. "I got angry at her for defending me against Leslie. She said that she wouldn't watch Leslie abuse me, and then I told her we were just having sex, and she didn't have the right to say anything about Leslie."

He stared at his hands. "I know that Leslie isn't a nice person, but she's not abusive."

Mara didn't reply, and Bishop looked up. "Do you think she is, Mara?"

She sipped at her cup of tea before saying, "You know that I love your mother, right?"

"Yes. I do too."

"I know you do," she said before reaching for his hand and squeezing it. "It's part of what makes you such a good man, Bishop. Roland and I are so proud of the man you've become."

He blushed, and she squeezed his hand again. "Your mama and I were best friends for many years, and I've kept quiet because I wanted to protect her and you. But she's not the same person she used to be, Bishop. Or maybe she is, and I just never really knew the real Leslie. I've kept the truth from you for too long, hoping that she would improve, that maybe she'd start to realize just how wonderful you were."

"What are you talking about?" Bishop asked.

"Your father didn't abandon your mother because he didn't love her anymore. In fact, he loved her deeply, but Leslie couldn't stop believing that he would stop loving her. She was so fearful that he would have an affair or that he would grow tired of her that she became, well, obsessed with discovering something that would prove her right."

"What?" Bishop said.

"Eventually, her paranoia and her refusal to believe that he would always love her drove your father away. She convinced herself that what she had suspected all along became true – he stopped loving her. After a couple of years, when it became apparent that Leslie was getting worse and that she couldn't properly mother you, your father started proceedings to gain full custody of you. Only…"

"Only then he died," Bishop said dully.

Mara nodded before reaching up to stroke his cheek. "Your father loved your mother, Bishop. Even after he left, he never dated anyone else. It was always just Leslie for him."

She turned his face toward hers. "You remind me so much of your father, Bishop. I could never tell you that before, but now – you need to know that he was such a good man. He loved you and your mother very much, and the greatest day of his life was the day you were born."

"All these years," he said.

"I'm so sorry, dearest. I should have told you before now, but I thought you and Leslie should have a relationship. I didn't want her to be alone, and I was foolish enough to keep hoping that she would eventually change."

"And now?" he asked.

"Now," she smiled a bit wistfully, "I see your love for

Ava, and I see your chance at real happiness, and I want you to have it. Even if that means giving up on Leslie."

She touched his shoulder. "I'm so sorry, Button. I'll understand if you hate me for not telling you the truth earlier."

Disbelief washed over him. How could Mara think he would ever hate her? He scrubbed a hand through his hair. "Mara, I don't hate you. I could never hate you. I spent most of my childhood pretending you were my mother and not Leslie. You came to all of my football games, and you packed an extra lunch in Mal's lunchbox for me every damn day. You showed up for parent/teacher interviews – hell, half the teachers at school believed you were my mother."

He took her hands. "Roland taught me how to shave and how to drive. He took me to baseball games and picked me up from parties in the middle of the night when I was too drunk to drive home. You bought me clothes for school and took me on family trips like I was your own kid. You helped me fill out the loan application for my first car, and you drove me to my first job interview. Everything I am, all the good things that have happened to me, is because of you and Roland, and I will never forget that."

He leaned forward and stared intently at her. "Leslie might be my birth mother, but you are, and always will be, my mom."

"Oh, Bishop." Mara started to cry.

Bishop hugged her hard. "Don't cry, Mara. I'm sorry."

"Roland and I love you and think of you as our child. And I'm so sorry I didn't tell you the truth about Leslie and your father sooner."

"I understand why you didn't," Bishop said as Mara grabbed a tissue and wiped away the tears.

"What are you going to do now, Button?"

"I don't know. Talk to Leslie, I guess, and then try my best to gain Ava's forgiveness."

"She'll forgive you, dearest. I know it. She's in love with you." Mara kissed his forehead, and Bishop smiled faintly at her as she pushed the plate of cookies toward him. "Now, have a cookie. You'll need the sugar rush if you're going to talk to Leslie."

CHAPTER 19

K at closed her laptop with a thud and drummed her
fingers on the desk. It was after five. Willow had
stayed home with Ava, Bishop left early, and Mal had been at
a client meeting for most of the afternoon. He'd texted her
five minutes ago to see if she needed him to come back to the
office, and she had hurriedly texted him back with a 'no need'
message.

Not that she would have tried to seduce him. Despite what
was happening, she had some self-control, but seeing him
would have brought on some excruciatingly uncomfortable
and embarrassing images. She didn't need to think about Mal
in any way other than the business partner that he was.

She rubbed at her forehead. Bishop had left before her
heat cycle had really got going, thank God, and she'd been
alone for the afternoon, ignoring the throbbing in her belly
and pelvis as her cycle intensified. She usually didn't go into
work the two days that her heat cycle lasted, but there was so
much going on with Bishop and Ava that she was the only
one left to take care of the day-to-day office responsibilities.

Her pelvis throbbed again, and she ignored the urge to slip her hand under her skirt and touch herself. She would not fucking masturbate at the goddamn office. God, some days she hated being a cat shifter. She really did.

Her monthly heat cycle seemed to worsen with every passing month, and she supposed she needed to bite the bullet and start taking the medication for it. She hated the idea. Some research suggested the medicine that helped curb the heat cycle made it harder for a shifter to conceive. While she wasn't interested in having kittens at the current moment, she eventually wanted to be a mother.

She used to be able to control it better, she thought grimly. She used to get by with just her vibrator, but lately, the thought of using it made her shudder. Her cat didn't want something plastic and fake. She wanted the real thing.

She bit her lip and then reached for her phone. She would call Mark. He was a tiger shifter, and he understood her need for release. Frankly, she hated to do it. It made her feel like a whore to call him up once a month for nothing but sex. It was ridiculous to feel that way. Plenty of single cat shifters did just that and had no problems with it. In fact, there was a local website for cat shifters that catered to that very thing. Female cat shifters connected with other shifters who were ready, willing and very able to help them out during their heat cycle.

Still, she wished bitterly for a moment that she was in a relationship. At least then, she would have someone to help her through the cycle. Her hands shook as she scrolled through her contacts and her cat made a hungry, mewling growl of need.

Patience. Mark will help us. Just wait, okay?

She waited, her hand clutching her leg, as the phone rang in her ear. She breathed a sigh of relief when Mark answered.

"Kat! How are you?"

"I'm good, Mark. How are you?"

"Couldn't be better. What's up?"

That's what she loved about Mark. He always got straight to the point.

"I'm wondering if you wanted to stop by my place for drinks tonight." She swallowed hard as her cat purred loudly.

"Oh, um, you know I'd love to, Kat, but I have plans for tonight."

"Maybe you could stop by after," she said.

He hesitated, and her cat yowled angrily at her.

Enough! Just wait!

"Is it your heat cycle?" he asked.

"Yes," she said.

"The thing is, I'm in a relationship now and, you know...."

Her cat hissed in fury, but she forced herself to sound cheerful. "Hey, that's great. I'm happy for you."

"Thanks, Kat. She's a fantastic girl – you'd like her."

"I'm sure I would. Listen, I'd better go, okay?"

"Yeah, of course. I'm sorry I can't help you anymore."

"Don't be. I'm happy for you. Good night, Mark." She ended the call and resisted the urge to throw her phone across the room.

Her hand inched under her skirt, and this time she didn't stop. The need pulsed through her like a living thing now, and she had to masturbate before going home. Her cat would have her in a bar and picking up a total stranger if she didn't.

She pushed her fingers past her panties and made a soft mew of need at the wetness she found there. She stroked her clit once, her entire body vibrating, before suddenly stiffening. The bell to the front door jingled, and she froze with her hand under her skirt as she sniffed delicately at the air.

"Hello? Anyone still here?"

"No, please God, no. Anyone but him," she groaned softly.

She stood and straightened her skirt with trembling hands. She would find out what he wanted and then make him leave, simple as that. She would keep herself under control and not think at all about what it would be like to pin him down and fuck him until neither of them could see straight.

She started toward the door to her office. She took a deep breath, and her pussy pulsed, and fresh wetness coated her panties. Taking a deep breath was a terrible mistake. It brought his scent to her, filled her entire body with it, and the pupils of her eyes turned to slits as her cat surged forward and took control.

RONIN GLANCED AROUND THE EMPTY RECEPTION AREA. There'd been no reply to his shout, and he frowned. The front door was open, so someone must still be here. Shrugging, he dropped off his timesheet on Willow's desk and glanced in Mal's office. It was empty, as was Bishop's, and he started toward Kat's office, stopping when she appeared in the doorway.

She leaned against the doorway, one hand on her hip, and smiled at him. "Hello, little bird."

"Hello, Ms. Frost."

"What are you doing here?" she asked.

"I forgot to hand in my timesheet this morning." There was something off about her. He could see it in the way she looked, in the way she looked at *him*. "Are you all right?"

"Yes, why wouldn't I be?" she said.

"You're acting differently."

"Am I?" She cocked her head.

"Yes."

She licked her lips, and his gaze dropped to her mouth. He twitched in surprise when she purred and ran her hand over her flat stomach.

"Come into my office. I need to speak with you about your work performance." She turned and disappeared into her office, her hips swaying enticingly.

He glanced around the empty reception area before following her into her office. "Ms. Frost? What's -"

He grunted in surprise when she grabbed him by his shoulders. She swept her leg against his, knocking his feet out from under him, and he hit the floor with a harsh thud. "What the hell?"

She pounced on him, her entire body vibrating and a low growl emerging from her throat. She straddled his hips before purring to him.

"Ms. Frost, what are you doing?" he asked as she took out the clip from her hair and leaned over him.

Her eyes turned a golden colour, and her pupils were dark slits. Lust shot through him when she pressed her breasts against his chest.

"I want you, little bird. And I know you want me. I can smell it."

She purred again before licking his cheek. He moaned as hot desire poured over him. Her purr loudened, and she reached for her shirt.

"Ms. Frost, wait." He took her hands, and she hissed at him.

"I don't know what's gotten into you, but I'm pretty sure that us sleeping together is not a good idea," he said.

"I don't care what you think," she said. "I want to fuck you, and I know you want to fuck me."

"Hey, I like a girl who takes what she wants as much as the next guy, but obviously, you're not thinking clearly. I'm your employee, remember?"

She ignored him and stripped off her shirt. He stared at her breasts, clad in a dark pink bra, and smothered his groan of need. "Bad idea, Ms. Frost. Very, very bad idea."

She kissed him hard on the mouth, shoving her tongue between his lips and stroking his tongue with a desperate kind of need. He returned her kiss, threading his hands through her hair as she nipped at his lips before biting his throat. He grunted at the feel of her sharp fangs, and she grinned at him.

"I'm going to fuck you, little bird, and you're going to lie still and let me. Do you understand?"

"Yes, ma'am," he said. He had no idea what the fuck was going on, but the feel of her mouth and the sight of her smooth skin had driven the reluctance straight out of him. Kat wanted to fuck him, and he'd have his damn man card taken away from him if he didn't give the woman what she wanted.

"Such a pretty bird," she said as she traced his cheek with one long nail. It was painted a bright red, and he sucked on her finger when she pushed it into his mouth. "My pretty bird."

He grinned at her before cupping her breasts through her bra. "Are we going to talk or fuck, Kitten?"

She snarled at him, and he gave her another cheeky grin. "I'm not afraid of a little pussy cat like you."

She hissed and dipped her head to kiss him again. They kissed deeply, their tongues battling for control, as he reached behind her and unclipped her bra. She shimmied out of it impatiently and then guided her nipple to his mouth. He sucked hard on it, and she purred loudly before rubbing her lower body against his.

He arched his pelvis and cried out when she quickly unbuttoned his jeans and pulled out his cock. She stroked it firmly, and he moaned.

"So pretty," she purred. "And all mine. Say it's mine."

"Whatever you say, Kitten," he gasped.

She tugged her skirt up around her waist. She wore a pink thong, and she pushed Ronin's hand away when he reached for the pocket of his jeans. She was already pulling the crotch of her panties aside and guiding his cock toward her throbbing opening, and he grabbed her hand.

"Hold up. We need a condom."

She hissed again at him, and he squeezed her bare thighs. "I get the impatience, but there's a condom in my wallet. Let me grab it."

She knocked his hand away and wiggled her hand beneath him. He lifted his hips, and she pulled out his wallet. She rifled through it, making a purr of triumph when she found the foil package and tossed his wallet aside.

She ripped open the package and rolled the condom onto his dick. He moaned at the feel of her soft hands, and she purred again to him before tugging his hands to her breasts. He cupped and kneaded them as she rose on her knees, pulled the crotch of her panties aside and thrust herself down onto his throbbing dick. He groaned, and she made a soft sound of excitement before rocking back and forth.

"Your pussy is amazing," he groaned.

She grinned fiercely at him, her eyes glowing brightly before pinning his hands against the floor and riding him like a woman possessed.

Her fingernails lengthened, and he cried out when she

released his hands and raked her nails down his chest, drawing thin lines of blood. The pain only heightened his pleasure, and he met each of her thrusts, their bodies slapping together as her purring grew to a deafening level.

She rubbed at her clit, and her entire body stiffened as she threw back her head and screamed her release. Her pussy tightened around him, and he shouted hoarsely before thrusting his pelvis upward as his orgasm rushed through him.

She collapsed against him, shuddering wildly and purring, and he stroked her damp back with the tips of his fingers as she buried her face in his neck. After a few moments, she lifted her head and stared blankly at him.

"Was it good for you, Kitten? Cause I gotta tell you – that might have been the best sex of my life." He grinned at her.

Her eyes returned to their normal colour. She scrambled off of him, shoving her skirt down and covering her breasts with her hands. "You need to leave."

"What?" He pulled off the condom and tucked his dick back into his pants.

"I'm sorry. You need to go, please." She shook wildly, and her face was pale. His confusion faded into concern.

"Kat? What's wrong?"

"Nothing. This was a mistake. Please go, please." she pleaded.

He grabbed his wallet and climbed to his feet. "Kat, let's talk for a moment and -"

"No!" she shouted. "This never happened. Do you hear me, Ronin? This never happened."

Unexpected hurt flooded through him, but he tamped it down and shrugged before strolling for the door. "Fine by me. Have a good night."

Bishop stepped into his mother's home and called her name. When there was no reply, he walked into the kitchen. She sat at the table, reading a magazine and smoking a cigarette. He sat down across from her.

She glanced up at him before looking at her magazine again. "What are you doing here?"

"I came to talk."

"About what? Your redhead whore insulting me?"

"Stop it. Don't speak about Ava like that," he said as he held on to his self-control by a thin thread.

"Why shouldn't I? She's a horrible little bitch, and you needed to see the truth."

"I'm not here to talk about Ava," he said.

"Then what? Stop wasting my time and get to the point," she said.

"I know the truth, Leslie."

"The truth about what?"

"The truth about why Dad left."

She butted the cigarette and lit another. "I don't know what you're talking about."

"Yes, you do. Mara finally told me what really happened."

Leslie snorted. "That wolf shifter has had it in for me for years. First, she takes away my only son and tries to turn him into her own. You'd think with six fucking kids, she wouldn't need mine, but no, she's a greedy little bitch who -"

"Shut your mouth about Mara!" Bishop roared as white-hot anger rocketed through him. Leslie flinched back, the ash from her cigarette falling unnoticed to the table.

"Mara has been nothing but good to me, and I won't hear you talk shit about her. Do you understand?" he said.

"What the fuck has gotten into you, Bishop?"

"I know the truth," he said. "I know how you drove my father away with your paranoia. I know that he loved you. I know that he died still loving you despite everything you had done to him."

"Your father was a liar and a cheater," Leslie spat. "And you're exactly like him, Bishop. You're going to destroy that redhead's life like your father destroyed mine. She should be thanking me for ending your relationship. Sooner or later, you'll do what your father did. You're useless and worthless – just like him!"

He stared wide-eyed at her, soaking in the anger and hatred that radiated from her in a steady scent before his shoulders slumped.

"Did you ever love me, Mom?" he asked. "Was there ever a part of you that loved me, even just a little?"

She snorted and sucked on her cigarette. "Don't speak so foolishly. I say what I do because there's no point in sheltering you from reality. I'm not doing you any favours if I try to pretend that your life is going to turn out sunshine and honey."

She took another puff and blew the smoke out before glancing back at her magazine. "While you're here, I need you to look at the upstairs toilet. It's acting up again."

He stood and walked toward the doorway.

"Where are you going? I said I needed you to look at the toilet."

"I love you, but I'm done, Leslie," he said.

"What? What do you mean you're done?"

He shrugged. "I'm done. Ava was right. You're abusive, and I'm tired of being shit on."

"Abusive? Are you fucking crazy? I never laid a hand on you, Bishop King," she said indignantly.

"Don't call me," he said.

"Bishop, wait!" she shouted. "You can't do this – I'm your mother!"

"No, you're not. Mara is my mother," he said. "Goodbye, Leslie."

CHAPTER 20

Praying like hell that Bria answered, Kat clutched her phone and breathed a sigh of relief when Bria picked up. "Kat! How are you?"

Her best friend was cutting in and out, and Kat held her phone away as a squeal of static went through it. "Bria? Can you hear me?"

"Kat? You're cutting in and out. The reception is terrible here!" Bria shouted.

"Are you having a good time?" Kat shouted back.

"Yes. I … and it's incredible and … my butt hurts."

"What?"

"I said… jungle… hot, and I fell and… hottie with a man bun rescued me."

"I can't hear you, Bria," Kat said.

"What's wrong? You sound… okay?"

"Everything's fine. Listen, I'll let you go. I'll see you in a few weeks, okay?"

"Okay!" Bria shouted past the static. "I love you and miss you, Kit Kat."

"Love you too, Bria," Kat said, but the call had disconnected.

She fell back on her bed and stared at the ceiling. Bria was making a pilgrimage with her family in the middle of the jungle. She'd been gone for nearly two months, and Kat missed her terribly.

She blew her breath out in a harsh rush. Her heat cycle had ended earlier this afternoon. Despite how busy it was in the office, she had called in sick yesterday and today. She couldn't go in, not with her heat cycle and not after what she'd done to Ronin. What if he came by the office again? Her cat would have him flat on his back and his dick deep inside of her before he knew what was happening.

She groaned and sat up, grabbing her purse and her phone before heading toward the door. What she had done to Ronin the night before last was inexcusable, and she was ashamed of her behaviour. She had lost control and forced him to have sex with her on the office floor. She slammed the front door shut and climbed into her car. She didn't have a lot of friends. Despite her outgoing nature, she was a very private person. What she wouldn't give to have Bria home so she could spill her guts to her.

Talk to Willow and Ava, her cat suggested.

Be quiet! I don't need your help!

Her cat hissed in reply before going silent. She wasn't ashamed at all about what they'd done to Ronin, and Kat had spent the rest of her heat cycle viciously denying her jaguar's cries to find Ronin and ride his dick into oblivion.

She pulled out of the driveway and headed down the street. She loved driving and typically found it very soothing, but her brain wouldn't stop yammering at her about her loss of control. She needed to suck up her pride and apologize to Ronin for what she did. Fuck, she didn't want to have that conversation. The odds of him asking Mal and Bishop to drop her from the firm was high.

Without realizing it, she had driven toward Mal's house. She parked in the driveway and rubbed delicately under her eyes for a moment before sighing and climbing out of the car. She needed to talk, she really did, and Willow was the closest person she had to a friend after Bria. She would just have to hope that, for once, Willow would keep the information to herself.

She waved at Garth sitting in a car across the street, and he nodded to her as she rang the front doorbell. The door opened, and Willow smiled at her.

"Hey, Kat. What are you doing here?"

"I was in the neighbourhood and thought I'd stop by and see how everything was going," Kat said.

"It's okay. Come in. Ava and I were just having some girl talk."

She followed Willow into the house and down the hall to the living room. Ava sat on the couch, drinking a glass of wine and staring moodily out the window, but she stood and hugged Kat when she walked into the room.

"I never said thank you for saving my life the other night, Kat. Thank you so much. I would have died if it hadn't been for you. If there's anything I can do for you – anything at all – just let me know, okay?"

A little uncomfortable by Ava's sincerity, Kat returned her hug. "Thanks, Ava. How are you feeling?"

"I'm fine," Ava said.

"She's lying." Willow poured Kat a glass of wine and handed it to her. "She's been miserable without Bishop the last four days."

"I heard what happened. I'm sorry." Kat sat down in the

chair by the fireplace. "Bishop's an idiot to choose his mother over you."

"He isn't. Family is important. I just wish that he could see how badly she treats him," Ava said.

Kat gave her a sympathetic look before taking a sip of wine. "Where's Mal?"

"Oh, he's upstairs playing with his kittens," Willow said.

"What?"

"Didn't I tell you? We rescued a couple of kittens, and they think Mal is their mother. They love him, and he turns into a big ball of mush whenever he's around them."

Kat grinned. "I don't believe it. Mal hates cats."

"It's true, I swear it. He cuddles them and plays with them. It's ridiculously adorable if you ask me," Willow said. "They hate my guts, though. I think they're jealous. The other day we were in bed having some awesome sex, and Dolly jumped on my back and scratched the hell out of me. I screamed so loud that I nearly deafened poor Mal."

Kat laughed, and even Ava smiled a little. Kat was suddenly glad she'd come over. Willow and her cheerfulness were precisely what she needed to take her mind off of Ronin.

"Anyway, Mal bandaged me up, and then we kicked the kittens out of the bedroom before we continued." Willow drank some wine. "Tell me what's wrong, Kat."

"What?" Kat said. "There isn't anything wrong. I just dropped by to check in on everyone."

"There's something wrong. My spidey senses are all a tingle over here," Willow said.

"Will, there's nothing wrong," Kat repeated. She had come over here thinking she would tell her everything that happened, but she'd lost her nerve. What if Willow told Mal?

She had worked hard to get where she was, and Mal and Bishop's respect was important to her.

"Do you believe her?" Willow asked Ava. Ava shook her head.

"I'm fine," Kat said.

"Yeah, as fine as Ava is. Why don't you want to tell us what's wrong?"

Kat hesitated, and Willow said, "I won't say a word to Mal or anyone else, Kat. I promise."

Ava nodded when Kat glanced over at her. "She means it, Kat."

Kat rubbed her finger along the rim of her wine glass. "I had sex with Ronin the night before last."

"Nice!" Willow said approvingly. "He's a bit too tattooed for my taste, but that dimple and his ass are rather fetching."

"Not nice," Kat said. "Not nice at all."

Willow leaned forward. "Not nice? Uh oh. Did he suffer from premature ejaculation? There's medication he can take for that."

Kat gaped at her. "Jesus, Willow! No, that's not what I meant. The sex was – well, it was incredible – but I really shouldn't have slept with him."

"Why did you then?" Ava asked.

"My heat cycle made me do it," she said.

"Heat cycle?" Ava said.

"Oh! Oh! I read about that on the "Shifter's Today" website," Willow said excitedly. "All female cat shifters – cheetahs, jaguars, tigers, lions – have what they call a monthly heat cycle. It's like a week of insane lust for anything that moves. Right?"

Kat grimaced. "Not exactly. It only lasts for two days."

"But you want to screw any man who looks your way, yeah?" Willow said.

"Yeah," Kat said.

"That sounds…distracting," Ava said.

"You have no idea," Kat said. "It's fine if you're in a relationship, your mate helps you get through it, but for a single cat shifter, it's pure torture."

"I thought there was a pill or something you could take for it," Willow said.

"There is, but there's been some suggestion that it can make us infertile. I want kittens at some point," Kat said.

She stared into her glass of wine. "Anyway, I normally don't go into the office during my heat cycle. I stay home and take care of the problem myself, or I have a friend who comes over and – you know."

"I do know," Willow said. "I've had some booty call experiences."

"It's been so crazy lately that I couldn't leave the office, and I thought I would be able to control it. Only, it's been getting worse as I get older. I called Mark, but he's in a relationship now."

"Ooh, bad luck," Willow said.

"Yeah," Kat said. "I was getting ready to leave when Ronin dropped by the office. I told myself to walk away, not to get too close to him, but my – my need was so bad by that point. I lost control. My damn cat took over, and I ended up riding him like a pony on the floor of my office."

"Remind me to call and make an appointment to have the carpets cleaned at the office," Willow said to Ava.

Kat flushed, and Willow smiled. "I'm sorry, Kat. I shouldn't tease."

"I feel terrible about what I did."

Ava leaned forward. "You shouldn't. You can't help it if your heat cycle makes you lose control. Besides, I'm sure Ronin didn't mind. He flirts with you like crazy."

"I forced him to have sex with me, Ava," Kat said miserably.

"Did he say no?" Willow asked with a serious look.

"He didn't say no, but he did remind me that it was a bad idea and that he was my employee."

"But did the words, 'No' or 'Stop', or 'Kat, I do not want to have sex with you,' come out of his mouth?" Willow asked.

Kat shook her head. "He said afterward that it might have been the best sex of his life."

Willow reclined against the couch. "Then stop acting like you forced him, Kat. He had a good time, you had a good time – it's all good."

"It isn't," Kat said. "I hate losing control, and I hate that I couldn't stop myself from having sex with him. He's a bird, for God's sake!"

"So, what?" Willow shrugged.

"I'm a cat, Willow. Bird shifters and cat shifters do not have sex."

"Obviously, they do," Willow said.

"If my mother found out that I slept with a bird, she'd have a meltdown," Kat said. "Katarina, how could you disgrace your family like that? Katarina, a bird is weak. Katarina, birds carry diseases!"

Willow burst out laughing. "I really want to meet your mom, Katarina."

"No, you don't. Trust me."

"Uh oh." Ava looked out the window before standing.

"What's wrong?" Willow asked.

Ava glanced at Kat. "Ronin's here. It looks like he's taking over for Garth."

"Shit," Kat said. "I need to leave."

She stood as Mal ran down the stairs.

"Mal? Honey, what's wrong?" Willow said.

"Mom called me. They took Grandpa to the hospital in an ambulance. They think he might have had a heart attack."

"Oh no!" Willow took his hand.

"I have to go to the hospital, Willow," he said.

"Of course. I'll come with you." She glanced at Ava and then Kat. "Kat, could you -"

"I'll stay with Ava," Kat said. "Go."

Ava gave Willow a quick hug. "He'll be okay, Will."

Willow and Mal left as Ava paced the room. "Kat, you can go. I'll be fine. Ronin's right outside."

Kat shook her head. "Nope. I'm staying with you. Now, sit down, and I'll make us both some tea."

GINGER SMOOTHED HER DARK HAIR AND STRAIGHTENED HER scrub top before staring at herself in the bathroom mirror.

"Okay, girl. Just go out there and act casual around the hottest man you've ever met in your life. And for God's sake, remember that you have a boyfriend who you love very much."

Do you, though?

Shut up!

She left the bathroom and walked down the hall to the nurses' station, where Fenton waited patiently.

"Ready to go?" he asked a bit gruffly.

"Just give me one more minute." She smiled tentatively at him before walking to curtain three and sticking her head through the opening. "Will, I was going to head out. Do you need me to stay?"

"We're good, Ginger. Thanks, honey," Willow said. She stood at the end of the bed next to Mal. His parents sat in chairs next to the bed, and his younger sister sat on the end of the bed, rubbing her grandfather's leg through the bedcovers.

"You're welcome." She patted Mal's grandfather's arm. "It was nice to meet you, Mr. Burke. They should have a room for you upstairs in the cardiac unit soon."

"Ayuh," he said tiredly. "It was nice to meet you too."

She squeezed Willow's hand before returning to Fenton.

"Is he okay?" Fenton asked.

"Yes. They think he's had a mild heart attack, but he seems to be stable now. He'll be having a CT scan soon, and they'll move him upstairs to the cardiac unit. He'll have to stay a few days, but I think he'll be fine."

"Good."

They walked toward the front doors of the ER, and Ginger smiled tentatively again. "Thanks for the ride home. Sorry you have to work so late." She glanced at the clock on the wall. It was just after eleven, and she wondered if Robbie had even gone to work tonight or if he'd called in sick for the third night in a row. He'd bought a new video game and spent the last two days playing it nonstop. He was going to lose this job just like he had lost the previous three. God, she had terrible taste in men.

"You okay?" Fenton asked as they stepped into the cool night air.

"Yeah, I'm good. Are you?"

"Fine." He scanned the dark sky and inhaled deeply before they moved away from the comforting lights of the hospital and into the dark parking lot.

"You're sad," he said suddenly.

She blinked at him in surprise. She'd been dating Robbie for nearly a year, and the guy still couldn't read her moods.

"How do you know that?"

"I can smell it on you."

"Really?" she said.

"Yes."

"That's kind of cool. And I guess pretty handy. You would know when to, like, cheer up your girlfriend or give her flowers or something." She groaned inwardly. God, why did she have to sound like such an idiot?

"I don't have a girlfriend," Fenton said.

"Oh."

"We broke up a couple of months ago," he said.

"I'm sorry. Was she a shifter as well?"

He nodded. "Cheetah shifter like me."

"Nice." She cleared her throat nervously. "So, do you ever date humans?"

"Once. It didn't go well."

"That's too bad."

He gave her a sideways glance. "You ever dated a shifter?"

"Oh God, no," she said and then grimaced at the look on his face. "But not because I don't think humans or shifters should date or anything like that."

He didn't reply, and feeling stupid, she said, "I think it's great when shifters and humans date. I just – a shifter's never, you know, asked me out. I don't, um, think I appeal to shifters. A kangaroo shifter who came to the ER with food poisoning told me that I smell funny."

She blushed furiously. Why the hell did she tell him that?

Her blush deepened when Fenton visibly inhaled. "You smell fine to me."

"Oh, um, thank you."

They were almost to his car, and she said, "You smell fine to me too."

"Thanks," he said before unlocking the car. He opened the

car door for her before stiffening. He lifted his head and sniffed the air.

"Ginger," he said urgently, "get into the car right -"

She jumped when a car backfired, her hand clutching at Fenton's arm. "Fenton, what – Fenton?"

The cheetah shifter staggered back against the car as blood bloomed on the front of his shirt. He slid down the car until he sat on the ground, and she dropped to her knees beside him as he stared at her.

"Ginger, run," he whispered.

"Just hold still." She yanked her scrub top over her head and folded it into a pad before pressing it against his chest. "Don't move, Fenton. You're -"

"Good evening, Ginger."

Her blood turned cold, and she looked behind her to see Sean Chambers with a gun in his right hand, standing in the shadows behind her.

"How are you, Ginger?"

"Mr. Chambers, please. I don't -"

"Shh," he said. "It's time for you to listen. I'll let you know when you should talk, okay?"

Fear made her throat dry, and her hands tremble. She nodded and continued to press hard on Fenton's chest. She stared at him in alarm when he tried to stand.

"Uh-uh, cheetah shifter. Don't move, or I'll put a bullet in this pretty little human's head," Mr. Chambers said.

He moved closer, smiling cheerfully at Ginger. "I need something from you, Ginger. You're going to tell me where my mate is."

"I don't know what you mean," Ginger said as her fear turned to terror.

Anger crossed his face, and he squatted next to her and traced her cheek with the warm barrel of the gun. She moaned as the light hit his face. His right eye was gone, and the skin around it was ragged and puffy. She stared into the gaping hole as he made a soft sound of disapproval.

"You know, I never really thought much of human weapons. Why would a dragon need a puny thing like this gun when he can breathe fire?"

"D-dragon?" she whispered.

He grinned at her. "They didn't tell you?" His chest glowed through his white shirt, and she watched with horrifying fascination as he turned his head and blew out a small burst of flame.

"Impressive, is it not, Ginger?" He traced the gun across her cheek again. "However, sometimes it's necessary for a dragon to remain hidden, I'm sure you know why, and I've realized that this puny little gun is actually quite remarkable. It took down your cheetah shifter rather easily, did it not?"

He glanced at Fenton. The shifter's face was completely white, and he breathed in harsh pants.

"Truthfully, I was aiming for you, Ginger. But I've never fired a gun before, and my depth perception seems to be a little off." He grinned cheerfully at her. "Do you like my new one-eyed look?"

"Mr. Chambers, please," she moaned, "he's dying."

"Oh, hardly." He rolled his remaining eye. "We're right outside of a hospital, and he does have healing abilities. If you're a good girl and tell me what I want to know, then I'll be out of your hair, and you can save the cheetah's life. He'll be just fine."

He cocked the gun and placed it against Fenton's temple. "But if you don't tell me, Ginger, then I'll have to shoot your rather dismal failure of a bodyguard in the head. And you and I both know that no amount of healing ability can save him from that."

"Please, don't," she whispered as tears streaked down her face.

"Tell me where Ava is, and both you and your cheetah shifter will live."

"I don't know where she is."

"Wrong answer, Ginger," he said.

His finger tightened on the trigger, and she moaned in fear. "No, wait! Mr. Chambers, wait!"

"Ready to tell me, Ginger?"

She nodded, and he smiled happily. "Good. One more thing, little lady. If you lie to me, if Ava isn't there, I will come back and burn you and your shifter alive."

He leaned closer to her, his breath smelling of sulphur and fire, and said, "Do you believe me, Ginger?"

"Yes," she said.

"Good. Now tell me where my mate is."

CHAPTER 21

"Fenton! Open your eyes! Fenton, look at me!"

Willow frowned at Mal. "Did you hear that?"

He nodded and patted his grandfather's leg. "We'll be right back, Grandpa."

Amos flapped his hand irritably. "Yes, I'm fine."

They slipped out from behind the curtain, and Willow gasped in dismay as they rushed Fenton by on a stretcher. Blood covered his chest, and Ginger, her hands soaked in blood and wearing just her bra and scrub pants, watched numbly as they moved him behind a curtain.

"Ginger! What happened?"

"Willow?" Ginger was trembling badly, and she stared blankly at her for a moment.

"Ginger, honey? Tell me what happened."

"Mr. Chambers, he – he was waiting for us in the parking lot. He had a gun, and he shot Fenton. He told me he would shoot him in the head if I didn't tell him where Ava was."

Willow's eyes widened. "Did you tell him, Ginger?"

When Ginger didn't reply, she shook her roughly. "Ginger! Did you tell him where Ava is?"

"Yes," Ginger moaned. "I'm sorry. He was going to kill Fenton."

"Mal?" Willow gave him a look of pure panic.

"Call Kat. Tell her to get Ava out of the house. I'll call Bishop." Mal reached for his phone, and Willow pulled her phone from her purse with her hands shaking.

KAT PEEKED OUT THE WINDOW. SHE COULD SEE RONIN'S CAR parked on the street, but the burnt-out streetlight made it too dark for her to see him. She sighed. She was being ridiculous. Now was the perfect time to march out there and apologize, but she couldn't bring herself to do it. The humiliation was too much.

Suck it up, Kat. You need to apologize - you know you do.

Yeah, she did, but –

Her phone rang, and she pulled it out of her pocket. "Hey, Will. What's up?" She listened silently for a moment before shouting Ava's name.

Ava appeared in the living room. "Kat? What's wrong?"

"We need to leave. Right now!" She shoved her phone back into her pocket and grabbed Ava's arm.

"Why? What's happening?"

"Let's go, Ava!" Kat hurried her toward the front door and nearly shoved her outside into the cool air.

She hustled Ava toward her car as Ronin appeared out of the darkness. "What's happening?"

"He knows she's here. He's on his way," Kat said.

"Shit." Ronin took Ava's arm as Ava made a soft moan of dismay.

"We take my car. It's faster," Kat said.

"Right." Ronin scanned the sky as Kat yanked her keys from her pocket.

"Fuck!" Ronin shouted, and then he shoved both Kat and Ava to the ground and threw himself on top of them.

A burst of flame lit up the dark, the night air rippled with heat, and Ava screamed as the dragon landed with a harsh thud on the front lawn. He stared balefully at them, one golden eye glowing in the darkness. His entire body trembled, and he shifted to his human form.

"Hello, my bride. Have you missed me?"

The three staggered to their feet, Kat and Ronin forming a protective barrier in front of Ava.

The dragon stared thoughtfully at Ronin. "Didn't I kill you already?"

"Leave now, and no one will get hurt," Ronin said.

Sean snorted laughter. "You're a brave bird, aren't you?"

His gaze shifted to Kat, and he scowled as his chest glowed and a brief flicker of flame erupted from his nostrils. "You're the bitch who took my eye."

Kat grinned fiercely at him, her fangs extending with a soft pop. "Come any closer, and I'll take your other one as well."

Sean laughed again before staring at Ava. "Are you going to let your friends die for you tonight?"

Ava paled. "No, I -"

"Be quiet, Ava," Kat said. "Leave, dragon. The human does not belong to you."

"You're wrong!" he snarled. "She is mine. Mine forever, and I will kill you, cat shifter if you do not give her to me."

Kat's body swelled, and her clothes ripped as she shifted to her jaguar form. She hissed at the dragon before glancing at Ronin. He nodded, and Ava cried out when the two shifters rushed toward the dragon.

Bishop waited impatiently at the red light. He was only a few blocks from Mal's house, and his stomach churned with nerves. It was late, Ava was probably already in bed, but he couldn't wait any longer to speak to her. Even though he had no real idea of what he would say to her.

He would simply say he was sorry, he decided, and hope that she forgave him. If she didn't, well, he deserved it for taking his pathetic excuse of a mother's side against her. He would tell her that he loved her and that he couldn't live without her, and if she –

His phone rang, and he grabbed it from the seat. "Hey, Mal. I'm just on my way to -"

He stopped, his eyes widening in horror as Mal spoke rapidly.

"Fuck!" He threw his phone on the seat and, ignoring the red light, stomped on the gas.

He tore through the dark streets, his heart racing with fear, and roared when he turned down Mal's street. He slammed on the brakes and threw open the door, snarling as his grizzly surged forward and he shifted.

Ava watched in terror as Sean shifted to his dragon form as Ronin jumped on him. The dragon slammed his enormous head into the bird shifter. Ronin flew across the yard, crashing into the oak tree and dropping like a stone to the ground.

Kat yowled with anger and leaped at the massive dragon. Ava screamed shrilly when the dragon caught the jaguar in his mouth. His jaws clamped shut, and there was a sharp crack as he snapped Kat's back and tossed her aside like a rag doll.

He hissed in triumph and turned toward Ava. "My bride."

There was an angry roar, and the grizzly charged out of the darkness. He wrapped his arms around the dragon's neck and dug his long, sharp claws into the thick hide.

The dragon screamed as Bishop's claws pierced through the scales. Ava dropped to the ground as a burst of flame shot out of the dragon's nostrils. The air was on fire above her, and she rolled away, screaming Bishop's name as the dragon tore at the grizzly with his sharp talons.

Bishop snarled with pain but hung on grimly to the dragon's neck until, with another squeal of agony, the dragon raked his claws down the grizzly's back and tore him away from his neck. He wrapped his talons around Bishop's body and flung him high into the air.

"Bishop!" Ava screamed as Bishop landed on the ground with a heavy thud.

The dragon stood over him, smoke drifting from his nostrils. "She is mine, grizzly shifter."

He drew a deep breath, his chest glowing as Bishop snarled up at him. Before he could release his flame, Ava darted forward and stood in front of Bishop. She held up her hands and gave the dragon a pleading look.

"Larry? That's your name, right?"

The dragon stared at her, and she swallowed her fear and forced a smile. "Larry, I'll go with you. Let my friends live, and I'll be your bride. That's what you want, isn't it? I'll go with you and I – I'll mate with you and have your children. We'll be together, forever."

The dragon took a step back. "You are trying to trick me."

"No," Ava said. "I'm not. You're right – I belong to you, and I want to be with you forever."

Her body shaking, she took a step forward and laid a tentative hand on the dragon's scaly front leg. "I belong to you, Larry. I know that now."

The dragon grinned, and she sucked in a shuddering breath before looking behind her. Bishop shifted to his human form, and she moaned at the deep slashes that covered his torso and back. Blood flowed down his body in steady streams, and she started to cry as Bishop tried to struggle to his feet.

"Don't!" she said.

"Ava, baby, no," Bishop said.

"I love you," she said as the dragon's talons circled her waist.

She watched Bishop grow steadily smaller as the dragon rose into the air before he flew away, his giant wings cutting through the air, and Bishop disappeared from her sight.

"KATARINA, LOOK AT ME."

His voice cut through the darkness, and she forced her eyelids open. She was in Ronin's arms, her naked body pressed up against him, and he smiled down at her. "Hi, Kitten."

"Ronin? I... I can't move. Why can't I move?"

The metallic taste of blood coated her mouth, and she could feel it dripping down her chin. Ronin kissed her fore-head. "You'll be okay."

"I can't feel my body." She moved her head. It was the only thing she could feel, and she stared wide-eyed at her body. Deep puncture wounds on her torso and legs bled heavily, but she felt no pain. "Ronin? What's happening? Why can't I feel anything?"

She stared up at him, her panic fading to puzzlement as she watched the tears slide down his cheeks. "Don't cry, Ronin."

"Close your eyes, Katarina," he murmured.

She stared at him for a moment longer before closing her eyes. He shifted her in his arms and said, "I'm sorry."

Agony sliced through her body. What was once numb was now hellishly aware of every puncture wound and broken bone. She opened her mouth to scream as Ronin's hard hand clamped across her mouth. She screamed and shrieked against his palm as the pain grew inside of her until everything else faded away.

Dimly, she was aware of soft pops and sharp cracks, and she shrieked again as a fresh bolt of pain ripped through her. Darkness appeared at the edge of her vision and, still screaming, she dove for it, sinking blissfully into its tight grip.

"Oh my God, Mal," Willow said.

Mal parked his car, and the two of them stumbled out onto the street. Bishop sat naked on the edge of the lawn, staring into the darkness, and Ronin sat under the oak tree, cradling a naked Kat in his arms.

"There's a lot of naked people in your front yard, Burke."

Mal turned to see Mr. Taylor, his eighty-three-year-old human neighbour standing next to him. He held a fire extinguisher and walked briskly to the fire that burned on the lawn and sprayed it. He set the fire extinguisher down and studied the sky.

"I saw a dragon tonight," he announced.

"Mr. Taylor, I -" Mal was at a complete loss for words.

"Should I be calling the cops, Burke?" The old man asked.

"Uh, no. We can take care of it, okay?"

"Okay." Mr. Taylor started toward his house and turned when Mal called his name.

"What you saw – it wasn't a dragon. I know it looked like one, but -"

The old man grunted. "Whatever, Burke. Next, you'll be trying to tell me it was a darthen lizard."

"Mr. Taylor -"

"Don't worry," he said with a scowl. "I'll keep what I saw to myself. Just be thankful Mrs. Perkins is visiting her daughter this week. That old cow can't keep her mouth shut about anything."

He climbed the front steps of his porch and disappeared into the house. Mal headed toward Bishop as Willow ran across the yard and knelt next to Ronin and Kat.

"Ronin? Is she okay?" she asked as she stared at the blood covering Kat's upper body.

"She's fine. Just unconscious," Ronin said.

"Where are her wounds?"

"They've healed already. She'll be fine, Willow."

"Are you okay?" Willow asked.

"Yeah."

"Good." Willow shrugged out of her jacket and draped it across Kat's naked body. Ronin pulled Kat closer and kissed the top of her head.

"I'll be right back, okay?" Willow said.

He nodded and kissed Kat's head again as Willow ran to Mal and Bishop.

Blood coated Bishop's back, but Willow could see the deep slashes covering his back already beginning to heal.

"Bishop? Buddy, are you okay?" Mal asked.

"He took her, Mal. I promised her I would keep her safe, and I let him take her," Bishop said softly.

"It's not your fault, Bishop."

"It is," he said tonelessly. "If I hadn't chosen Leslie over her, I would have been with her tonight. I would have kept her safe. Instead, she's gone and -"

His voice broke, and he swiped at the moisture on his face. "Kat is dead."

"What?" Mel said as he glanced at Kat and Ronin.

"The dragon broke her back. I saw it. I *heard* it. She's dead, and Ava's gone, and it's all my fault."

"Honey, Kat's not dead," Willow said as she touched his shoulder.

"She is."

"No, honey, she isn't. I promise. I just checked on her, and she's fine. She's already healed."

"That's impossible," Bishop said.

"She's healed," Willow repeated. "Tell us what happened."

"He was about to kill me, and Ava offered her life in exchange for mine. She said she wanted to be with him and that she would be his mate," Bishop said. "I've lost her."

"No, you haven't. We'll find her and get her back, Bishop," Mal said.

"It's too late."

The utter despair in his voice sent shivers down Willow's back, and tears dripped down her face as she sat down beside him. "Don't say that, Bishop."

He didn't reply, and Mal made an impatient grunt when his cell phone rang. He yanked it from his pocket, glanced at the screen, and put it on speaker. "Kaida? Can I call you back?"

"Do you know where Bishop is? He's not answering his phone," Kaida said.

"He's here with me," Mal replied. "Kaida -"

"Good. Can I speak to him?"

"This isn't a good time. Chambers found Ava, and he's taken her. We have no idea where she is."

"Fuck!" Kaida said. "The dragon's clan is here. They're scenting for him now. It shouldn't take them long to find him. Can you bring Bishop to our clan?"

"We're on our way." He ended the call and clasped Bishop's shoulder. "Bishop, we need to go."

"I'm not going anywhere," Bishop said.

"Bishop! You heard Kaida. His clan is here, and they're searching for him. We have a chance to save her," Mal said.

"It's too late," Bishop repeated softly. "She'll be dead before they find him. You know that, Mal."

Willow jumped to her feet, and Mal flinched when she slapped Bishop as hard as she could across the face. "Snap out of it, you big dumb bear!"

She rained blows on the grizzly's chest and shoulders. "The woman you love is out there with a fucking dragon! And you're going to sit here and feel sorry for yourself because you couldn't save her? Oh boo-fucking-hoo! You have the chance to save her now! Are you really going to leave her to her fate?"

"Willow, I -"

She punched him again and then cursed in pain before grabbing her hand. "Get off your giant, stupid ass and go and save your mate before I kick you in the balls!"

Bishop stared silently at her before lumbering to his feet.

"That's better," Willow snapped. "Mal, let's go."

"You're not coming with us, Willow."

"Like hell, I'm not, Malcolm Burke! Ava's my best

friend, and I'm not getting left behind on this rescue mission. Do you hear me, or do I have to kick you in the balls as well?"

"No, honey." He stepped back and covered his crotch as Ronin joined them, holding Kat in his arms.

"Kat?" Bishop touched her arm gently.

"She's okay. I'll take her inside and get her warmed up," Ronin said.

Mal nodded. "We're going after Ava."

"Good luck," Ronin said gravely before carrying Kat into the house.

"Grab some clothes, Bishop." Willow glared at him. "We're leaving in two minutes."

CHAPTER 22

Bishop jumped out of the truck and stared at the circle of four men and three women. They stood in the middle of the clearing, holding hands with their faces pointed toward the dark sky.

"What are they doing?" Willow said.

Mal had driven them to the city's outskirts and into the woods that surrounded them. They'd followed a gravel road that turned into a dirt road to a small community of cabins hidden in the large trees.

"They're scenting for him." Kaida had joined them, and she briefly rubbed Bishop's back.

"Scenting?" Willow frowned.

"Dragons have a special ability to sense their clan members." An old woman stood next to Willow. She was over six feet tall, and her hair, pure white with threads of green throughout it, hung to her waist. She wore a red t-shirt and black yoga pants with the word 'juicy' written across the butt in bright yellow letters. "Hello, Bishop."

"Hello, Gram."

"It's good to see you again, bear shifter." She kissed Bishop's cheek before staring at Willow and Mal.

"Hi, I'm Willow, and this is Mal," Willow said.

"Hello, human. Hello, wolf shifter." The old woman sniffed at Willow's hair before turning to stare at the group of elders. "Do not despair, bear shifter. They will find their clan member, and you will see your mate again."

Bishop didn't reply, and Kaida rubbed his back again. "She will be okay, my bear."

One by one, the men and women in the circle released their grip on each other's hands. Cadmus stood behind them, and the eldest of them turned and spoke quietly to him. He nodded before bowing and retreating to where Bishop and the others stood.

"They've found him," he said.

Bishop breathed a sigh of relief as Cadmus smiled at him. "He is not far. He has taken your mate into these very woods."

"Let's go," Bishop started forward, and Kaida gripped his arm.

"My bear, you cannot go with us."

"I'm going!" Bishop snapped. "She is my mate, Kaida."

"I know, but they will not allow others to see -"

"Hush, Kaida," Cadmus said. "The bear shifter and his friends will come with us."

"Cadmus? Are you sure? You know what they will do to him. The others shouldn't -"

"Enough. I have made my decision, and the other clan has agreed to it," Cadmus said.

The circle of elders moved into the trees, and Willow took Mal's hand. He squeezed it reassuringly as they followed Bishop and the others.

AVA LANDED ON THE GROUND WITH A SOFT THUD. THE dragon had dropped her before landing, and she scrambled to her feet as he shifted to his human form.

He smiled at her and held out his hand. "Come, my bride. I will show you our new home."

She hesitated and then took his hand, allowing him to lead her into the large cave that he had dropped her in front of.

She stared into the cave, her stomach heaving at the pile of bones and fur that littered one side.

"Well, what do you think?" Larry smiled eagerly at her.

"It, um, it's lovely," she said.

"A little bare at the moment, but do not worry. I will give you all the comforts of home that you desire."

"Right," she said.

He pointed to a fallen log that was dragged into the cave. "Sit, my bride. Make yourself at home."

She sat gingerly on the edge of the log as he moved to the back of the cave and pulled out a dark cloak from a trunk. He wrapped it around his naked body before returning to her and sitting beside her.

She stared at the hole where his eye used to be, and he shrugged. "You will grow used to my battle scars."

"Mr. Chambers, I -"

"Larry, remember?" He smiled at her, and she forced herself to return his smile.

"Larry, are you sure that I'm the right mate for you? Dragons don't mate with humans, remember?"

He scowled at her. "That is a ridiculous rule created by the ancients. Why should dragons not mate with humans?"

"Well, you want to stay hidden, don't you?"

He shrugged. "It matters not to me whether humans know

of our existence. We have survived for thousands of years. Humans are no match for us. No one is. You see that now, don't you?"

"Yes."

"There are others who believe as I do, you know," he said. "They believe that dragons and humans could coexist. That we could mate if we so desired."

He studied her curvy body, his eye glowing in the darkness. "And I do desire, Ava."

She shuddered all over before sliding away from him. "Why did you choose me?"

"Because you are so lovely, my bride." He took her hand and squeezed it. "You are kind and sweet, just like she was."

"Who?"

"Alannah. She was my mate before you."

"What happened to her?" She needed to keep him talking.

His brow darkened. "She rejected me. Another fooled her into believing that he was her mate. Even after I killed him, she would not believe that we were meant to be together."

Smoke drifted from his nostrils, and she swallowed down her fear as he smiled again at her. "But it turns out she was right all along. We weren't meant to be mates. You and I are mates."

She didn't reply, and he moved closer, putting his arm around her and drawing her up against him. "I know you think you love the bear shifter, my bride, but once you are in my bed, you will forget all about him. I promise you."

"I do love him," she said. "Please, if you love me, Larry, you'll let me be with my mate."

"I am your mate!" he shouted and then made a soothing noise when she cringed away from him. "Don't be frightened of me. I won't harm you."

"You killed Brody," she said.

"An unfortunate accident, and frankly, that was kind of your fault. If you had not made me so angry by seeing another male, I would not have felt the need to dispose of him. He's dead because of you, my bride."

"You didn't have to kill him," she said defiantly.

"I did. You should be thankful that I let your bear shifter live. Do you see how much you mean to me? I am willing to sacrifice my happiness for yours, to deny my very nature, just to please you."

"That's very kind of you." She glanced to her right as Larry stared moodily into the darkness. A large rock rested against the log, and she reached down slowly and wrapped her fingers around it.

"It was, wasn't it?" He touched the ruined crater where his eye used to be. "I'm regretting that now. The bear's scent is all over you. I know you have been in his bed, and I will admit I find that thought displeasing. I am tempted to go back and kill the shifter for even touching you."

"No," she said as fresh terror washed over her. "Don't leave me, Larry. Please."

He smiled at her. "How quickly you become attached, my bride. That makes me so happy."

He clapped his hands briskly. "Come, we will mate so that I may put a child in your belly."

"Um, I'm kind of tired, and I -"

"Do not think of denying me, Ava. I am your master now, and you will obey me in all things," he said. "Now, I don't have a bed as of yet, but I promise you I'll find one in the next few weeks. Until then, you will have to grow used to the ground."

He glanced away at the trunk. "I suppose I could put some of my clothes down for you. Would you like that, my bride?"

He turned toward her, and Ava slammed the rock directly into his face. His nose broke with a sickening crack, and he tumbled off the log as she scrambled to her feet and darted to the mouth of the cave. Larry roared with anger, and she screamed and fled into the trees as a burst of flame emerged from the cave.

"You bitch!" he shouted.

Her heart pounding and fear flooding her mouth, she ran blindly forward. She could hear the dragon crashing and lumbering behind her, and she forced herself to run faster. She couldn't see a damn thing, and she cried out when she ran into the thick trunk of a tree. It knocked her off her feet, and, dazed, she stared in amazement as the tree trunk trembled and moved.

"What the hell?" She climbed to her feet and made a harsh moan as the clouds parted and bright moonlight flooded through the trees.

"No, oh no." She stared upward at the seven dragons who studied her in the moonlight. The one she had run into leaned down and sniffed at her hair as she stood frozen.

"Please," she whispered.

"Ava!"

She froze and then cried out with happiness when Bishop appeared. He yanked her into his embrace and kissed her hard on the mouth. "Honey, are you okay?"

"Wh-what are you doing here?" she asked.

"I'm so sorry. I love you," he said.

"I love you too," she said and then started to cry. Bishop pressed her against his massive chest then wrapped his arms around her. The seven dragons moved silently past them as Kaida, Willow, and Mal crowded around her and Bishop.

"Willow?"

"Oh my God, Ava." Willow was crying, and she pressed her forehead against Ava's. "I was so afraid, honey."

"Are Kat and Ronin okay?" Ava asked. "Kat - her back - I think I heard…."

"They're both fine," Bishop said.

"How did you find me?" she asked.

Bishop still held her tightly, and her ribs ached from the pressure, but she clung to him as Kaida said, "The elders found him."

"AVA!"

The dragon's scream echoed through the forest, and Ava trembled as Larry, blood trickling from his broken nose, stumbled into view.

"It's okay, baby," Bishop said. "He can't hurt you now."

Larry stared at the seven dragons as they silently surrounded him. He dropped to his knees and said, "Forgive me, my clan."

"You are beyond forgiveness." The largest dragon's voice rolled out like thunder.

"She is my mate." Larry's remaining eye stared at Ava. "Tell them, Ava. Tell them you are my mate."

"I'm not your mate," she said.

"No!" he screamed. "She belongs to me!!"

"You have broken the rules of our clan. Your punishment is death," the elder said.

"What? Wait…no!" Larry began to swell as the seven dragons inhaled deeply. Their chests glowed brightly, and Kaida touched Bishop's arm.

"Take her away from here, right now," she said.

Bishop lifted Ava into his arms. He moved swiftly through the trees as Mal and Willow hurried along behind them.

"Bishop?" she said.

"Don't look, Ava," he said grimly. Exhausted and still afraid, she buried her face in his chest.

"Willow, turn away," Mal said.

"Mal -"

"No, Willow. Do as I say," Mal growled.

Willow turned and stared into the trees as Mal put his arms around her.

The four of them stood silently until the night air lit up with bright flame, and the screaming began. Ava jerked in Bishop's arms, and he kissed her forehead as the smell of burning flesh drifted to them.

"Mal?" Willow's voice was thin with fear.

Mal hugged her tightly. "It's okay, honey. Close your eyes."

As Larry's agonizing screams echoed throughout the woods, Ava clung to Bishop.

He killed Brody, she reminded herself grimly. *He tried to kill Bishop, Kat, and Ronin, and he would have killed you eventually.*

"It's okay, baby," Bishop murmured in her ear before kissing her forehead again.

After a long while, the screaming stopped, and Kaida appeared in front of them.

"It's over," she said.

"Thank you," Bishop said.

"Take your mate home, my bear."

Bishop nodded as Ava reached out and grasped Kaida's hand. "Thank you, Kaida."

"Take good care of him," Kaida said.

"I will," Ava said.

THE SHRILL RING OF HER CELL PHONE WOKE KAT. SHE SAT UP, nearly falling off the couch, and clutched at the blanket that covered her as she looked around blearily. Her phone sang its shrill cry again, and she reached for her purse that sat on the floor beside the couch. She fumbled it out and answered it. "Mal? Are you okay?"

She listened intently as Ronin entered the room. He waited, a look of relief crossing his face when she smiled.

"Thank God. Yes, he's here with me. We're still at your place, but I'm going to head back to my own house. Yes, I'm perfectly fine. No, I'm okay, really."

She listened and then smiled again. "Yeah, I know. I'll talk to you tomorrow."

She ended the call and stared at Ronin. "They're okay. They found the dragon and Ava, and she's not hurt. Other members of his clan destroyed the dragon."

"Thank Christ." Ronin scrubbed his hand across his face before collapsing in the chair next to the fireplace.

Kat wrapped the blanket around her and swung her feet over the couch. Drying blood covered her, and she grimaced. "What the hell happened?"

"You don't remember?"

She thought back. "Not really. I remember trying to take that damn dragon on and being in his mouth. There was pain and then…."

"And then what?" Ronin said.

"I don't remember," she said. "I remember the pain, and you were holding me."

"I held you while your body healed itself," he said.

She frowned. "What was wrong with me?"

"Puncture wounds from the dragon's teeth, probably a few broken ribs. I'm not entirely sure."

She touched her side through the blanket. "I've never healed that quickly before. I'm not a bear shifter."

He shrugged. "Maybe you're better at healing than you think."

"Maybe," she said. "Are you hurt?"

"Nah. Got my head knocked against a tree, but I'll live."

"Good." Her extra set of clothes was piled neatly on the arm of the couch, and she picked them up.

"I found them in the trunk of your car," Ronin said.

"Thanks. Mal and Willow are on their way home. I'm going to get dressed, go home, and shower for about a thousand years."

He grinned at her. "Do you need some help washing your back, Kitten? I'd be happy to volunteer."

She flushed. "Ronin, I – I need to apologize."

"For what?"

"For the other night."

"Well, it was kind of rude of you just to kick me out afterward, but I get it. I had just rocked your world. That takes some time to get used to," he said teasingly.

"No, that's not it, I -"

"Ouch, Kitten. You could at least pretend I rocked your world."

"No! The sex was great, really, it's just that – well, I was in heat, and that's the only reason I slept with you."

"You were in heat," Ronin said slowly.

"Yes," she said as shame burned in her belly. "Every month, a female cat shifter goes into heat and -"

"I know what a heat cycle is," he said.

"Then you know why I did what I did," she said. "I'm sorry. It was inappropriate, and I shouldn't have attacked you like that. It's not an excuse, but my usual, uh, friend who helps me through it is in a relationship now, and you were, well, you were just in the wrong place at the wrong time."

"So, you only fucked me because you were in heat," he said.

She flushed again. "Yes, I'm sorry."

"Bullshit."

"Excuse me?"

"Bullshit. You want me, Kitten, and you're just using this 'in heat' thing as an excuse."

"I am not," she said. "Relationships of a sexual nature between an employer and employee are inappropriate, and I'm -"

"You going to tell Mal and Willow that?" he asked.

"What they do is none of my business, and besides, Willow is Mal's mate," she replied. "But I'm not going to sleep with an employee."

"You already did, Kitten."

"Stop calling me Kitten," she said through gritted teeth. "Look, I'm sorry. I don't mean to hurt your feelings but what happened between us was because of my heat cycle and only because of that. I don't – I don't sleep with birds."

"Bigot," he snorted.

"I am not!" She glared at him.

"Whatever." He stood and walked to the door. "I get it, Ms. Frost. The idea of sleeping with a mere bird makes your hackles rise, and you're horrified that you're attracted to me."

"That isn't it," she insisted.

"Do you need me to drive you home?" he asked with a scowl.

"No, I'm fine."

"Good. See you later, Ms. Frost."

"Ronin, wait. Are you – don't say anything to anyone about us sleeping together, all right?" she said.

"I don't kiss and tell, Ms. Frost. Besides, we can't have everyone knowing the jaguar shifter fucked a bird, can we? Your reputation would be ruined."

"Ronin, I -"

He walked out of the room, and she collapsed against the couch as the front door slammed shut.

"Well, fuck," she muttered.

"ARE YOU SURE SHE'S OKAY?" GINGER HELD HER PHONE TO her ear as she stared at the motionless Fenton and listened to Willow. "Thank goodness. Tell her I love her, okay, Willow? And tell Mal that they moved his grandfather to the cardiac unit, and he's doing well."

She listened and then nodded. "Yes, he's out of surgery. The doctors got the bullet out. It lodged in his lung, but they said his body was already starting to heal itself as soon as they removed the bullet. They think he'll be fine in a day or two."

She touched Fenton's hand lightly. "I love you, Willow. Thanks for calling."

She slipped her cell phone into her pocket and picked up Fenton's hand before leaning over him. "Fenton, can you hear me?"

His eyes fluttered open, and he stared blearily at her.

"Ava's okay. Mr. Chambers found her, but Bishop and the others saved her. She's fine, and he's – he's dead."

"Good," he muttered tiredly as his eyes slipped shut.

She sat down on the chair beside the bed and continued to hold his hand. She really should leave him and go home. Robbie would be worried about her.

No, he isn't. You were done work four hours ago, and he still hasn't bothered to find out where you are.

She studied Fenton's face before standing and brushing her hand across his cheek. "Fenton, I'm going to -"

His eyes popped open, and he stared at her. "Hurts."

She rubbed his shoulder. "I know, I'm sorry. Is there someone you want me to call? A family member?"

He shook his head wearily. "No. I don't have anyone."

"You have me," she said.

"Please stay. Will you?"

She smiled at him. "Yes."

CHAPTER 23

"Better?" Bishop asked.

"A thousand times better." A towel wrapped around her, Ava sat down beside him on the edge of the bed. "I thought you would join me in the shower."

"You should eat. I made you a sandwich."

"I'm not hungry," she said.

He stared at the plate in his hand. "You should eat, Ava."

"I will later." She combed her fingers through her wet hair as Bishop set the plate on the bedside table. He was acting strangely, and it was freaking her out a little. He loved her, he had told her he did in the woods, but there was a nervousness radiating off of him that made *her* nervous.

Unable to stand the silence, she said, "Will you tell me what's wrong?"

"I told Leslie I was done with her," he said.

She stared cautiously at him, not entirely sure how to respond.

He glanced at her before staring at his hands again. "You were right. She is abusive, and I should never have taken her side over yours."

"Bishop, it wasn't about taking sides. I didn't like seeing her hurting you," she said.

"She won't hurt me again."

"Are you sure that cutting her out of your life is what you want?" She supposed she should have been happy, but Bishop looked so miserable that guilt flooded through her. If he abandoned his mother because of her and only her, he would eventually resent her for it.

"You think I shouldn't have?" he asked.

"I don't know what you want me to say, honey," she said. "I don't like the way Leslie treats you, but I also don't want you not to have anything to do with her because of me."

"It's not because of you. I mean, what you think is important to me, but…."

She took his hand and squeezed it lightly.

He kissed her knuckles and then traced the freckles on the back of her hand. "She lied to me, Ava. All these years, she lied to me about why my father left. She said he stopped loving her, that he had affairs and that I was exactly like him and would do the same thing. I spent years telling myself that I was like all the other bear shifters. I didn't want a mate or a family. It's why I've never had a real relationship or – or let myself fall in love. I was terrified that I would hurt my mate the way my father hurt my mother."

"Oh, honey, you wouldn't do that," she said.

"You're right. I wouldn't. And it turns out that my father didn't either. Mara told me the truth after she saw how much I loved you. She told me that my father loved Leslie and that he never stopped loving her, but that her paranoia and her distrust eventually drove him away. He died still loving her."

She touched his cheek, and he kissed the palm of her hand. "I'm so sorry for what I said. I didn't mean it. I pushed you away because I was certain that I would hurt you and that my mother was right, and I wasn't meant to mate with someone for life."

"And now?" she asked.

"I love you, Ava," he said. "I know we haven't known each other for very long, but you are my mate. And I promise I will love you until the day I die."

She should have been freaking out. Despite all the time they'd spent together, there was still so much she didn't know about Bishop, and he already believed she was his mate. She should caution him that it was too soon and that they needed to slow down and get to know each other better.

She would have said all those things if she wasn't completely in love with him. Everything about this moment felt utterly and completely right to her, and she would be a fool not to realize it.

She cupped his face and smiled at him. "I love you too, Bishop King."

He pulled her into his arms and buried his face in her neck. "I'm so sorry."

"Stop it," she said. "You don't need to apologize."

She tugged on his hair until he lifted his head, and she could press a soft kiss against his mouth. "You belong to me."

"Yes," he said. "Always."

She kissed him again, tracing her tongue along his lips, and he made a harsh groan of need before opening his mouth. She slipped her tongue inside, exploring his mouth delicately as he tugged the towel away from her damp body and then pushed her onto her back. He kissed the cluster of freckles on her right breast, and she moaned and urged his mouth toward her nipple. He sucked it into an aching hardness as her pelvis repeatedly arched against him.

"Bishop, don't stop," she pleaded when he lifted his head.

God, she loved his naughty grin. "Every freckle, Ava. I'm

going to kiss every single freckle on your delicious body, and then and only then will I make you mine."

"I need you right now," she said.

He cupped her breast before plucking lightly at her swollen nipple. "Patience, my love."

She scowled at him, and he leaned down to kiss her wrinkled forehead. "I love you, Ava."

"I love you, Bishop."

"Hello, Ava."

"Bren! How are you?" Ava stopped in the hallway of the hospital and shook Bren's hand.

"I'm good. Are you happy to be back to work?"

"I am. Mind you, this is my first shift back," she said with a small smile.

He glanced around the empty hallway. "I don't see any security detail."

"Oh, right. Well, it's been a while since we've seen Mr. Chambers, so I wanted to get things back to normal. You know," Ava said. Shit, could he tell she was lying?.

"I'm here to talk with you about Mr. Chambers," Bren said.

"Oh? Did you, um, find him?" she asked.

Bren shook his head. "No, we haven't. Not a trace of him."

Ava didn't reply, and Bren studied her carefully. "We will find him, Ava."

"I know you will," she said.

"I have to admit, I find it strange that Mr. King is so willing to let you return to your normal life without knowing exactly where Mr. Chambers is."

"Oh, well, it's not completely normal. I'm still staying with him, and he, uh, still drives me to and from work." Ava hid her fidgeting fingers behind her back and vehemently wished she was a better liar. While she had known that sooner or later Bren would show up, she was feeling wholly unprepared. She should have come up with a better story, she realized belatedly.

"I have a theory about Mr. Chambers. Do you want to hear it?" Bren asked.

"Sure."

"I think that your Mr. King took care of the problem."

"No, he didn't," she said.

That came out more naturally because it wasn't a lie. Bishop hadn't done anything to Larry. It was his clan who'd killed him.

"Are you sure about that?" Bren said.

"Positive, Bren. Bishop didn't do anything to him."

"Brody's sister calls me every day, wondering if I've found his killer yet," Bren said.

Ava winced. Since Brody's funeral, she hadn't spoken to Diana, and a wave of guilt washed over her.

"Are you certain you have no idea where Mr. Chambers is?" Bren asked.

"Yes," she said.

"If Mr. Chambers shows up again, I trust that you'll call me?" Bren said.

"Of course, I will. I, um, still have your business card."

"Good." Bren hesitated before leaning down and kissing her on the cheek. "Take care of yourself, Ava."

"Thank you, Bren. You too."

She watched him walk away, fighting down the ridiculous urge to call him back and tell him everything. Bren was human, and his father was a powerful man with a powerful hatred for shifters. Besides, he wouldn't believe her anyway if she told him that Sean Chambers was a dragon and was roasted alive by his clan members for failing to follow their rules. As guilty as it made her feel, it was better and safer for Bren if he didn't know. Still feeling guilty, she headed back to the ER.

"KAT?" WILLOW POPPED HER HEAD INTO KAT'S OFFICE.

"What's up?" Kat asked without looking up from her monitor.

"Your mom just called the office. She wants to know if one – you're deliberately ignoring her text messages and two – if you're blowing her off for coffee."

"Shit! I completely forgot!" Kat pushed away from her desk and grabbed her purse. "Did she say if she was still at the coffee shop?"

"She is, and she says you have three minutes to get your butt down there. I told her it wouldn't be a problem with your fast-as-lightning feet." Willow eyed Kat's shoes. "Of course, those heels might slow you down a few seconds."

Kat smiled distractedly and raced out of the office. She flew down the stairs and out the front door of the building. She hadn't grabbed her jacket, and she shivered in the cool air as she dodged past humans and shifters and sprinted around the corner. She stopped at the door to the coffee shop, smoothing down her dark hair and straightening her shirt before stepping into the crowded shop. Her mother sat at a table in front of the large front window. Kat hurried over to her, kissing her briefly on the cheek before sitting down.

"Hello, Katarina."

"Hello, Mother. I'm sorry I'm late."

"Forgetfulness is a habit you get from your father." Her mother sipped at her tea as she pushed a paper cup across the table. "I got you a skinny latte. I know you're watching your figure."

Kat tamped down the urge to roll her eyes. Her mother was obsessed with dieting and maintaining her body and convinced that Kat was also. "Thank you, Mom."

"You're welcome, Katarina." Her mother took another sip of tea. "You know, sweetie, you really shouldn't wear green. It washes you out, and you'll never find a man if you look like a vampire."

"I told you, I'm not looking for a man."

"Did you know that Mrs. Henderson's youngest daughter is engaged? She's seven years younger than you, and she's getting married." Her mother carried on as if she hadn't replied.

"Angela's only getting married because she's knocked up."

"Katarina, please. You know I hate it when you're crass. Besides, what's wrong with having kittens? Children will take care of you when you're old, you know."

"Mom, do you think we could talk about something other than me dying old and alone? Work is going well. We've taken on five new corporate clients and will probably be adding another three before the end of the month. The business is really starting to take off," Kat said.

"That's so nice, sweetie. I'm glad to hear it." Her mom smiled at her. "I met the nicest young man at the library the other day. You know how I've started volunteering there every Monday? Well, he's been in a few times now. He's studying to be a lawyer. A lawyer, Katarina!"

"Good for him." Kat sipped at her coffee.

"His name is Lester, and he's twenty-eight. He's still

living with his parents, but the poor boy is trying to save some money while he's in school."

"Mm-hmm," Kat said. "Sounds like a nice guy."

"Oh, he's so nice! He's a tiger shifter, and he's got the cutest crooked tooth. It adds character to his whole face."

"I'm sure it does."

"Oh, and I know for a fact that he doesn't have a girl-friend right now," her mother said.

"Maybe he's gay."

"Katarina! He isn't."

"You don't know that."

"Actually," her mom gave her a sly look with just a hint of guilt, and Kat groaned out loud, "I do know he isn't gay. I happened to mention I had a single daughter, and once I showed him your picture, he was extremely interested in meeting you."

"Mom, you have got to stop showing strangers my picture. Please."

"Lester isn't a stranger," her mom said. "He's a perfectly nice boy who -"

"Hello, Kat. Hello, Mrs. Frost."

Bishop, holding Ava's hand, stood beside their table, and Kat breathed a sigh of relief as her mother smiled at him.

"Bishop! It's so good to see you."

Bishop bent and kissed her cheek. "You as well, Mrs. Frost."

"Who is this then?" Her mother stared at Ava's and Bish-op's clasped hands.

"Mom, this is Bishop's girlfriend, Ava Lewis. Ava, this is my mother, Eleanor Frost," Kat said.

"It's nice to meet you, Mrs. Frost."

"It's lovely to meet you. Don't you have the prettiest hair?"

"Thank you," Ava said.

Eleanor smiled at Bishop. "I never thought I would see the day where you would have a girlfriend, Bishop."

Bishop kissed Ava's knuckles gently. "Ava's one of a kind, Mrs. Frost."

"I'm so happy for you. Now, with Mal mated to that chatty receptionist and you with your lovely Ava, we just need to find someone for my Katarina. Wouldn't you agree?"

"Oh, um…" Bishop glanced at Kat, who shook her head at him.

"We're keeping her pretty busy at work lately, so, you know…." Bishop trailed off as Mrs. Frost made a soft noise of displeasure.

"So, it's fine for the two of you to find your mates, but my Katarina has to be alone?"

"Mom, that isn't what he said," Kat said.

"No," Bishop said. "Kat absolutely can date. But she's pretty busy, and she doesn't have much time…" He gave Ava a 'holy shit, get me out of here' look.

"Mrs. Frost, it was so lovely to meet you, but I need to be at work soon, so we'd better get in line for some coffee," Ava said smoothly. "Kat, we'll chat soon, okay?"

"You bet," Kat said.

The two of them joined the line of people as Eleanor crossed her legs and smoothed her skirt over her knees. "I never thought I'd see Bishop with someone. Bear shifters aren't the dating type."

"He's very happy," Kat said.

"Oh, I know. It's just odd that a bear shifter would date anyone, let alone a human." Her mother paused. "Tiger shifters, on the other hand, they're known for making excellent mates."

"Yes, Mother, I know," Kat said.

"All I'm saying is that – oh!" Her mother made a startled growl when a man wearing a plaid jacket and a ball cap nearly fell against their table.

He pushed himself upright and stared blankly at Kat. He was sweating profusely, Kat could see the patch of wetness soaking through the collar of his jacket, and his eyes were completely bloodshot.

"Excuse me, I'm sorry. I didn't mean to -"

The man's apology broke off into a coughing fit. He buried his face in the crook of his elbow and coughed steadily as Kat's mother stared at him in alarm.

"Sir? Are you all right?" Kat asked.

He nodded as he continued to cough. Her mother hissed, and the hair on Kat's arms stood up when his coughing turned into a long, low howl. The buzz of conversation in the coffee shop stopped, and both the humans and the shifters stared at him as hair sprouted on his face and his body rippled.

"Sir?" Kat said loudly as her mother leaned back in her chair and hissed again.

His low howl cut out, and he stared shamefully at her as the hair faded from his face. "Oh, my goodness, I'm so sorry. That just, um, that was embarrassing."

"It's fine," Kat said. "Do you need to sit down?" She had no idea what was happening with the coyote shifter standing in front of her, but it was evident he was sick.

He shook his head. "No, thank you. I just need to use the washroom. Excuse me."

He staggered to the back of the store as Eleanor, her face wrinkled with distaste, made another soft hiss. "Coyote shifters are the worst."

"Stop it, Mom. He's ill," Kat said.

"So, when would you like to meet Lester? I could give him your cell number on Monday."

"Mom, I'm not interested."

"Why not? Honestly, Katarina, it's like you *want* to be single," Eleanor said.

"So, what if I do?" Kat asked. "I'm focusing on my career and -"

"Career? Sweetheart, working at a security firm isn't a career."

"I'm a partner at the firm. I have responsibilities that I take very seriously, and I -"

"I know, sweetie." There was more than a hint of exasperation in her mother's voice. "I understand that you're very proud of your job, and your father and I are proud of you, but there are plenty of women who balance a career and a family. We want you to be happy."

"No, you want grandkittens," Kat said.

"What's wrong with that? Your sister is showing no interest in having kittens yet, and your brother certainly isn't going to give us any, not with the way he consorts with a different woman every week. You're the stable one, sweetie, and if you would just give me a chance, I know I could find a nice boy for you."

"Mom, I don't need your -"

The door to the bathroom flew open with a loud bang, and Kat twisted around in her seat. The coyote shifter stumbled out into the hallway. He had removed his jacket to reveal his sweat-soaked t-shirt. His body rippled again, and Kat stood and started toward the man.

"Sir? You need to calm down." The illness was bringing on his shift, and she kept her voice steady as the shifter stared at her with haunted eyes.

"Help me," he whispered.

"I will. We're going to call an ambulance for you, but you have to calm down. Shifting isn't going to help."

"Can't stop," he moaned before clutching at his head. He pointed his face to the ceiling and howled piercingly. Several of the customers in the coffee shop cried out and cringed away, plugging their ears as the coyote shifter fell to his knees.

A porcupine shifter knelt next to him and placed a hesitant hand on his back. "Mister? Are you okay?"

The coyote shifter growled, and the porcupine shifter squealed in pain when the coyote bit him on the arm. He tore a chunk from the man's forearm, and the shifter screamed again and beat at the coyote's face. He was starting to shift, his quills piercing through his skin with harsh pops, and Kat winced when he fired his quills directly into the coyote shifter's face and chest.

The coyote shifter howled in anger and lifted the porcupine shifter over his head. Quills shot everywhere as he tossed the man down the hallway like he was a bag of feathers. The porcupine shifter hit the exit door with a hard thud and crumpled motionless to the ground.

The coyote shifter fell to his knees again and made a gagging noise. He vomited blood and yellow bile as his body heaved and twisted. With another piercing howl, he shifted completely.

Kat stared in shock at him. The man was a coyote shifter, she could smell it, but she had never seen a coyote shifter like him before. His body was three times the size, and his muscles bulged obscenely as he crouched on the floor. His snout was elongated, and his fangs were twice as large as usual and protruded from his mouth.

He lifted his gaze to her, and she took a step back as her cat hissed in fear. His eyes were bright red, the pupils tiny circles of black in a sea of red, and thin trickles of blood oozed from the corners and down his cheeks.

"What the fuck?" Kat said as frightened screams rang out in the coffee shop.

She took another step back as the coyote shifter growled at her. His body tensed as he prepared to jump, and her cat surged forward.

Too late! Her mind screamed frantically as the coyote leaped at her.

There was a roar, and Bishop, in his grizzly form, slammed into the coyote before he could land on Kat. He drove the animal into the wall and roared again in triumph when the coyote fell to the floor.

The coffee shop rapidly emptied as people shoved and pushed their way out the door. Bishop backed away, growling under his breath. The coyote shifter laid limply on the floor, and Bishop sniffed cautiously at it.

"Thanks, big guy," Kat said shakily.

Bishop chuffed in reply before glancing behind him. Ava stood near the counter, and she gave him a faint smile. He made a low rumbling noise, and she nodded.

"I'm fine, honey."

He walked toward Kat, and she squeezed his shoulder through his thick, dark fur. "Thanks again. What's wrong with him?"

Bishop snorted as Kat's mother joined them. "Is that a coyote shifter? He looks so strange."

"He is," Kat said. "But he's much bigger than he should be, and his eyes were red, and he wasn't -"

The coyote shifter stirred on the floor, and Kat threw her arm around her mother and backed up. As the coyote shook his head and climbed to his feet, Bishop made a warning growl. The coyote snarled in return, saliva dripping from his mouth to splatter on the floor.

"Bishop, he's gone crazy," Kat said. "Be careful."

Bishop moved to the left as the coyote sniffed the air. He stiffened before turning his head to stare at Ava. He grinned, his fangs cutting his lips until blood poured out of his mouth.

He took a step toward Ava, and Bishop roared with anger and swiped the coyote across the back with one massive paw. It drove the coyote to his stomach, blood spurting from the four deep gashes, but he bounced back to his feet immediately. Ignoring the blood gushing from his wounds, he snarled at the giant grizzly as Bishop rose to his back feet.

"Bishop, watch out!" Ava screamed as the coyote lunged at the grizzly.

"Holy shit!" Kat shouted. She had never seen a coyote shifter take on a grizzly before, and she stepped protectively in front of her mother as the coyote landed on Bishop. His weight drove Bishop backward, and Ava screamed in horror when both the grizzly and the coyote smashed through the large front window and into the street.

"Bishop!" Ava shouted before sprinting for the window.

"Ava, no!" Kat grabbed Ava's arm and pulled her to a stop as Ava turned and twisted in her grasp.

"He'll tear you apart!" Kat shouted. "Come this way!"

They ran out the door of the coffee shop and into the street. A crowd of people had gathered, and Kat screamed at them to get back as the coyote scrambled away from Bishop. He inhaled deeply and howled again as he eyed the humans standing around him.

Bishop climbed to his feet, shaking the shards of glass from his thick fur, and, with a short howl, Kat shifted to her jaguar form. She joined the grizzly, and they stalked toward the coyote. He stared hungrily at the humans, and the crowd of people gasped when he took a step toward them.

What the fuck is happening? Kat thought. The coyote shifter had gone insane in the goddamn coffee shop, and if she and Bishop didn't stop him, he would cut a bloody path through the frightened humans.

Moving as one, they circled the coyote and blocked the crowd of people with their large bodies. Bishop roared again in warning as Kat hissed and bared her fangs. The coyote ignored them. His attention was solely on the humans behind them, and Kat tensed, preparing for a fight, when the coyote lowered his head and crouched to the ground.

He sprang forward as gunfire rang out, throwing the coyote shifter backwards. He landed on the ground, sliding headfirst into the brick wall of the coffee shop.

Kat whipped her head to the left. An older man with short grey hair in a t-shirt and jeans stood a few feet away from them. He lowered his gun and stared at the two shifters for a moment before pulling a badge from his back pocket. He flashed it at the crowd.

"Police, step back, please."

He moved cautiously toward the fallen shifter as Kat and Bishop followed him. He booted it lightly in the hindquarters, training his gun at the creature as Kat sniffed his prone body. Blood poured from the coyote's chest, and Ava joined them and touched Bishop's shoulder lightly.

"Is he dead?"

At the sound of Ava's voice, the coyote reared up, snarling and howling.

"Shit!" The police officer shouted, and Kat flinched when he shot the coyote three times in the head.

Blood and brains splattered the wall of the coffee shop as the coyote shifter collapsed on the sidewalk.

"Jesus Christ, I am getting way too fucking old for this shit," the cop muttered. He crouched and examined the coyote carefully before staring at Kat and Bishop. "What the fuck is this?"

"A COYOTE SHIFTER TOOK DOWN BISHOP," MAL SAID IN disbelief.

Bishop frowned at him. "He was unbelievably strong, Mal. And big."

"Grossly big." Kat tapped one nail against the boardroom table. "I've never seen anything like it."

"Maybe it was a combination. Like half coyote and half, I don't know, bear," Willow suggested.

"That was no bear," Bishop said.

"Besides, you can't get a combination of shifters," Mal said. "Even if two different types of shifters mate, their offspring is always one or the other."

"On 'Mysteries of the Shifter' the other night, there was a wolf/leopard shifter," Willow said solemnly.

"That show is trash, Willow," Mal said. "Besides, that was nothing but a wolf shifter who dyed his fur yellow and painted some damn spots on his body."

"Okay, fine, there aren't any shifter hybrids," Willow said. "But what was up with the super coyote?"

"I have no idea," Kat said. "But he was also incredibly aggressive. He would have killed the humans if Bishop hadn't stopped him."

"How's the porcupine shifter?" Willow asked.

"He'll live," Ava said. "The paramedics took him to the hospital. They think he might have a concussion, and the bite wasn't healing yet, but I guess porcupine shifters don't heal as quickly as other shifters. Plus, it was a pretty bad bite."

She turned to Kat. "How is your mom?"

"She's fine," Kat said. "She couldn't wait to tell her bridge club all the gory details."

Willow stood as the phone rang. "Well, I guess we'll never know. That off-duty cop took care of it."

Mal and Kat followed her out of the boardroom as Bishop rested one big hand on Ava's knee. "Are you okay?"

"I'm fine." She brushed her hand across his cheek. "My favourite grizzly protected me."

He leaned forward and kissed her, and she sucked on his bottom lip for a moment. He groaned into her mouth, and she grinned and leaned back when he went to cup her breast. "I have to be at work in ten minutes."

"You could call in sick," he suggested. "Spend the day in my office with me."

"You mean spend the day naked and bent over your desk," she said with a laugh.

"I love the way you think, Ava," he said, and she laughed again before kissing him lightly.

"Drive me to work?"

"Of course. I love you, honey."

"I love you too, Bishop."

Keep reading for an excerpt from Book Three in the Shifters Series, "Katarina and the Bird".

KATARINA AND THE BIRD

(THE SHIFTERS SERIES BOOK THREE)

Kat swallowed the last of her whiskey, grimacing at the taste, before tapping the bar with one pointed fingernail.

Porter ambled over with the bottle of whiskey. "You sure you should have another, Kat?"

She squinted at him. "You're not my mother, Porter."

He laughed. "No, I'm not. But you're not driving home, Kat. Hand over your keys."

She scowled at him. "I don't need to give you my keys, Porter. I'm not stupid – I'll call an Uber."

"Okay," he said and poured her another.

She made herself sip at this one rather than downing it and ignored the sounds of Tori and her best friend Lori giggling. Lori had shown up at the bar twenty minutes ago and immediately glommed onto Ronin like he was a piece of lettuce.

Christ, the entire bar was filled with rabbit shifters, and all of them were horny for the damn bird.

Not just the bunnies, her cat pouted.

Shut up.

She finished her drink and slid off the barstool. She weaved unsteadily as she made her way to the ladies' room. She ducked into the stall and used the toilet. As she was buttoning her jeans, the bathroom door opened, and her cat hissed when she heard the high-pitched giggling of the rabbit shifters.

"Oh God, Tori, you were right. He is so dreamy," Lori said.

"I know, right? My shift is over in an hour. Are you up for taking the bird home?" Tori asked.

"Oh, hell, yes," Lori said. "The kids are with their dad tonight, so my night is free."

"Good. But listen, my kids will be at home, so you need to keep it down."

"Sure, no problem," Lori giggled. "But you'd better tell the bird that too. The two of us are going to knock his tail feathers off tonight."

Kat's nails lengthened, and her cat hissed angrily. She stopped herself from tearing open the stall door and showing the horny little bunnies what happened to females who tried to take what was hers.

Not yours!

Yes, mine! Her cat hissed.

"How do my tits look?" Tori asked.

"Fucking fantastic, how about mine?" Lori said.

"Gorgeous," Tori said. "Okay, we gotta get back out there. Porter will have my head if I stay in here much longer."

Kat heard a high-five and clenched her fists again as the two rabbit shifters left the bathroom. She escaped the stall and washed her hands before staring at herself in the mirror. Her cheeks were bright red, and her dark hair had started to escape the clip. She scooped it back into place with hands that trembled lightly and clipped it securely.

Go home, Kat. You're drunk.

Yes, that was an excellent idea. Besides, did she really want to watch Ronin leave with the bunnies?

No, she didn't.

Kat pushed open the bathroom door, stopping in surprise when Ronin stepped out of the men's room. They faced each other in the hallway, and she frowned when Ronin, his voice uncharacteristically somber, said, "You've had too much to drink, Kat."

"I'm fine," she said.

He shook his head. "You've been tossing back whiskey like it's water. I think you've had enough."

She snorted. "Thanks for the advice."

"I'm serious. Let me give you a ride home and -"

"I don't think so, but thanks."

"Kat, wait." He grabbed her arm as she weaved past him, and her nostrils flared as fresh lust filled her belly.

She turned and shoved him against the wall, and he groaned when she rubbed her entire body against his.

"Kitten, what -"

"Shut up," she muttered before rubbing her face against his neck. She grabbed his wrists and pinned his arms against the wall above his head before rubbing her body against his again. She rubbed against him repeatedly until he was panting, and she could feel his erection against her belly with every slow stroke of her body against his.

She rubbed her cheeks against his face, relishing the feel of his warm breath against her skin.

"Jesus, Kat, you are killing me over here," he groaned.

She ignored him, and he made a harsh gasp, his entire body arching against hers when she licked him from the base of his neck to his mouth. She licked his lips before licking the rough stubble on his chin. She purred and turned around, sliding her body up and down his as he cupped her waist. She ground her ass against his cock, and he made another harsh groan as his fingers tightened.

"If you don't stop doing that, I'm going to fuck you right here in the hallway," he warned in a hoarse voice.

Her cat yowled with excitement, and she ground her ass against his dick again.

"I warned you, Kitten," he muttered before turning her and yanking her against his hard body. His hands gripped her ass, and he squeezed hard as he lowered his mouth toward hers. Before he could kiss her, Porter walked down the hallway.

"What the hell?" he said.

Kat tore herself away from Ronin as her cat hissed her disapproval. She stumbled down the hallway, shaking off Porter's hand when he reached out to steady her and hurried back to her barstool.

She sat down, her hands shaking badly, and stared at her empty whiskey glass. Jesus Christ, what was she thinking?

Ronin sat down at his table, and her hands fisted around the glass when Lori immediately joined him. The rabbit shifter's nose twitched rapidly, and she took a step back before glancing at Kat. Even through her shame, Kat felt the hard bite of satisfaction when Lori took another step back and stared in disappointment at Ronin.

"What are you doing, Kat?"

Porter was back behind the bar, and she refused to look at him. "Another whiskey, Porter."

"No. You're cut off. What are you doing?" he said.

"I don't know what you mean."

Her cat hissed angrily. After her initial hesitation, Lori

was back to pressing her ample chest against Ronin's arm and giggling madly. Another hiss escaped her mouth when Tori passed by them and dragged her hand across Ronin's broad back.

"Bullshit," Porter said as he glanced at Ronin and the two rabbit shifters. "Wolves aren't the only ones who mark, Kat."

"We don't mark like wolves," she said.

"No, not usually, but you can mark if you're really riled up. Ronin's twenty feet away, and I can smell you all over him. Does he know you marked him?" Porter said.

"It was an accident, and besides, it doesn't seem to be affecting his game any," she said.

"Why the hell did you mark him? I've never seen a cat go after a bird before," Porter said. "Does he know you're a cat shifter?"

"Yes," Kat said. "And I told you – it was an accident."

"Sure, it was," Porter said with a small grin.

"It was," she insisted. "He's my employee."

"What is up with the security firm and marking their employees? First Mal and now you," Porter said. "You guys are going to get a reputation."

"Oh my God." Kat buried her face in her hands. "I am losing my damn mind, Porter."

"Maybe what you need is a wolf to distract you from your lust for birds," Porter said with a grin. "You know that little bird could never handle your claws, Kat."

She glared at him, and he held his hands up defensively. "Okay, okay. I'm just teasing. For some weird reason, I know you don't find me attractive in any way, shape, or form. I'm mostly over it."

"Fuck," Kat groaned before rubbing at her temples. They were starting to ache from the alcohol, and she started a little when a hand dropped onto her back.

"You okay, Kat?"

"Hey, Judd. Yeah, I'm good." She smiled faintly at the bouncer. He was a bear shifter and a good guy, if not a bit of a player.

"You don't look so good," he said.

"Just a bit too much to drink. I think I'm going to call it quits," she said as Porter took her empty glass. She fumbled out her credit card and handed it to Porter as Judd rubbed her back.

"Why don't you let me give you a ride home, Kat?"

"That's nice of you, Judd, but I can't impose."

"I don't mind," the bear shifter said. His hand still circled her back as Porter frowned at him.

"Judd, she's drunk."

"I know," Judd said. "I'll behave myself, for God's sake, Porter."

"Will you?" Porter asked.

The bouncer growled at him. "What the fuck kind of guy do you think I am?"

"I know you're a good guy, but you've had a crush on Kat for a long time and sometimes -"

"Can the two of you please stop talking like I'm not here," Kat said before taking her credit card back from Porter and shoving it in her purse. "Just because I'm drunk doesn't mean I'm going to automatically fuck Judd."

Judd flushed. "I didn't think that, Kat."

"Yeah," she said, "I know. Listen, it's sweet of you to offer, but I'll take an Uber home."

"I really don't mind," Judd said before curving his arm around her waist and hugging her briefly. "You should probably have someone make sure you get tucked into bed safely."

"Move your arm before I move it for you."

The terse demand made all three of them stare in surprise at the bird shifter standing next to the bar.

"What did you say?" Judd asked as his arm tightened around Kat's waist.

"You heard me," Ronin said. All trace of his usual good humour had disappeared, and he gave the bouncer a dark look. "I'm driving Kat home tonight, so do us both a favour and stop drooling on her."

"Ronin, don't," Kat said.

"Yeah, Ronin, don't," Judd repeated softly.

"Last chance, big guy," Ronin said.

Something in his voice made Judd stiffen, and he dropped his arm before taking a step toward him. "You're awfully brave for a bird shifter."

"Let's go, Kat," Ronin said. He held his hand out, his gaze never leaving Judd's.

"Hold on. Kat and I are old friends. I'm sure she'd much rather have me drive her home and tuck her into bed than a fragile little bird like you," Judd said.

"Talk about her bed again, and I'll break your jaw, you idiot mouth-breather," Ronin said.

"Oh, you just made a big mistake, little birdie," Judd said.

Kat cursed and slid off the barstool as Judd rushed Ronin. The shift was happening, her cat yowling to be free and help the bird shifter. Ronin was strong and brave, but he was a bird and no match for the angry bear. She'd seen Judd take down a thousand-pound bull without breaking a sweat.

Before she could shift, Judd, snarling under his breath, swung at Ronin. Kat's mouth dropped open, and her cat stared in silent surprise as Ronin dodged the blow easily and grabbed Judd's arm when the force of his swing knocked him off balance. He wrenched Judd's arm up behind his back, and the bear screamed shrilly as there was a loud crack.

Ronin pulled again, and Judd dropped to his knees, snarling and growling viciously as Ronin leaned over him. "I've broken your arm, but I did make a promise to break your jaw, didn't I?"

"Ronin, stop," Kat said quickly as she staggered toward them.

"I'm going to let you go, and you're going to stay right where you are until the lady, and I leave. Do you get me?" Ronin said to Judd.

The bear shifter snarled at him, and Ronin yanked his arm higher. "Do you get me?"

Judd screamed again before nodding his head. "Yes! Yes!"

"Good." Ronin dropped his arm. Judd stayed on his knees, and Ronin held his hand out to Kat. "Let's go, Katarina."

ABOUT THE AUTHOR

Elizabeth Kelly was born and raised in Ontario, Canada. She moved west as a teenager and now lives in Alberta with her husband and a menagerie of pets. She firmly believes that a person can survive solely on sushi and coffee, and only her husband's mad cooking skills prevents her from proving that theory.

For more information about Elizabeth, check out her website at

www.elizabethkelly.ca

facebook.com/EKellyBooks

twitter.com/ElizabethKBooks

instagram.com/elizabethkelly_author

amazon.com/Elizabeth-Kelly/e/B00EOHZ0MS

bookbub.com/authors/elizabeth-kelly

Katarina and the Bird (Book Three)

Porter's Mate (Book Four)

Bria and the Tiger (Book Five)

Rosalie Undone (Book Six)

The Dragon's Mate (Book Seven)

Rise of the Jaguar (Book Eight)

The Draax Series

Reign (Book One)

Rule (Book Two)

Rebel (Book Three)

Harmony Falls Series

Sweet Harmony (Book One)

Perfect Harmony (Book Two)

Forbidden Harmony (Book Three)

Redeeming Harmony (Book Four)

Individual Books

The Necessary Engagement

Amelia's Touch

The Rancher's Daughter

Healing Gabriel

The Contract

A Home for Lily

Saving Charlotte

Shameless

The Fairy Tales Collection

Broken

An Unlikely Seduction

Holiday Romance

The Christmas Wife

The Christmas Rescue

The Christmas Nanny

The Christmas Boss

Sordid Games